The Sound
of
Bluebirds

M.L. Mercy

AOS Publishing, 2024
Copyright © 2024

M.L. Mercy

ISBN: 978-1-990496-74-5

Cover Design: Jessica James

Visit AOS Publishing's website:
www.aospublishing.com

For Carlye

For being a constant in a world of inconsistency.

Prologue

"Where are we going to find our joy today, Baby Blue J?" My mother's voice sounds gentle and angelic as she perches herself on the edge of my bed, softly rubbing my back to wake me from my sleep.

My four-year-old eyes slowly open to a sunlit room, glowing through my light blue curtains. My heart feels full in these moments. I turn my head to look at my mother's big brown eyes and caramel waves of hair that hang around her face. My hair and eyes are the same colour as hers; maybe that means I could be an angel, too, someday? I think to myself.

"With the flowers and the birds!" My tiny and tired voice croaks as my brown eyes widen at the thought of walking through a rainbow of coloured flowers and watching the bumblebees and butterflies circle the petals.

"Then that is where we will find our joy," my mother smiles back at me before shutting the door behind her as she leaves my bedroom.

I wake up with a slight ache in my heart. It's the same ache I feel anytime I remember my mother. She's been gone for over twenty years; one would think this feeling would have numbed itself by now, but it still hurts.

I sit up and find myself alone in the dark, stale air of my bedroom. There are still hours before the sun will rise for the day, so I flop back down onto my rumpled sheets. I reach to the other side of the bed and run my hand over the cool, undisturbed cotton covering. Being alone in the king-sized bed usually never bothers me, but for some reason, it's bothering me tonight.

Chapter 1

Josh

"That is the stupidest thing I have ever heard!" My brother Isaac's booming voice bombards the room.

I look up from the screen I'm mindlessly swiping on to see Rob, our youngest brother, on the receiving end of Isaac's words. Both men are sitting on the other side of the giant square coffee table that separates the seating area in our father's living room. We're waiting for my father and middle brother, Landry, to make their presence known so we can get this day over with.

My father's house is an overly large one dripping with expensive furnishings and unused rooms. The living room has large oak cabinets surrounding us. Some hide the extensive entertainment unit while others hold an entire bar, featuring top-shelf liquor from all over the world. Fresh flowers decorate the room; none are in season, nor are they native to our area—so I can imagine their price tag. My father has expensive taste. I think it's to help hide his questionable morality, but hey, what do I know?

I can hear the leather sofa squeak under Rob's legs as he shifts back in his seat, preparing to make his rebuttal to Isaac.

"All I'm saying is that Steph Curry is a better shooter than Michael Jordan. Look at the stats, Isaac. The numbers don't lie,"

Rob says while shoving his phone towards Isaac, urging him to read the screen.

I can't help but roll my eyes at my two brothers arguing about basketball again. I'll admit that I'm usually in there with my own basketball opinions, but not today. Today, I woke up in a bad mood, and I know I will go to bed in one, too.

I reach up and tug at this stupid bow tie around my neck. I feel like it's choking me. As Landry's groomsmen, Isaac, Rob, and I are all dressed in matching suits. However, the groom himself has yet to make an appearance.

In total, there are four Hayles brothers: my brother Isaac and I are from my father's first marriage, while my half-brothers Landry and Rob are the children from my father's second marriage. My father didn't waste any time before marrying again after my mother died when I was eight years old. Landry and Rob arrived shortly thereafter.

At thirty-three years old, Isaac is the oldest of David Hayles' sons. Being two years older than me, he is the spitting image of my father. With a tall frame, dark features, an unforgiving face, and an attitude to match, his dominating presence is notable. I can see clearly now as my youngest brother, Rob, who's only twenty years old and much physically smaller than Isaac, begins to recede back from Isaac as their argument continues.

Standing a couple of inches over six feet, Isaac and I are the same height. We also share our wide frame, though my hair is a lighter shade of brown, and my eyes aren't quite so dark. My mother used to tell me I had teddy bear eyes, which I loved at the time, but never mentioned to anyone now.

Then there's my brother, Landry. Simply, the thought of him makes my stomach turn and my head pound. Landry, who is in his early twenties and the groom we are all waiting for, has been the bane of my father's existence since the day he was born. Honestly, I have always had a soft spot for Landry and watched with sadness more than once as he royally messed up his life. But not today. There's no sadness or pity for Landry today, even though I know he's feeling like shit about his upcoming nuptials in approximately one hour.

Landry is marrying well-known Brighten socialite Lindsay Preston. Landry and Lindsay were never a couple before they became engaged. In fact, Lindsay was in another long-term relationship when she became Landry's fiancé—with me.

Lindsay and I had been in a serious relationship for about a year when she and Landry slept together while I was on a business trip. However, I didn't find out about it for several weeks after it happened. It took the same amount of time for Lindsay to find out she was pregnant and for my father to arrange their engagement.

Neither Lindsay nor Landry told me about the turn of events. It was my father and Isaac. After being summoned home from my trip on short notice for an important family meeting, I was shocked to find out that I had not only lost my girlfriend but was also going to be an uncle. The shock was substantial, to say the least.

It's hard to find the words to express how angry I was when my father informed me of the news, and while he said he understood my anger, no sympathy was given. Being the mayor of the city of Brighten, my father wanted no scandal and no drama surrounding Landry and Lindsay's relationship. Thus, I would not cause a scene and would accept what had happened without so much as a face-to-face confrontation with Lindsay. My father also had a very important relationship with Lindsay's family, as they were large donors to his political campaign. Hence, Lindsay was off-limits. Landry, however, was free game.

Overall, I felt okay with not having to confront Lindsay. Even though we had been together for a year, I never loved her. Our relationship was easy in that she was a good enough lay and a socially acceptable partner in the eyes of my father. Everyone assumed Lindsay and I would eventually get married, and we probably would have had the situation with Landry never happened. Getting over Lindsay was easy—it was Landry's betrayal that broke my heart.

Over the years, Landry and I had our ups and downs. Rebellious to the core, Landry was constantly pushing our father's limits. Landry was a masochist, continuously putting himself in harm's way, either at the hands of my father or his own. That was until he found Hollynd.

Hollynd had been Landry's girlfriend for all of last year. When they were together, Landry was a different person. Of course, there were times when they struggled due to Landry's self-destructive habits, but overall, he was better. Being around a couple like Hollynd and Landry was bittersweet. Their love for each other radiated throughout the space they occupied. It was overwhelming at times. While I was happy that my brother had found such love, I was also jealous. Lindsay and I never had that sort of connection. Hell, I had never had that sort of connection with anyone, ever.

When I found out Landry had gotten Lindsay pregnant and that they were to be married, aside from being angry over his betrayal to me, I was also livid over his betrayal to himself. He and Hollynd were technically not together when he slept with Lindsay, but I knew that he was still in love with her. In fact, I know that he's still in love with her right now, even as he gets ready for his wedding to another woman.

I had only confronted Landry once about what he had done. It was the same day I found out about him and Lindsay. This was also the last time I had seen him face to face—until today.

Today, my father is forcing me not only to attend this wedding but also to participate as a groomsman. Though I'm trying to pull off the best nonchalant demeanour I can at the torturous event, I can feel a silent rage slowly circulating through my veins. I don't know if it's the reality of the situation or if it's the fact that I haven't slept well in weeks, but I feel unsettled and volatile. Several drinks and an easy bridesmaid may be in order.

* * *

When someone like David Hayles enters a room, it's hard not to take notice. His bullish presence takes up so much space that breathing can sometimes feel like a struggle. A certain chill fills the rest of the space. I knew he was there before he made a sound—this is what life was like with my father.

My father walks into the room, passing by my chair, and walks straight towards Rob.

"Robert, where is your brother? Why isn't he downstairs yet?"

Rob shifts uncomfortably in his seat as my father stares coldly at him, waiting for a reply.

"Um, I'm not sure. Do you want me to go and get him?" Rob says, clearing his throat.

My father shoots a glance in my direction, and a slight twitch from the corner of his lip betrays him.

"No. Joshua, please go and get Landry," my father's voice hisses in my direction.

I roll my eyes with an annoyance that I have no intention of hiding from the room. My father is such a sadistic bastard. I know he gets his kicks from torturing his sons, especially Landry. Of course, he would ask me, the estranged brother and wrongfully done party, to be the one to fan the flames of Landry's misery.

In the chair opposite of mine, I can see Isaac trying to contain his amusement for the situation at hand.

"Fine," I grumble, rising to my feet and storming out of the living room.

Making my way up to Landry's bedroom on the second floor, my annoyance with this entire situation, no, the annoyance of my entire life, is growing. The whole situation is straight out of a bad episode of *Dr. Phil*. My only solace is knowing that by this time tomorrow, I will be on a plane to Elmerson, and far away from the newlyweds and my father.

Having the opportunity to work with the renowned defensive team at Boulder Crest Law on a high-profile case was an opportunity I could not pass up. Working alongside Richard McKay benefited my career greatly, even if it cost me my girlfriend. When Richard asked me to stay on for the next big case they had coming up, I graciously accepted the long-term position.

As for today, I will watch this shitshow go down, and tomorrow, I will return to my other life, far away from my family. Only this time, I will return to my life as a single man. Elmerson is home to many gorgeous women who are just waiting for a rich, successful, handsome man to pay them some attention. I realize this might sound arrogant, but hell, being nice has gotten me nowhere. It's time to stop with the feelings crap and take what I want. A relationship is not what I want right now. A good romp in the sack, however, that I could do.

I knock on Landry's bedroom door twice, both going unanswered. Instead of trying a third time, I let myself into the room without an invite. By now, my frustration has risen ten-fold. In the two-thousand-dollar tuxedo, my father picked out, I see my younger brother sitting on the floor, leaning against the bed. Landry is the tallest of the four sons, but he doesn't look like it as he slouches down on the floor. His hair is almost black. Usually, Landry's face and ears are full of piercings, though I don't see a single one right now. Dad must have told him to take them out—he can be such an asshole. We all know Landry is suffering enough right now. It's obvious just by looking at him.

Landry doesn't bother looking up as I enter the room and tower over him. His eyes remain focused on the white gold band in his hand.

"What the hell are you doing?" I break his concentration on the ring.

I can see the look of desperation in Landry's dark blue eyes—he looks like a man about to succumb to ruin. For a moment, I almost feel sorry for him—almost.

Landry stands, meeting me face to face. The hand that was holding the ring is now clenched tight. like he's holding onto it for dear life.

"I thought you'd given the rings to Rob already?" I ask while gazing down at the harden fist.

Clearing his throat before he answers, Landry nods. "Yes, I gave them to Rob."

"Then what is that ring for?" I gesture towards his hand.

"It's nothing," Landry answers quickly before shoving the ring into the inside pocket of his blazer.

"Well, Dad wants you downstairs now," I mumble before heading towards the bedroom door.

"Josh, wait." Landry stops me before I can leave the room. I turn around to face my brother, watching him wince uncomfortably. "I know we haven't talked one-on-one since you found out, but I wanted to say…"

"No, Landry," I abruptly cut off his mumbling words. "I have no interest in listening to a goddamn word that you have to say. The only reason I'm here is because Dad demanded that I attend. Don't think for one second that I'm here because I want to be, and don't think for a goddamn second that I am upset because Lindsay is getting married. What I am angry about, however, is that I can't even trust my own brother anymore. Not that I trusted you much before, what with your habit of messing up every chance you get. Believe me when I say, little brother, that you fucked up *huge* this time! But you already know that. Stop trying to apologize to me."

With that, I turn and exit the room before Landry can respond. I'm not interested in hearing what he has to say. What I am interested in is heading straight to the nearest source of alcohol and having a stiff drink—and that is precisely what I do when I arrive back in the living room.

Chapter 2

Courtney

Swipe card, work cell, and name tag, I whisper to myself. The Valemont, Elmerson's most prestigious hotel, does not take kindly to its employees forgetting these items.

Today marks my one-month anniversary as part of the evening concierge team. While I have been an employee of The Valemont for over a year, my promotion from *Front Desk Agent* to *Evening Concierge* was a serious accomplishment for me. I worked my ass off last year in hopes of moving from the front desk to the concierge. Pulling extra shifts, going above and beyond for guests—all in hopes of landing this position. Now, I'm part of the two-person concierge evening team, with shifts running from three p.m. to eleven p.m.

Ever since I was little, I've been fascinated by five-star hotels. The glamorous ambiance and the allure of a luxurious life that was absolutely nothing like my own held a special place in my dreams. It was like an alternate reality, where everything you ever wanted was available to you. My eyes would sparkle whenever I saw a hotel like this in movies or, if I was lucky, in passing as we made our way to some budget-friendly place my parents could afford.

Hotels like this can be found in every beautiful city in the world. From Paris to Rome, New York to Tokyo— growing up, I wanted to be a part of this world and away from the small town I was raised in—a town where boredom and tragedy cultivated my childhood. Moving to Elmerson last year was my first step in the many I intended to take.

I toss the rest of my personal items into my locker, clicking the lock shut before heading out to begin my shift. Before I leave the staff room, I stop at the full-length mirror to give myself a once-over. I smooth out my black pencil skirt, which lands at the top of my knees, and make sure my burgundy blouse is tucked in tight. Both the blouse and skirt are very form-fitting—thank goodness for control top nylons. I reach up and brush the tips of my shoulder to ensure no loose hairs are stuck on the fabric of the fitted black blazer. I almost always begin my shift wearing the blazer but often lose it mid-shift, getting too hot from running around looking after guests.

My chestnut brown hair is pulled into a tight ponytail, and my long bangs are parted to the side and tucked behind my ears.

My faux pearl and diamond earrings, a treat for myself when I got promoted, and my black two-inch heeled pumps polish off the ensemble.

Satisfied with my appearance, I walk briskly towards the lobby. My feet move swiftly over the gray and black tiles. My heels click behind me as I cross the large entryway, the chandelier twinkling high above me. Black wingback chairs with gold piping are placed throughout.

Outside the front doors, I see Rick and Kel, the bellhop and valet attendants, laughing while waiting for guests. Rick is leaning against the row of gold luggage carts while Kel gestures about something wildly with his hands.

Upon entering the lobby, I see my dear friend and co-worker, Liv—Olivia to everyone else. Liv is preparing to take over the evening shift at the front desk as the daytime attendant is wrapping up his shift.

Liv looks up from the large marble desk, and I wave. She waves back and offers her beautiful smile, her light blonde hair draped over her blazer.

I continue towards the concierge area, between the front desk and the bank of elevators. While the concierge desk looks the same as the front desk, with the same dark wood base and marble top, it is about half its size.

When I arrive at my area I see Brenda, the daytime concierge clerk, tidying the space to end her shift. Brenda has worked for the hotel for fifteen years and has been an incredible mentor to me as I transitioned into this position.

"Good afternoon, love," Brenda smiles at me as she logs out of the computer, stepping away from the desk. "Are you ready for a quiet evening? There are only fifty-three arrivals tonight: thirty-two in the standard rooms, nineteen between bronze and silver, and only two in the gold suites."

The hotel consists of three hundred and forty-two guest rooms, which are further divided into room types. While most rooms are standard guest rooms, meaning they are one large area holding the bed or beds, televisions, and desk all in one space, the rest are suites.

"Well, I guess it's Sunday night, and we never get many guests in the suites on Sundays. Have you received any special requests for the suite arrivals yet?" I ask Brenda as I casually begin to flip through the list of arrivals. While everything we do is through the computer system and our phones, we always have hard copies of the guests printed every few hours. If you don't, you will learn to do it after you've experienced a power outage in a hotel.

While we provide services for all guests, the suite guests are always our top priority. Like most service industries, the more you pay, the more you get. Thus, my first task will be noting any special requests for our incoming guests. After discussing the requests with Brenda, she continues to tidy her workspace.

"Has Milo arrived?" I ask Brenda.

"Not yet, but you know Milo, he's never here until the very last minute."

"That's why he likes working with me so much. He knows I'll arrive early to learn everything we need to know, so he doesn't have to worry about it." I quip. "He's lucky he's so darn charming," I continue saying before the sound of Milo's voice rings through our area.

"Did I hear someone say charming? Well, ladies, here I am," Milo says with a mischievous grin.

It's hard not to smile back at Milo—as disorganized as he can be, he makes it so easy to like him. Not to mention that he's extremely good-looking, and the concierge role is entirely in line with his image. Milo's dark blond hair is always perfectly styled, and no single strand is out of place. His strong jawline is always shaved smoothly, and his brilliant smile can bring both men and women to their knees. Having known Milo for a year, I know he chooses either or sometimes both.

However, I can't complain about the company I get to keep every night at work. Aside from his handsome demeanour, Milo is very professional and good at his job. I am fortunate to be working alongside him most nights. Milo has been working here for the last two years. He's currently trying to earn his golden keys through the *Les Clef d'Or*, an international organization of concierges. Becoming a member requires immense dedication, which Milo takes very seriously.

Although I have been only working in this position for a month, Milo has already asked me if apprenticing with the *Les Clef d'Ors* is something I'm interested in. While it sounds like an excellent group and a very fulfilling goal, I don't have the time for the commitment.

In addition to full-time work, I'm taking several online courses as I work towards my degree in Hospitality Management. Hopefully, one day, I will be running the show, and maybe if I work hard enough, it will be a hotel in an exotic location abroad. That's not to say that Elmerson is not an exotic city, but it's not my forever. Somewhere out there is the dream I have for my forever. I can't quite see it yet, but I can feel it.

"I was just saying you wouldn't show up until the last minute," Brenda says to Milo while she checks her watch.

"Brenda, I would hate to show up too early and surprise you. I'm doing it for you. I know how much you love to be right," Milo teases Brenda, who shakes her head and laughs.

"You are such a brat, Milo. Honestly, Court, I don't know how you put up with him."

"Because she loves me too much," Milo says with a wink, and I roll my eyes.

Brenda gives us a quick wave of goodbye. "Alright, you two, have a good night and I'll see you tomorrow."

"So, what's happening tonight?" Milo asks, his fingers tap rapidly onto the keyboard in front of him.

"Not much. I think it's going to be a slow night. However, we do have two people booked into the gold suites. One is a couple coming in for their anniversary. The husband called yesterday and requested champagne on ice and a dozen red roses delivered to the room before their arrival."

"Did Brenda order the flowers?" Milo asks, not stopping to look up from the computer screen.

"Yes, her note says they will be delivered by five-thirty."

"Okay, and what time does the couple arrive?" Milo quizzes me.

It's typical for Milo to grill me like this at the beginning of each shift since I'm still in training. To be honest, I don't mind. I want to do this job well, and I am fortunate to be learning from the best.

"They're supposed to arrive at seven."

"How long are they staying?"

"Two nights."

"And what are their names?"

"Mr. and Mrs. Peterson."

That's another thing management expects of their staff: guests must be greeted by their proper names. While it's impossible to learn the names of all the guests, especially if we are completely booked, we are expected to know the names of all platinum and gold suite guests. We try to remember the rest of the guests, but we also have cheat sheets on each floor in the housekeeping supply room. If you know what room that person belongs to, you can quickly look up their name.

"And how many years have the Petersons been married?" Milo continues his interrogation.

"Thirty years."

"Very good. Who is the other gold suite guest checking in tonight?"

"Mr. Joshua Hayles. Single occupant."

"How long is he staying?"

"Long-term. Reservation notes say he is here for work; the company is paying. Booked for four weeks but says that it may be extended."

"What company does he work for?"

"Boulder Crest Law Firm."

This catches Milo's attention—he looks away from the computer screen and turns his swivel chair in my direction.

With one eyebrow arched up, Milo smirks. "A single lawyer, you don't say..."

I roll my eyes again. "It says he's a single *occupant*, not that he's single. Besides, you know the rules about *engaging* with the guests."

"Not to get caught?" Milo continues with his mischievous smile.

"Aren't you supposed to be my supervisor? Not the guy trying to corrupt the new concierge clerk."

"Oh, girl, you're adorable," Milo grins. "Not to mention that I don't think you need me to corrupt you."

"What's that supposed to mean?" I ask innocently.

"I've heard stories about you and a certain someone from the kitchen. Does the name 'Kai the sous chef' ring a bell?"

Instantly, my cheeks begin to burn with embarrassment. How did Milo know about me and Kai? Well, not that there is a me-and-Kai, exactly. It's more like a hookup once in a while.

"From the colour of your cheeks, I'll take that as a yes," Milo laughs a little too hard.

Still embarrassed, I turn to walk away from Milo and bump a tray of papers off the countertop and onto the floor. This causes Milo to roar even harder. Thank goodness there aren't any guests around yet.

"Aw, Court, I'm only teasing you."

"I know that," I reply. "You just caught me off guard."

"That, and you are a super klutz," Milo notes and I can't help but nod along as I finish picking up the papers from the floor.

"Okay, back to business. Does Mr. Hayles have any special requests?" Milo asks once he finishes giggling.

"Not that I noticed."

"Okay, well maybe if we're lucky, he will be a low-key long-term guest. Sometimes these rich business guys can be demanding."

"Right," I agree. "There are nineteen arrivals in the other suites too. There is nothing too major for special requests for these, either. Some extra towels and stuff like that, so I will email housekeeping right away."

"Great. Once the flowers arrive, can you take them up to the Petersons' suite and get them in water right away? You remember where the vases are kept on that floor, correct?"

I nod.

"Okay, then you will have to go back up around six-thirty to prepare their champagne and ice. We don't want to do it at the same time as the flowers, or the ice will be melted by the time they arrive."

"So, basically, you are going to make me do all the running around tonight while you sit at the desk?" I tease Milo. "Look at me, my heels are too high for this shit."

"Hey, that's not my fault. Don't they hurt your feet?"

"No, I'm used to them, and I'm just kidding about running around in them. I'm a pro at it. Once when I worked at the front desk, I accidentally gave a guest the wrong key. I had to sprint up the stairs to beat the elevator before they walked into someone else's room. I ran up four flights with these babies." I point down to my shoes. "And I made it in time."

"Wow, that's impressive."

"I know," I say as I lift my right foot back towards my butt and wink before I turn to leave to straighten up the lobby. This allows me to chat with Liv at the front desk if she's not busy.

I adore both my job and my coworkers. Although I anticipate a quiet night, my stomach still tingles with excitement. In hospitality, you never really know where the night can take you.

Chapter 3

Josh

I dig my fingertips over my temples, trying not to flip out on the Uber driver who picked me up from the airport over a half hour ago. If he hits another pothole, I swear I'm either going to punch him in the back of the head or throw up all over the black leather seat. I was hoping that by the time my short flight was over, I would have lost most of the hungover nausea I had been battling all day. Thankfully, last night's wedding reception was mostly a blur.

I spent the minimal amount of time required at the wedding reception for my brother and ex-girlfriend. Though I could see my father's cold glare stare me down as I darted out the back of the ballroom shortly after the reception concluded, I was not in the mood for mingling—even less so for pretending to be happy for the new couple. Not to mention the schmoozing that would be in order when speaking to my father's "friends"— in reality, the uppity assholes are truthfully just useful for campaign contributions. I couldn't imagine a worse evening. Of course, the countless shots of whisky I consumed, which led to throwing up in the garbage can outside the hotel after chain-smoking four cigarettes while some chick from the bar pranced around me like a kitten, didn't help my evening. Waking up hours later with said kitten sleeping naked beside me and not even knowing her name was the evening's rock bottom. This had led to my ultimate demise—a slow, painful death in the back of an Uber whose driver was committed to hitting every pothole in sight.

Finally, we arrive in front of The Valemont hotel. As I exit the car, I'm greeted by a lanky bellboy whose name tag reads *Rick*. His eyes are wide with needy servitude, and he is no doubt looking forward to the eventual tip. Despite my annoyance with my Uber driver, I can't help but soften my expression at the eager bellboy.

"Good evening, sir. My name is Rick. Please allow me to get your luggage."

I nod and walk towards the hotel's rotating door. As I enter the lobby, I immediately notice the upgrade in the accommodations since last fall. It seems the better you perform with Boulder Crest Law, the better the perks.

Last year, we worked on a significant case involving an embezzling CFO and his mistress for months. The guy had stolen millions from his company, and it was my job to prove he hadn't. I won the case, naturally. Now, we are preparing for the trial of the CEO of the same company.

Honestly, I'm happy to be back in Elmerson—hours away from my narcissist father, overbearing brother Isaac, newly married brother Landry, and meek brother Rob. One of the things I loved most about working out of town was being free from all the baggage that comes along with my family and its name, and even though it was my family name that initially caught the eye of Richard McKay, it was my work ethic that had him requesting me back. The thought that I can be whoever I choose to be when no one is looking over my shoulder makes me giddy inside.

My thoughts trail off as I watch this scowled face, albeit stunning woman, in high heels trying to shift a black wingback chair from one wall to the adjacent one. She then proceeds to stare at it intensely with her arms crossed, only to move it back to its original place. Honestly, she's giving this chair placement too much thought. However, I find it amusing to watch her wiggle the oversized chair in her high heels as her brow furrows fiercely and the tip of her pink tongue nudges out from her soft pink lips. When she finally seems satisfied with the chair, she immediately begins shifting the flowers on the side table beside the chair. She just doesn't quit moving. She reminds me of a hummingbird zipping around a garden, looking for the perfect nectar.

I turn my attention away from the amusing woman and take in the prestigious lobby. The glow from the chandelier overhead emits a warm atmosphere throughout the space. A light hint of chlorine mixed with an air freshener penetrates my nose, telling me there must be a pool in the hotel. At the end of the lobby, I see the entrance to a restaurant and lounge. Both are currently filled with patrons, reminding me that it's close to supper time, and I've hardly eaten. My stomach grumbles slightly as the scent of garlic from the restaurant wafts towards the lobby. I notice the furniture mover is gone as I turn right and make my way to the front desk to check-in.

I'm greeted at the front desk by a perky blonde attendant whose smile is as big as her blue eyes.

"Good evening, sir. Are you checking in with us this evening?"

"Yes, it's under Joshua Hayles."

"Of course, Mr. Hayles. I need a piece of ID and a credit card, and we will get you all set."

I hand her my cards and watch her quickly type away on her computer. Within seconds, she hands my cards back to me with that same bright smile. God, her job must be exhausting if she has to act this happy all the time.

Behind me, Rick appears with my luggage sitting atop a gold trolley. Perky Olivia instructs him where to take the bags, and he takes off ahead of me.

Meanwhile, Olivia continues her nonstop information about the hotel's amenities, restaurant, spa, and pool hours, and honestly, I stop listening. I'm distracted by a clicking sound behind me on the tiled floor. I turn back to see the same tiny hummingbird-like woman I saw in the lobby; only now is she carrying a huge bouquet of red roses. She's already passed me when I turn around, but my eyes happily settle on the curve of her backside in her tight black skirt. I can't help but notice a slight sway in her hips as she walks—her long, dark ponytail swishing along with it.

For a moment. I feel a slight twitch as I watch her head towards the elevators at the end of the hall. I shake off my body's tingles as this woman is way too young for me to be checking out. She must be somewhere in her early twenties at best. As for me, a man in his thirties, she probably thinks I'm as old as I think she is young.

Finally, front desk Olivia hands me my keys and directs me towards the elevators. The swerving curvy girl is gone again, and I can't help but be disappointed. Having her as an elevator companion wouldn't be the worst thing.

It isn't long until the elevator has lifted me up to the fourteenth floor. Walking through the sliding gold doors, I'm greeted by a beautiful bouquet of fresh, white lilies sitting on a small table. Immediately, my thoughts go to my mother, who adored lilies. Anytime she saw them, she would be quick to point them out. As a boy, I remember her joy anytime she encountered the beautiful flower. As I stare at the pinkish-white petals, I remember pushing my little nose so far into the flower that yellow powder would sprinkle my nose. My mother would say that it was a flower kiss and should be seen as good luck. A small smile forms in the corner of my lips before I'm reminded of the lilies laid out on top of my mother's casket.

I shake all thoughts of my mother from my mind and turn right down the long hallway. The corridor matches the lobby's black and grey colour palette, with accents of burgundy and gold on the carpet. My eyes are drawn to the wall sconces that sparkle down the hallway, lighting my way most luxuriously.

I finally reach room 1403 and fumble around the pocket of my blazer for the key card I had only received from the front desk minutes before. When I locate the card and swipe it against the lock, the door only flashes a red light. I try it again, feeling annoyed, and still, nothing happens but the single red light.

I hear a door further down the hallway click closed. Looking up, I see the woman I had been watching in the lobby. Her face looks like a porcelain doll, smooth and pristine, which makes her pink lips look even more vibrant. These features aren't the ones that make my breath hitch; her eyes are. They are large round pools of deep blue, the deepest I have ever seen.

When she notices me staring in her direction, she immediately straightens her posture and releases the most exquisite smile.

"You must be Mr. Hayles."

I clear my throat, not expecting to be dumbfounded simply by a hotel employee. "Um, yes."

"Are you having trouble getting into your suite?" She is now standing only a few feet away. "I would be more than happy to assist you, Mr. Hayles. Unfortunately, we haven't met yet, so I need to see your ID before I unlock the door for you."

Now that she's close to me, I can read her name tag, which says 'Courtney—Concierge,' and I can smell vanilla wafting off her. She smells good, but not good enough to make me forget that I'm locked out of my room, and now I must produce my ID again. Meanwhile, Courtney is still talking, and I can feel my previously taken headache pain reliever wearing off.

"I apologize for the inconvenience, Mr. Hayles, but we want our guests to be as secure as possible. It will just be this once, I assure you. Now that we have met, I won't have to worry about you trying to sneak into any hotel rooms. Not that I'm saying you look like the type of person that sneaks into hotel rooms, but I mean that..."

"Stop talking!" I growl, and Courtney steps back in shock.

Eventually, I locate my ID and hand it over to her without looking up from my wallet. Am I frustrated and annoyed? Yes. Do I feel bad for overreacting and snapping? Also, yes.

She checks the ID quickly and returns it to me without saying a word. In one swift motion, she pulls out her key card and swipes it over the lock, causing a click and a green light to appear.

"I apologize for the inconvenience, Mr. Hayles. I will have new key cards delivered to your room promptly," Courtney says briskly before heading straight down the hallway. I can't help but watch her body walk away. Once she turns the corner, I enter my suite and notice all my luggage has been placed near the entrance.

The suite is enormous, and much like the hotel's public areas, it's draped with black and gray. The front of the space contains a living room and office area. A couch and side chair are placed against the wall, opposite the giant television and gas fireplace. At the far side of the space, a large balcony window overlooks the city.

Closest to me is a desk, lamp, and office chair. A large armoire is between the office area and living room—peeking inside, I find a mini fridge, microwave, coffee machine, and a fully stocked mini-bar.

The bedroom with a king-size bed is just off the living room. There is another television mounted on the wall across from the bed. An enormous bathroom, steam shower, and jetted tub are attached to the bedroom.

I loosen my tie and kick off my shoes as I wander around the room. While the effects of the hangover seem to have faded, except for this dull headache, I'm exhausted from the day. There's nothing I would like more than to have a hot steam shower, pour myself a drink, order room service, and watch basketball on TV—and that's precisely what I intend to do.

Chapter 4

Courtney

Ugh! What a jerk that man is. I bet he thinks because he's so good-looking that he can speak to people like garbage and demand they stop talking. I'm marching towards the front desk across the lobby to get Joshua Hayles' keys re-coded. Luckily, there is no one at the desk except for Liv. Tossing the malfunctioning key cards onto the marble countertops, Liv flashes her light blue eyes my way.

"Woah, what's got you all riled up?" Liv asks.

"Room 1403's keys aren't working."

"Oh, 1403. Yes, the sexy lawyer that just checked in," Liv raises her eyebrows at me while reaching for the plastic cards. "Did you get a chance to check him out?"

"I did. However, it was hard to notice anything good about him while he was being an ass."

"Why? What happened?" Liv's eyes widen.

"He told me to stop talking! I was simply trying to apologize because he was locked out of his room. Of course, I had to ask for his ID since I didn't know who he was, which I also apologized for, and he yelled at me to stop talking!" I can feel my blood pressure rising as I retell the story.

"Okay, I have to know something. Were you babbling? Because, babe, you and I both know that you tend to babble. Especially when you get all flustered."

I bite my lip and feel my cheeks heat in embarrassment.

"Well, maybe a little, but he still didn't have to be a jerk about it."

"You're right, but admit it, he made you a little bit flustered."

"Maybe a little," I admit to my friend, who's now sliding the new keys over to me. "He is kind of good-looking," I smirk.

Liv lets out a belly laugh. "Come on, he's more than a little good-looking. He's gorgeous, I mean, for an old guy."

"Why, how old is he?" I ask out of curiosity.

"Thirty-one. I looked at his birthday when he checked in. He's a Scorpio, by the way."

"Maybe that's why he's so grumpy," I indulge Liv and her fascination with astrology. "Anyway, I better get these keys up to him before he calls down here to yell at me some more."

"Good luck," Liv smiles as I leave the front desk.

Before returning to the fourteenth floor, I stop by the concierge desk to see if Milo would mind taking the keys upstairs to Mr. Hayles' room. Unfortunately, when I get there, I find Milo in an intense search for tickets to the sold-out Michael Bublé concert. A VIP guest of ours, who will be in town that night, is looking for tickets.

It's common for guests to have such requests for us at the concierge desk, and we always try our best to accommodate them. Lucky for this guest, Milo is the master at problem-solving and accommodating guest requests, no matter how difficult they may be.

Since Milo is preoccupied, I find myself back on the way up to the fourteenth floor to disturb his majesty in 1403 once again.

Moments later, I'm knocking on Mr. Hayles' guest room door with the new keys in hand. At first, he doesn't answer. I assume he hasn't gone anywhere; I wait a moment before trying again. When I'm in the middle of my second round of knocking, the door flies open—I'm met with the same stupid, good-looking Joshua Hayles I met earlier, except this time, he's only wearing a towel. I can't help but take a moment to gaze over his chest, which is defined with muscles and shadowed with dark hair. His hip bones slightly protrude over the soft white towel, which is only held together by his firm grasp.

I turn away quickly, again embarrassing myself in front of this man.

"Mr. Hayles, I'm sorry to bother you again. I brought your new keys." I hold out my hand while still avoiding looking in his half-naked direction. "I'm so sorry to disturb you, but I didn't want you to be without keys and…"

Again, I'm interrupted by his booming voice. "Courtney, stop talking!"

Forgetting that I'm turned away on purpose, I look back to meet his eyes, which are the richest brown I have ever seen, "How do you know my name?"

Taking the keys from my hand, he replies, "It's on your nametag."

"Of course," I blush. "Have a good night, Mr. Hayles."

"And stop calling me Mr. Hayles," he demands as I turn to leave.

I take a deep breath before I turn back and reply to this insufferable man.

"How shall I address you, sir?" I ask with a slight tone of annoyance in my voice.

"By my name, Josh." His voice is serious and deep, and this causes my skin to tingle. We stare at each other, neither breaking the gaze of the other.

Finally, I'm able to pull myself from this spell and produce a slight smile.

"Of course. Have a good night, Josh," I say more quickly than I intend to.

I walk away from Josh's room, and his door shuts behind me.

Glancing at my phone, I notice it's almost time to prepare the ice and champagne for the Petersons, who will arrive shortly. I immediately begin this task hoping that it will distract my mind from returning to the image of the chest, the hip bones, the stern voice, and the man in 1403.

Chapter 5

Courtney

For the last two weeks, I have done everything possible to avoid Joshua Hayles. Between my embarrassment at seeing him in a towel and liking it a little too much and my conflicted feelings of dislike for his arrogance, I'm quite willing to let Milo take over tending to Mr. Hayles.

This week has felt painfully long, and it is only Thursday afternoon. We have a busy weekend ahead of us at the hotel, but this evening is quieter. This gives all the departments in the hotel the chance to get ready for a full house and ensure the property is in tip-top shape.

My assignment is to replenish the fresh flowers throughout the hotel. While this is usually a different department's job, the flower delivery came in later than usual today, and I volunteered to take it over.

The hotel has a variety of flowers throughout the floors, and these arrangements may change with the seasons. This task is probably taking longer than it should. I am distracted by the sweet scent from each bouquet placed on the black cart I'm rolling through the building.

I have been stopping at each floor for the last hour and replacing the old flowers with new ones. I can feel the ache in my feet as the doors to the fourteenth floor open, and I push my almost empty cart through. With the second to last display in sight, I double-check my list to ensure I have the correct arrangement for the floor. White lilies are always displayed on the gold suite floor.

I empty the old, slightly wilted lilies and replace them with the bright, new ones. Their scent, which has always reminded me of hot dogs for some reason, permeates my nose. Happy with the display, I turn to continue onto the last floor when my sore ankle gives way, and I stumble towards the table. My hip jams into the smooth edge of the marble top with enough force that the fresh lilies wobble and topple over. With the flowers falling to the floor and a stream of water chasing them on the edge of the table, I hang my head in defeat.

As I lower myself onto my knees carefully, the plush gray carpet squishes against my skin. One by one, I begin to pick up each lily, trying not to let the flashback in. I press them hard against my tightening chest as orange dust clings to the fabric of my black blazer. With each second that passes, distant memories are becoming more and more vivid. I repeatedly try to shoo them away, but despite my best efforts, they bombard my thoughts mercilessly.

Instantly, I'm transported back to the day of my brother's funeral, carrying an armful of fresh lilies towards the front of the church. Walking slowly because my leg is stitched up and bruised from the accident, I can still hear my mother's wailing cries from the pews. Dylan is holding my arm and walking with me at our slowed pace. He is also severely battered from the accident, though we are considered the lucky ones, as my brother's lifeless body lies in the white casket at the front of the church. I'm carrying my once-favourite flowers, which I now loathe with every part of my being. My brother is dead, and I hate these flowers.

I shut my eyes tightly, cursing away the memory overtaking my brain. Forgetting that I'm on the fourteenth floor of The Valemont, I can feel my breath becoming shorter in panic, just like it did that day in the church.

"Courtney," a voice echoes from above. "Are you okay?"

I look up from the carpet I'm still sitting on, though my eyes are foggy.

"Hey, hey, it's okay," he says, and I feel a hand press down on my shoulder.

The man kneels beside me, and I realize it's Josh. The scent of his spicy cologne overtakes the scent of the lilies, and I am transported out of the church.

"Oh my gosh, I'm so sorry."

Professional replaces my initial panic as I frantically clean up the mess.

"Courtney, stop!" Josh's voice commands. "Just stop for a second and breathe."

With his hand still on my shoulder, Josh inhales deeply to demonstrate.

"You're okay, Courtney. Just breathe."

This time, I listen and relax my body, causing some of the flowers to fall from my arms and back onto the floor.

Josh picks up one of the fallen flowers and looks at it carefully.

"What happened?"

"I spilled the flowers, and then..." My words trail off, and we sit in silence for a moment.

"Lilies were always my mother's favourite flower. The white ones especially," Josh speaks softly.

"They used to be mine, too."

"What do you mean, used to be?" Josh sets the flower down and looks at me.

"They remind me of someone I lost a while ago. We used lilies at their funeral."

"I see." Josh's eyes are gentle and compassionate, and my heart rate slows. "I can understand that. They were used at my mother's funeral too, but I don't know…she loved them so much that it's hard not to think of that when I see them."

"I'm glad we display lilies on this floor, then," I smile slightly but look away from his eyes.

"Me too."

We sit together among the scattered lilies, neither of us speaking. The spilled water slowly drips off the edge of the table.

"I better get this cleaned up," I comment and begin to clear the flowers yet again. Josh starts to assist me.

"You don't need to do that, Mr. Hayles."

"I told you, it's Josh," Josh mumbles while standing up and offering his hand.

"Right, I'm sorry. It's a force of habit. Thank you for helping with this," I wave my hand over the mess. "You don't need to stay; I know you are very busy."

Josh clears his throat. "You're right. I am. But I…" He stops mid-sentence and stares at me longer than expected. "I wanted to say I'm sorry the flowers upset you. I hope one day you give them another chance."

Before I can respond, Josh turns abruptly and walks toward his room. I continue to stare in amazement. That person was nothing like the Josh I had encountered a couple of weeks ago.

I spend the next few hours perplexed over the interaction I had with Josh, and occasionally, I feel a slight grin creep across my face.

It's Friday evening before the long weekend, and we are entirely booked. The front desk is fully staffed tonight with four attendants on duty, which works well for Milo and me—we usually need help from the front desk once all the arrivals have checked in.

The concierge desk phone is constantly buzzing with requests from guests. Some are looking for last-minute dinner reservations or tickets to local shows. Others are specialty requests—items unavailable through housekeeping, the spa, or our restaurant. These are always the most unusual requests. Tonight, a guest staying in one of our Platinum suites has called down for three unique French dishes. *Oursins*, *tête de veau*, and a*ndouillette* have all been requested to be found, ordered, and served in the suite tonight. First, I googled the dishes, and honestly, I wish I hadn't—urchins, cow brain, and pig intestine. I'm on the phone with the city's only authentic French restaurant, trying to arrange the order.

As the restauranteur and I debate between prep and pick-up times, I look up from my seat at the concierge desk to see Josh Hayles stroll up and lean casually against the marble top. Though his lean may be casual, his brows are furrowed, and the rest of his face wears a scowl to match. He must have just arrived from work since he's still in a perfectly fitted black suit.

However, his tie has been loosened slightly, and I can see that the top button of his dress shirt has also been opened. Despite his demeanour, Josh is still handsome beyond belief. He is so attractive that I miss the final wine recommendation for pairing with urchins.

I offer him a slight smile when our eyes meet and motion that I will only be another moment on the phone. After our strange encounter yesterday with the lilies, I expected our interactions to be more pleasant, but judging by the look on his face at this moment, I may be mistaken. Internally, I'm cursing Milo for not being at the desk right now so he could help Josh. Josh looks miserable, and I don't want to be on the receiving end of his wrath.

When I finally finish my call with the restaurant, I turn towards Josh and plaster a smile on my face.

"Josh, how may I assist you?"

Josh's dark eyes burn into me with precision. I cannot for the life of me figure out what he's thinking until he speaks. "I have some dry cleaning that needs to be sent out."

"Yes, of course." I nod as I quickly grab a notepad to mark down the request.

"Also, can you make a reservation for me at the restaurant for tomorrow evening?"

"Absolutely. How many guests and for what time?"

"Party of two, for eight o'clock."

While I'm writing down the reservation information, I can't help but wonder if this is a date. The thought of arranging a date for Josh makes my stomach turn, which is entirely ridiculous.

"Do you have any requests regarding the location of your table? For example, should I request a corner booth?" I'm fishing for information.

"No, anywhere is fine."

"Is that everything, Josh?" I look up to see his eyes, which aren't as narrowed as they were when he came up to the desk.

Something in his face softens as a small smile forms over his perfect, full lips. I cannot help but smile back.

"Yes. I appreciate your help, Courtney." Hearing him say my name in his deep voice causes the spontaneous combustion of sparks to zap through my body.

"Of course, Josh. I'll send someone up to retrieve your dry-cleaning this evening, and I will text you the confirmation of your reservation for tomorrow night."

Josh taps his fingers onto the countertop with a slight nod before walking towards the elevators.

I stare as he walks away. However, my concentration becomes interrupted when Milo appears beside me. I didn't even notice his return. Milo turns his head to see what I'm staring at so intensely.

"It's hard not to watch a man like that walk away, is it?" Milo says as he sees Josh walking away from the desk.

"Absolutely," I agree, never allowing my eyes to leave the tall man at the end of the hall until he vanishes into an open elevator.

***

Four hours later, my shift is finally over. It's been a hectic, long day at the hotel, and I'm relieved I have the day off tomorrow. I will be able to catch up on some work at home, both household and schoolwork if I don't allow myself to drink too heavily tonight.

I'm currently squished in a red vinyl-covered booth at Caspers, a pub only a few blocks from the hotel. This is the go-to spot when the Valemont staff decides to go out. The pub is moderately busy for a Friday night. The jukebox drowns out most of the noise from the corner pool tables. The Eagles' "Take it Easy" rings through the air.

Tonight, there are ten hotel employees at Caspers. Staff from several departments are gathered around the corner table, including Liv, who's seated to my right, and Kai to my left. Kai's arm is casually slung over my shoulders as he laughs with Kel the valet attendant across the table.

Kai and I have been "hanging out" for a couple of months. We always have a lot of fun together when we decide to hang out, though it's almost always mainly physical.

Kai is a couple of years older than me and has worked at the hotel under our head chef, Alex, for three years. After getting to know each other during evenings like this one, Kai and I hit it off almost immediately—his charm and good looks drew me in. With his dirty blond hair, always dishevelled after being in a hot kitchen all day, and his baby blue eyes, Kai could pass as a Hemsworth brother.

While I have always enjoyed my hookups with Kai, he clearly stated that he was not the relationship type. Honestly, though, after the disaster of my last relationship, I am okay with Kai's reluctance to be anything more than friends with benefits.

Suddenly, I feel Kai's hand pull me in tighter as I finish the last sip of my martini.

"Babe, tell them about the French dishes you had to order for that guest earlier," Kai urges me to retell the story of the cow brains and intestines and how plating them for the guests almost made me sick.

I retell my story to the large group, with plenty of moans and gags erupting from the table. It's become a tradition amongst the staff to see who can come up with the craziest guest story from the week.

As I pick up the skewer of olives from my glass, my favourite part of the drink, Liv, elbows me.

"Hey, let's go to the bar for another drink."

I nod in agreement and scoot out from the rounded bench.

Once we are free from the hotel crowd, Liv and I head to the bar. We walk past the server attending to our table and who we could have ordered another drink from instead of leaving the booth. However, I know for a fact that Liv has a crush on the bartender, so she always insists on ordering our drinks from him in person.

When we reach the bar, I test the wooden top with my hand before I lean against it. Nothing worse than a sticky countertop.

"Hey, girls, I'll be just a sec," the tall bartender with dark hair, Buddy Holly glasses, and plaid shirt calls towards us.

"No problem, Chase," Liv shouts towards the man currently popping the tops off a row of five brown beer bottles.

While we wait for Chase to take our order, I turn around and scan the bar. Most of the tables are filled with laughter, though the odd one seems to be engaging in intense conversations. That is until I set my eyes on the table in the far corner. The man's dark, narrow eyes meet mine as he casually sips from his glass. His tablemate, whose back is towards me, stares at the football highlights from a nearby hanging TV.

I immediately recognize the face as the guest from 1403, Josh. He has changed out of the work clothes I saw him in earlier. He's now in a tight, fitted black T-shirt instead of his white dress shirt and tie. He looks equally sexy in both.

I give a small smile, unsure if he even knows who I am. However, when his large hand raises, gesturing for me to come over, I know he has recognized me.

"What are you waiting for? Go over there." Liv nudges me on my back, but I don't move. "Good God, woman, when a man like that waves you over, you go!" Again, when I don't budge from my spot, Liv pushes me harder.

Catching me by surprise, Liv's force causes me to stumble forward. I look up and see a grin on Josh's face. Embarrassed, I tuck my hair behind my ear, finally free from the tight ponytail I usually sport. Feeling less than professional in my ripped, light denim jeans, red T-shirt, and black Converse, I slowly approach Josh's table.

When I arrive at the table, Josh motions for me to sit down without saying a word. Though I'm hesitant to do so, I pull out the chair between Josh and his friend at the round table. When Josh's friend notices me sitting, he offers me a bright smile.

"Hey, how ya doing? I'm Peter Kirk," the cute red-headed guy with bright green eyes extends his hand towards me.

Josh shifts in his seat and clears his throat.

"Yeah, sorry. Peter, this is Courtney..." Josh's voice trails off, as he doesn't know my last name.

"Morgan," I fill in the silence.

Peter and I quickly shake hands before Josh continues.

"Peter and I work together at the law firm. Courtney works at the hotel I'm staying in."

"Well, it's great to meet you, Courtney. What do you do at the hotel?"

"I work in the concierge department," I reply to Peter while stealing a glance at Josh, who seems to be content simply watching the exchange.

"Interesting. Tell me, how much of a pain in the ass is Josh as a guest?"

I open my eyes wide at Peter's comment and allow the awkwardness to sink in as Josh glares at Peter.

"Oh, no, Josh is a great guest," I reply, converting myself into Concierge Courtney instead of two-drinks-deep Courtney.

"Ah, I'm just giving Josh a hard time. I keep telling him he needs to loosen up." Peter smiles as Josh finishes his drink and sets the glass on the table.

"You're getting the next round," Josh grumbles at Peter. "Courtney, tell Peter what you want."

"Oh no, that's okay," I say quickly.

"Courtney, tell him what you want." Josh's tone is now demanding.

"Um, just a vodka martini, please," I say to Peter, who's now rising from his seat.

"You bet, Courtney. Josh, the same?"

Josh nods, and Peter heads to the bar to retrieve the drinks.

I glance quickly towards the bar to see if Liv is still there. She is conversing with Chase with such intensity that I could be over here on fire, and she probably wouldn't even notice.

"You look different," Josh mumbles, breaking my thoughts on Liv and Chase.

"Oh, I changed after work." I look down at my casual clothes. "I don't really want to go out in a pencil skirt and heels," I laugh awkwardly.

"I like your work attire. It makes you look older," Josh notes seriously.

"Yeah, I guess." I look down at my fingers, fidgeting on my lap.

"You're nervous. Why?" Josh asks.

I look up at him, not really knowing what to say. Should I tell him he's intimidating and that I don't know how to act around him?

"Well, we're not really supposed to socialize with guests, so I guess I feel weird about that."

"Is your boss here, Courtney?"

"No," I reply quietly.

"Then, what's the issue? Have a drink with me and tell me about yourself."

Now I am dumbfounded. Why does Josh want to know more about me? I'm not even sure he likes me, let alone wants to hear about my life. I wonder how much he has had to drink. Why in the world would someone like Josh want to know someone like me?

"Why?" I look up at Josh inquisitively.

Josh rests his forearms on the table and leans in towards me. With his brows furrowed, he looks intensely into my eyes.

"Honestly, I don't know."

Before I reply to the strange statement, Peter returns with our drinks. Setting a martini down in front of me, I grab it quickly and take a large gulp.

After setting down Josh's drink, Peter doesn't bother rejoining us. I hear him say something about going to check on a woman he saw sitting alone at the bar. By the time I set my drink down, now already half gone, Peter has disappeared.

I can feel the liquor flowing through my limbs.

"How long have you worked at the hotel?" Josh asks.

"Just over a year. I started at the front desk but moved to the concierge position a month ago."

"Are you enjoying it?"

"I really am. I get to meet the wildest and weirdest people. The requests we get at the concierge desk, seriously, don't even get me started. Though most people are great and a lot of fun— well, not all of them, some can be miserable.

"Eventually, I would love to be a general manager of a hotel one day. Maybe once I finish school and I have a bit more experience, I can start applying for managerial positions, but that's a long way off." I know now that the alcohol is taking effect as I'm rambling to this man. I am also gesturing with my hands far more than usual.

I can see Josh smirking slightly into his glass as he takes the final sip of the brown liquor. Suddenly, I realize I may have stuck my foot in my mouth when I mentioned the miserable guests.

"Oh, I wasn't talking about you when talking about guests. I was speaking generally." My lips continue moving, though my brain screams at them to stop.

Josh's smirk turns into a full-blown smile. I don't think I've ever seen him fully smile before. It's nice, like, really nice. It makes his entire face glow and soften.

"You know you reminded me of a tiny hummingbird the first time I saw you zipping around the lobby," Josh laughs as he takes another drink.

"A hummingbird?" I ask with confusion. "I don't understand."

"You don't need to understand; it's just what I thought of when I saw you. It amused me."

I look away quickly with a shy awkwardness.

"Your cheeks are red, Courtney," Josh finally says through his grin.

Red cheeks—another sign that I've had too much to drink and that I'm thoroughly embarrassed. I look down at the olives pierced with a toothpick in my drink and stir them slowly.

"How old are you, Courtney?" Josh's smile fades.

"Twenty-two," I answer quietly, like it's a secret or something.

Josh replies with nothing but a *hmm* sound.

"And you're in school and you work full time?" Josh continues with his interrogation.

"Yes, but my classes are online, so I don't have to be on campus."

"Are you from Elmerson originally?"

"No, I grew up in Greensly, which is a small town about three hours from here. It's up north by the border."

"And your family's still there?"

"Yes. Um, I'm sorry, is this the Spanish Inquisition?" I blurt out after the question about my family: a topic I really don't want to discuss right now, or any time for that matter.

"I'm sorry. I guess it's just the lawyer in me. Trying to get all the facts."

"Maybe I should start grilling you. Let's see how you like it?"

Josh's smirk returns. "Go for it, but first, let's get another round."

Josh waves a server over to our table and orders us each another drink and two shots called 'Southern Blues.' As we wait, I begin my line of questioning.

"Do you like it here in Elmerson?" I start with an easy question.

"Yes, it's better than Brighten, anyways," Josh replies, his hands folded in front of him. I can see the veins in his thick forearms as they rest on the table, and I'm trying my hardest not to stare.

"Is that where you're from, Brighten?"

"Yes."

"Do you have family there?" Again, I go for a basic question, though I'm hoping he slips in something about not having a wife or girlfriend there. Though I know I shouldn't care because it's completely moot.

"Yes, I have family there," Josh answers matter-of-factly, giving me no other information.

"Well. that's pretty vague," I comment as the server returns with our drinks and places them on the table.

"What do you want to know?" Josh asks, handing me my shot glass, and I sniff the liquid— it smells like blueberries.

"Tell me about your family. Are you close to them? Do you miss them?"

"Well, my father's an asshole, my mother's dead. My older brother is a dick, and my youngest brother is too sweet for his own good. Then there is my middle brother, who recently married my ex-girlfriend, who is pregnant with his child, who was conceived while she and I were still dating. So, to answer your questions—we are not a big, happy family, and no, I don't miss them."

My mouth is agape as I listen to all the information Josh casually blurts out. I don't even know what to say. I stare wide-eyed at him while he lifts his shot glass towards me, looking for a *cheers.*

"Come on, Tiny Bird. Bottoms up," Josh says, waiting for me to respond.

I lift my glass to clink it against his and drink down the liquid. Josh does the same and we sit silently as I process all the information Josh disclosed about his family.

"Josh, what the hell is wrong with your family?" I finally blurt out.

Josh bursts out laughing, which is the first time I've heard him do that too.

"Seriously, that's messed up," I shake my head. "Is that why you're so grouchy all the time?" The alcohol has taken over all my common sense, and the words tumble out of my mouth.

"I knew you were talking about me earlier when you mentioned miserable guests," Josh shoots a glare at me. Even in my drunken haze, I can feel his eyes burning into me. "You really think I'm grouchy?"

His golden-brown eyes bear a hint of sadness, and I instantly regret saying anything.

"No, not really. Maybe you're just really serious? Which makes sense since you have a very serious job," I babble, trying desperately to backtrack my stupid remarks.

Josh shifts his wooden chair towards me at our rounded table until he is close enough to reach up and tucks a piece of my dark hair behind my ear.

"I can be funny too, sometimes," Josh whispers to me.

I cannot bring myself to say anything as I take in his features up close. Features like his dark stubble that covers his solid jaw or the odd strand of grey that peaks through his brown hair.

"I'm sure you can," I reply through my now very dry mouth.

Josh reaches over to my fresh martini, waiting for me beside my empty shot glass. With a quick swoop of his hand, Josh grabs the stick of olives and quickly shoves them into his mouth.

"You did not just eat my olives, Hayles!" I burst into laughter and shock.

Josh smiles slyly as he chomps down on the olives and flips the empty toothpick between his fingers.

"That's what you get for calling me grouchy," Josh smirks and looks at me with deviousness, and something in my heart jumps.

Chapter 6

Josh

I shouldn't be flirting with this woman. I keep trying to remind myself that she's only twenty-two, which makes her nine years my junior. This thought keeps popping into my head as the salt from the vodka-soaked olives coats my tongue.

Courtney holds her fake, angry scowl at me. She's so goddamn adorable. From the moment I saw her earlier from across the bar, I couldn't stop watching her. When she was at the table on the far side of the bar with other staff, most of whom I recognized, but not all of them, it was her smile that kept my eyes wandering back to her. It's so bright and vivacious. It's also so alive. She was too far away for me to hear her laugh, but I can recall its infectious nature after hearing it ring through the lobby my first week here. I have been able to ignore her for the most part until yesterday evening. Seeing her in that panic state on the floor of the hallway hit me hard, and I'm not entirely sure why. It took everything I had not to scoop her up and take her in my arms. At the time, I wasn't sure what the root of her pain was, but I could feel it radiating off of her. It's a feeling I've felt before in my youth. It's a feeling I feel now, sometimes.

When Courtney and the blonde girl from the front desk finally left the crowd at the table and went to the bar, I felt excited and nervous. I couldn't resist beckoning her over here when we made eye contact. The way she leaned against the bar with her long dark hair flipped over her shoulders, her tight T-shirt and denim jeans that hugged her perky ass so perfectly, I was mesmerized. She was the most breathtaking image of casual I have ever seen.

I have spent most of my adult life dating women like my ex-girlfriend/sister-in-law Lindsay, who was always dressed in ridiculously expensive attire, always trying to portray an image of a Barbie doll, women who will do whatever they have to alter their physical appearance if it means they can hide their inner selves just a little bit more. Admittedly, I have slept with more than my share of these women, and it wasn't terrible. However, that's all it was: physical attraction and satisfaction. There was no spark beyond a quick carnal screw, and frankly, I was getting bored.

Tonight, however, I feel something. A stir inside me, a small tingle of something I haven't felt for a long time. Maybe not since my days in university when I still thought there was more to relationships than a quick turnaround time from one to another. Tonight, I feel giddy and carefree. This girl's presence and youth are contagious. I feel lighter. I'm not sure what it is, but I like it.

"Are you actually hungry?" I ask the girl whose olives I just stole.

"Nah," she replies. "I was giving you a hard time. I couldn't let you get away with stealing my olives and not give you a bit of a guilt trip." Courtney leans over and bumps her shoulder against mine.

Our eyes catch each other for a moment, but the moment is overtaken quickly as the background music switches songs and "Honey" by Måneskin begins to beat throughout the bar.

"Oh my God, I love this song!" Courtney exclaims and begins to sway to the music in her chair.

"I don't even know this song," I say as I listen to the unfamiliar notes. It must be something new—I'm so out of the loop of pop culture and anything trendy.

"It's Måneskin. They are so good! How can you have never heard of them?"

"I'm into more old-school music," I say, trying to brush off the fact that I have no idea what's considered cool anymore. "Music from a time when it was actually good."

Courtney rolls her eyes at my old-man remark and stands up from her chair. She slaps her hand onto my shoulder, and shivers instantly run across my body.

"Come on, then. Let's go to the jukebox and find some good old music." Courtney shines her smile at me as I get up to follow her to the nearby jukebox.

The crowd in the bar has started to thin. I see Peter is at the table in the corner with the girl he was eyeing earlier. I also glance across the way to Courtney's former posse, still drinking and laughing, except for the blonde front desk girl. I have no idea where she went off to.

We stand side by side when Courtney and I arrive at the jukebox, lit with fluorescent-coloured lights. Close enough that if I dropped my hands to my side, which are currently crossed against my chest, I would undoubtedly graze her fingers.

"Okay, so I'll pick a song for you, and you pick one for me. No peeking at what the other person selects. Deal?"

"Alright," I agree, pulling out a handful of loose change from the pocket of my jeans.

Courtney carefully gazes through the songs as the lights from the machine glow against her skin. When I see a smile creep across her face, I know she must have found her selection. I hold my hand out towards her so she can grab some change. Her fingers fumble around through the money and continuously graze the palm of my sweaty hand. These tiny touches are causing my heart to pound.

"Turn around, and no looking," Courtney bosses me once she has the money needed for one song.

I turn around as instructed while she inserts the money into the slots. I can hear the coins tumbling into the machine.

"Okay, you can turn back. We still have a minute left on the current song, and then yours should be up. I tried to pick something from your generation." Courtney gives me a wink and giggles, so I have no doubt it will be something ridiculous.

"Should I be afraid?" I ask.

"Oh, definitely."

The current song begins to fade out, and the jukebox makes the next selection. Instantly, the bar begins to buzz with a yelling female voice.

"Now tell me what you want, what you really really want" screams through the speakers.

Instantly, Courtney spins towards me with a wide-open grin and eyes filled with excitement.

"Did you seriously put on The Spice Girls?" I ask as I recross my arms and lean against the wall beside the jukebox.

"Yeah, I did! Aren't they from your era?"

"How old do you think I am?" I ask in shock.

"It doesn't matter. The Spice Girls are awesome. You remind me of a Baby Spice fanboy. Am I right?" Courtney now stands in front of me.

"Nah. I always preferred Posh."

"Really?" How come?"

"I don't know. The dark hair and sharp features." The words fall out of my mouth as I reach up and touch the ends of Courtney's dark hair hanging over her shoulder. *What am I doing?*

"Huh. I would have thought you were a blonde-hair-girl kind of guy," Courtney mutters as her cheeks blush, although her eyes never leave mine.

"Nope. Never had any luck with blondes," I reply as I twirl the strands of her hair through my fingers.

I push myself up from the wall and gently let go of Courtney's hair.

"Now, let me show you what good music sounds like."

I step around her and move in front of the jukebox. I already know what sound I want to pick. I knew from the moment I saw it listed when we first came up here. I insert my money and make my selection before moving back towards Courtney, who has taken my place against the wall beside the jukebox.

"You are going to learn a valuable lesson about music in just a moment, and once you experience it, you'll never go back to this crap." I wave my hand in the air as the Spice Girls sing their final few lines.

There's a moment of silence before Keith Richards' guitar comes on, followed by Mick Jagger's crooning voice.

"I'll never be your beast of burden. My back is broad but it's a-hurtin'" rings out from the jukebox.

"Is this The Rolling Stones?" Courtney asks while tilting her head to the side as if raising one of her ears would help her hear better.

"Of course. How do you get better than The Stones?"

I watch as Courtney's body begins to sway to the song. I can tell by the look on her face that she is enjoying it.

I can't help but reach my hand out towards her. Instantly, she reaches her hand and takes mine. I pull our clenched hands to the center of my chest, and Courtney moves closer to my body. My other hand tucks itself under her hair and rests on the nape of her neck. Her skin is so goddamn smooth. It takes a moment of hesitation before I feel her other hand rest on the side of my hip. Courtney's body is tense at first, but soon I feel her relax.

Slowly, our bodies press together as we gently sway to the song. We move further away from the wall, and I turn in front of the jukebox. There isn't a space to dance here, but no one seems to notice or care.

With my head towering over hers, I can smell tangerine coming from her silky hair. Courtney's forehead rests against my chest for a moment before she tilts it up towards my face, which automatically tilts down towards hers. We stare intensely into each other's eyes, and I feel my grip on the back of her neck tighten with desire while I release her other hand, pressing it against my chest. I can't help but raise my hand and place it on the edge of her jawbone as my thumb moves toward her mouth and gently grazes her bottom lip.

It's all I can do not to devour her with my lips. Even when I remind myself of our age difference and that this could seriously mess up her job, the thought of tasting her sweet mouth overpowers everything.

A figure appears behind her before I can lower my head to hers. I look up and see a guy, about six feet tall, with his fingers hooked into the belt loops of Courtney's pants, pulling her away from me.

Courtney steps back from my body, and I instantly miss her touch.

"Come on, babe. We're leaving," the skinny guy with dirty blonde hair says as he pulls Courtney towards him.

Hearing him call her "babe" infuriates me. Who is this guy? Does she have a boyfriend? If she does, she shouldn't have been over here all night with me. An image of Lindsay, my cheating ex-girlfriend, flashes through my brain, and my anger increases.

I stand up straight and take a step back. Courtney's eyes are moving between this guy and me.

"Oh, um, Kai. I didn't know you guys were still here," Courtney says while still looking between us two.

"We're all leaving now. Meet us at the door if you're coming with us, Court. We're going to get tacos, and then I'm crashing at your place." Kai slaps Courtney's ass before turning away.

"Sorry, that's just Kai from the kitchen," Courtney looks at me with embarrassment.

I clear my throat and shake my head. My disappointment is measurable.

"You should go with your friends. It's getting late, anyway."

"Oh, okay," Courtney says hesitantly. "Thanks for the drinks and…" Her voice trails off.

"Yep," is all I manage to say before turning away and walk towards Peter's table, leaving Courtney standing there on her own.

I don't allow myself to turn back. Not even for a second. When I tell Peter I'm leaving, I notice the crowd of hotel staff, including Courtney, have disappeared. After I pay my tab at the bar, I head outside and begin the walk back towards the hotel.

The night air has cooled off significantly, and I wish I had a jacket.

As I round the corner about a block from the hotel, I hear voices hooting and hollering. Across the street I see the hotel staff that had just left the bar gathered around a taco truck. Courtney is easy to spot for two reasons—one is her red T-shirt, and two, Kai has his arms wrapped around her with his face nuzzled into her neck. The same neck I can still feel on the palm of my hand.

So, she has a fucking boyfriend. I shouldn't care at all. She's too young, she is clearly a tease, and in a couple of months, I will never have to see her again.

Chapter 7

Courtney

It's been two days since the night at the bar with Josh, and I haven't seen him. The day after our drunken moment by the jukebox was my day off work, and to be honest, I spent most of the day in bed, hungover. Aside from feeling like garbage from drinking too many martinis, I was frustrated with how things ended with Josh that night.

After we left the bar, I spent the next half hour thwarting Kai's best efforts in trying to come home with me. I wasn't in the mood to be with Kai that night. Instead, I went home alone, downloaded "Beast of Burden," and listened to it until I passed out.

For two days, my mind has been in an endless loop—replaying the night with Josh. Even as I update the restaurant directory in our system as Milo tends to the guests, I have to remind myself to stay focused.

It's been a quiet evening so far, which isn't unusual considering it's early Monday evening. We expect business guests this evening, but since they are probably still at work, they haven't arrived at the hotel for check-in yet.

I can't keep myself from glancing up occasionally to see if Josh has arrived back at the hotel, nor can I shake this anxious feeling. Judging by the abrupt end to our night and the cold look in his eyes when he walked away from me, has left me feeling slightly panicked. Not that I've never angered a guest before, but I don't think of Josh as just another guest.

An hour later, the directory is finally up-to-date. Milo has returned from his errand, and we are both sitting behind the desk, discreetly on our phones, waiting for the next task to arise.

"Excuse me," a booming voice fills the space as Milo and I look up at the large figure above our desk.

At first, I plaster on my best customer-service smile until I realize it's the man I've been waiting to see for the last two days. My smile fades as my heart begins to race.

"Josh. Hi," I say as I rise off my chair.

Meanwhile, Milo shoots me a quick glare, undoubtedly because of my casual tone.

"Mr. Hayles," Milo turns to Josh and stands beside me. "How can we help you this evening?"

"I need a reservation in the restaurant at eight for two guests."

"Yes, of course," Milo answers since he's the only person Josh looks at. I'm clearly being ignored and feel like an idiot just standing idly by.

"Anything else, Mr. Hayles?" Milo asks after making a quick note about the reservation.

"No, that will be all for now." Josh taps the countertop lightly with his hand before turning and walking away towards the elevators.

"Have a good evening," I call in his direction to see if he will acknowledge me. He doesn't.

I spend the next few hours performing any duties that come up under a mask of pleasantness—in reality, I'm livid and remain in this mood over the next several hours. To try to blow off steam, I head towards the lobby to tidy up the space and maybe shoot the shit with Rick and Kel if they're not busy.

While fanning out the newest edition of *Travel Plus*, I catch a glimpse of Josh in my peripheral vision. He's still wearing his suit from earlier, which is navy and tailored to perfection. He's walking towards the lobby doors, but stops abruptly as a gorgeous woman walks through the doors towards him. She is tall, with long, red hair that lay in ringlets over her shoulders. The woman is wearing a long, black dress jacket, paired with at least a three-inch heel—she could be a supermodel. Josh and the mystery woman stand face to face for only a moment before he leans in and presses a soft kiss on her cheek, as she does the same to him.

They both turn towards the restaurant entrance, which is not too far from the magazine stand I'm fiddling with. Josh places his hand on the woman's lower back, and I instantly feel nauseous.

As they walk toward me, I turn back towards the magazines and silently pray that he doesn't notice me. I feel completely inadequate and naive for thinking there might have been anything between us the other night. This is the type of woman Josh would be with— Ms. Supermodel, not the clumsy concierge girl.

I'm waiting until I hear their shoes clicking away before I turn around, only the sound seems to be getting louder before it stops abruptly.

"Excuse me, Courtney," Josh says my name in a monotone voice.

I cringe at the thought of having to talk to him and his date but turn with my brightest grin on display.

"Yes, Mr. Hayles. How can I help you?" Suddenly, the thought of saying his first name seemed like something I wasn't privy to anymore.

"Could you please take Ms. Russel's jacket up to my room while we have dinner?" Josh smiles at me with his mouth, but it doesn't reach his eyes.

"Oh, the restaurant has a coat check for your convenience."

"Yes, I realize that. However, it would be best to leave it in my room rather than have us drag it around later. Don't you agree, Isabelle?" Josh turns from me and looks at the red-haired woman, who giggles at Josh's question.

"Yes, Joshua. I think that sounds like a wonderful idea," she replies with a sweetness in her voice that makes me want to gag on the spot.

The woman begins to take off the black jacket to reveal a very tight black dress cut low enough to reveal a slight pop of cleavage. It's not trashy-looking; it's a beautiful dress for a beautiful woman. I hate them both, nonetheless. Isabelle hands me her jacket, and I lay it carefully on my outstretched arms. I can tell by the fabric that it's an expensive item.

"Very well, then," Josh says before lifting his arm to signal to his date to take it. They both turn away from me without another word. That is, until Josh turns back slightly, just enough to look at me, dumbfounded with his date's stupid coat.

"Oh, and Courtney," Josh calls back to me. "Maybe put a bottle of wine up there as well. Red." Our eyes meet for a moment before he casts an arrogant smirk at me and turns back to his date as they walk into the restaurant.

Anger fills my body as I take a deep breath, trying to remind myself that I'm at work and he is a guest. Even though there are moments when a guest needs to be told to fuck off, it's not something I can actually do. Instead, I walk out of the lobby to the elevators to take this dumb jacket up to Josh's room—when he and Ms. What's-her-face head up there for the rest of their date, it will be waiting for her, hung with care.

I deliver the jacket before ordering the bottle of wine from the lounge. When I enter Josh's empty room, I take a moment to inhale deeply. It smells like him, and I'm taken back to being pressed against his chest with his hand on my neck.

I allow myself to remember for a second because even that short amount of time causes the butterflies in my stomach to emerge. I head towards the closet through the doorway and hang up the black jacket.

Before I exit Josh's suite, I glance around to the areas I can immediately see—the office area and the living room. Both are left tidy, though there are traces of Josh everywhere. The random tie lying on the desktop. The empty tumbler on the coffee table next to an iPad. A single white lily by the iPad—of course. I let out a sigh of acute sadness.

I left Josh's room to prepare the wine and glasses as Josh requested. I can't believe I'm basically setting up his room for him so he can get laid. The thought makes my stomach turn, though it shouldn't. I shouldn't care in the slightest.

When I finish with Josh's requests, I check the time to see how much longer I have left in my shift so I can get out of here and, hopefully, get Josh out of my head.

I head back down to the main floor to see what needs to be done next. Since it has been a quiet night, Milo suggests we catch up on some inventory in the backroom. He says one can watch the desk and the phone while the other goes to the back. Usually, I detest doing the inventory job, but tonight, I volunteer wholeheartedly. I would love nothing more than to hide out for the rest of the night and not witness Josh and his date head upstairs after their dinner. I think again of his little smirk, and I'm disgusted.

Finally, it's eleven, and it's time to go home. This has been the longest shift ever, but I'm grateful I didn't see Josh again for the rest of the night.

After changing into light denim jeans, a white T-shirt, and a grey hoodie, I grab my backpack and head out for the night. Despite it being February, we are having an unusually warm spell right now, for which I'm so thankful. I hate having to trudge home in the snow in heavy outerwear.

When I exit the staff door on the side of the building, I expect to feel a breath of fresh air hit my face. Instead, the first thing I notice is a whiff of smoke from up the ally. I can tell almost instantly that it's cigar smoke. When I look closer at the man smoking the cigar, I notice it's Josh—however, he looks nothing like the man I had seen only a few hours before.

He's no longer wearing his navy suit but rather in grey sweatpants and a maroon hoodie. His hair, which had been combed to perfection earlier, is now messy as if he had just showered. He's leaning up against the side of the hotel. I wish I didn't have to walk past him to get home, but unfortunately, this is the street that leads to my apartment. I was fortunate to find a place so close to work when I moved here. I'll admit, it's more like the size of a room than an apartment, but its location is ideal, and it is within my price range.

I slip my hands into my pocket and lower my head, hoping that maybe he won't notice me as I walk by.

"Going to find your boyfriend?" Josh's voice grumbles as I approach.

"Pardon me?" I stop abruptly. "What are you talking about?"

The happy, professional demeanour I had earlier has all but disappeared. I'm tired and frustrated after a long night of stressing over the very person in front of me.

"Your boyfriend. Are you going to see him?" Josh takes a puff from his cigar.

"Are you talking about Kai?" That's the only possible person he could be referring to, and of course, this comes back to the other night. "Not that it's any of your business, but Kai isn't my boyfriend. Why do you even care?"

"I don't like women who flirt with other men when they are with someone else. It infuriates me."

"Look, this problem you're having right now is your issue, not mine. Kai isn't my boyfriend; he's my friend." I look at Josh with annoyance, oozing out of every pore. "If you don't mind, I'd like to go home to bed, Mr. Hayles."

I begin to walk away, but Josh's voice stops me again.

"I asked for white," he says.

"What?" I glare at him in confusion.

"The wine in my room. I asked for white."

My mouth drops in shock. I know for a fact that he said red because I remember comparing his thing for redheads with his love for red wine.

"You did not ask for white wine. You asked for red, and I delivered it. Speaking of reds, where is your date, Josh? Don't you need to get back to her?"

"She left," Josh replies as he tosses his cigar butt to the ground and stomps on it with his black Nike shoe. "Turns out she didn't like red wine."

"Well, then, I guess you shouldn't have asked for red wine," I use the same matter-of-fact tone Josh uses.

Josh stands up from leaning against the wall and slowly walks towards me. Before I can say anything, we are face to face.

"So, he's not your boyfriend?"

"No," I say, and I feel my voice shaking slightly.

"Then why did he call you 'babe' and slap your ass?"

I roll my eyes before answering. "Because in the past, there have been times when we have hooked up. But we're not together; we're just...whatever."

Josh lowers his head towards me, and I can smell the cigar mixed with his cologne coming off his clothes.

"I don't like that," Josh grumbles.

"It's not your business, though, is it?" I counter his comment.

"Would you like it to be my business, Courtney?" His words come out as a raspy whisper as his hand moves up to my shoulder.

I lift my head to meet his brown eyes, looking back at me. I open my mouth to speak, but I don't know what to say.

"Courtney," Josh whispers.

"Josh," I whisper back.

"I don't know why, but I really hate Kai."

"Okay," I reply as I feel my legs stretch up to lift my face even closer to his.

Josh's hand slides off my shoulder onto the back of my neck, the same spot he held onto the other night when we were at the bar.

"You're too young for me," Josh says, though it's barely audible.

"Josh."

"Yes?"

"Shut the hell up," I demand still using a whispering tone.

I barely stop speaking before Josh pulls me hard by the back of the neck and rams his lips into mine. Kissing him feels like no other kiss I've ever experienced before. His lips are strong, and now that he's in the moment, there is no hesitation in his actions.

There's a slight stubble that rubs against my skin. It burns, but I like it. I raise my hand and press my palm to his jawline. Suddenly, I feel Josh's tongue slipping past my lips with eagerness. God, this man knows what he's doing.

My other hand no longer hangs loosely at my side but now rests on his hip bone. As he pulls me into his body tighter, I can't help but release a slight moan, which is quickly followed by a wave of embarrassment.

Josh doesn't seem to notice or mind because he's still devouring my lips with his.

"This is a bad idea," Josh mutters, his lips still attached to mine.

"The worst idea," I agree, though not pulling away in the slightest.

"I'm too old for you."

"I could lose my job," I admit.

"We should stop."

"Yes," I agree.

"I don't want to stop, Courtney," Josh confesses in return but then slowly pulls back. "But I should. I'm sorry."

I lower my hand from Josh's face and take a step back. I can still taste him on my lips when I lick them.

"Why are you sorry?"

Josh slips his hands into his pockets and looks down at the ground. "Because it was inappropriate. I should know better. I don't want to take advantage of you."

I can't help but laugh.

"I can decide who I want to kiss, and I want to kiss you. Even though you drive me crazy."

"I drive *you* crazy?" Josh's eyes widen with shock.

"Yes. You are moody and bossy. Oh, and pouty when you get jealous," I say and give him a wicked smirk.

Josh doesn't grin back but rather stares down at me with a scowl.

"Which way do you live so I can walk you home?"

"You don't have to walk me home, Josh. I can go by myself."

"You're not walking alone in the dark by yourself. I want to make sure you get home safe."

"I do it every night."

"Well, that's ridiculous. Let's go."

Josh stands up straight and furrows his brow as he waits for me to take the lead. I roll my eyes and begin walking in the direction of my apartment.

"Are you going to chaperone me home every night now?"

"I might," Josh says as he keeps pace with me.

We walk in silence. This is the first time since I moved here that someone has offered to walk me home to ensure I arrive safely. It's unsettling to receive this type of caring. I have been trying hard to be completely independent, but now I feel conflicted. Not that I mind his company, but I have been enjoying my independence very much since I left Greensly over a year ago.

Moving to Elmerson was my chance to start again, get away from the guilt and pressure placed on me by my family and Dylan. For the first time in six years, I have been free to be myself and do what I want, and I will not let some guy tell me any different. No matter how stupidly hot he is.

Chapter 8

Josh

I'm sitting at my large, black desk at the Bolder Crest Law Office. In front of me is a stack of folders awaiting my attention, but I can't seem to concentrate on anything. The tiny brunette with pale skin and piercing blue eyes pressing her lips against mine has taken up a permanent residency in my mind.

I shouldn't have kissed Courtney last night. I don't know what I was thinking. What I should have done is what I normally do. Finished supper with Isabelle, taken her back up to my room, slept with her, and sent her along her way. I know for a fact that she would have been up for that—I could tell throughout supper how she continuously licked her lips and reached over to circle my palm with her finger.

When she returned to my room with me because her jacket was up there, and she tried to kiss me, I stopped her without a second thought. However, when she offered to give me a blowjob, I couldn't refuse. After she finished, I gave her some lame-ass excuse about an early meeting, and I sent her off without even bothering to open the red wine I had Courtney bring up.

I smile when I think about Courtney, who was all fired up when I said I had asked for white wine. Honestly, I had no clue what kind of wine I asked for, but God, seeing her fired up did something to me.

We didn't speak much when I walked her home last night. When we finally reached the small white building a few blocks away, Courtney turned quickly, saying I could go. I think she was embarrassed to have me see where she lived. There was no doubt that the building had seen better days. It was white, though the paint was chipping badly, showing the building's original brown in some spots. The concrete steps that led up to the main door were cracked. The area itself didn't look too shady, but this building was a disaster.

We parted ways without another kiss, which was probably for the best. Except now, kissing her again is all I can think about.

I wonder if she will be working tonight. Even if I only get a glimpse of her in the lobby, I'll take what I can get. I don't want to do anything to jeopardize her job since I know how important it is to her.

I don't know what's wrong with my head right now. I force myself to focus on the files in front of me. I have to prep for this case; it's why I'm in Elmerson—to work on a big case, get a big bonus, and get away from Brighten for a while. I need to keep my head in the game, and pursuing a woman will not benefit my long-term plan—it will only be a distraction.

By the time I arrive back at the hotel, I'm utterly exhausted. Once I composed myself, I was able to get a ton of work done. My eyes are killing me from staring at my computer screen for the last five hours. I plan to order room service, take a hot shower, and do nothing else for this evening. I usually try to fit in a workout or a run in the evenings, but tonight, I can't. I will have to get up early tomorrow morning to make up for the workout I'm missing.

I walk through the lobby and immediately scan for Courtney. I had decided earlier that whatever was going on between us could go no further—but that doesn't mean I can't look, right? Unfortunately, I don't see her as I walk past the concierge desk and continue toward the elevators without hesitation. I wonder if she has the day off work?

The answer is presented to me when the doors open to the first available elevator. The doors slide open to reveal Courtney standing in her perfectly pressed burgundy blouse, tight pencil skirt, and her hair twisted tight in a smooth bun at the back of her head. When our eyes meet, a small smile forms on her lips. She steps out of the elevator but pauses at the door, instinctively reaching her arm back to hold the door from closing before I step inside.

"Good evening, Mr. Hayles," her sweet voice says as I walk past her.

I can smell her perfume, which reminds me of a sweet apple orchard. I take a moment to bask in the smell before responding. I imagine grabbing her arm and pulling her into the elevator with me, wondering how much time alone we would have before the cart arrives on my floor.

"Ms. Morgan," I reply as I step into the elevator and press my floor button.

Our eyes meet briefly before Courtney releases the doors, and they slowly move to a close. Once the cart begins to move, I realize I have been holding my breath. I lean back on the elevator wall and close my eyes for a moment. I must get this woman out of my head.

I've spent the entire evening in my room trying to occupy my mind with basketball on TV and takeout from a local noodle house. My goal is to avoid Courtney at all costs. It's unfair for me to lead her on, knowing this can't go any further.

I check the time on my phone while the sounds of the post-game show rumbles in the background. It's 10:45 p.m., and instantly, I think about Courtney getting off work in fifteen minutes and walking back to her apartment alone in the dark. I shake the thought from my mind and think about the countless nights she has done this before. She doesn't need me to take care of her. On the other hand, I really want to take care of her. I want to make sure she gets home safe, and if I'm honest, I want to be near her.

I continue my internal debate for another five minutes before I drag myself off the king-sized bed and get dressed to meet Courtney at the side door she left through the night before.

I pull on the pair of jeans lying on the end of my bed and grab a T-shirt from the dresser drawer. Shoving on my black Nikes and tossing a black jacket over my green T-shirt, I head out of my room.

I check the time when I get around the side of the building. My phone reads 11:02 p.m. Assuming Courtney will be changing after her shift again, I lean against the wall and swipe through some apps on my phone while I wait for her.

Ten minutes pass by when I hear the door creak open, and Courtney walks into the alleyway. She's dressed very similarly to how she was yesterday, but instead of a hoodie, she's wearing a dark gray knitted sweater that hangs well below her waist. She has on a pair of black knitted boots, too, the kind with rubber soles. Her same backpack is slung over her shoulders.

I stand tall when she turns, greeting me with a bright smile.

"Hey, you're not smoking tonight," Courtney observes. "What are you doing out here?"

"I'm going to walk you home again," I say as I clear my throat.

"Josh, I don't need a chaperone. I'm a big girl. I'll be okay," Courtney rolls her eyes.

I shake my head. "I'm not here to be your chaperone, Courtney. I'm here because I want to make sure you're safe."

"So, a chaperone?" Courtney mocks me.

"Let's go," I shake my head and begin to walk in the direction of her apartment.

We walk side by side down the street, lit up in an orange glow from the streetlights overhead. At first, we walk quietly down the empty sidewalk. I can tell she is nervous because her fingers keep fidgeting with the cuffs of her sweater.

As we round the first block, the smell of deep-fried food lingers in the air. Instantly, my stomach rumbles.

"Are you hungry?" I ask Courtney as the lights of a nearby diner come into view.

"A little," Courtney replies.

"Want to stop for something to eat at this diner?"

"Sure," Courtney says, a small smirk emerging.

We walk towards the diner in silence.

It's a twenty-four-hour restaurant. The entire place smells of old coffee. There are only a handful of other patrons here—one booth with an older couple and three individuals sitting up at the counter. I lead the way to the back of the diner and slide into an empty booth, where the bench is covered in red faux leather seats and a white table. Courtney takes the seat across from me.

"You're quiet," I comment as she unbuttons her heavy sweater to reveal a teal shirt underneath.

"I'm just a little nervous," she replies quietly.

"How come?" I ask with one eyebrow raised.

Before she can reply, our server walks up to our booth. She is an older lady with gray curly hair. Wearing black dress pants and a white T-shirt, her name tag reads Olive, and she looks as bitter as one, too.

"What can I get you?" The server asks us, but her eyes do not leave her paper pad.

"I'll have a coke, please," Courtney says.

"Coffee for me," I answer. "We'll need a few more minutes with the menu," I mention as Olive has already started to walk away.

"We better pick out what we want by the time she returns with our drinks because I'm not sure she'll be back after that."

Courtney smiles at my remark as her deep blue eyes scan the plastic-covered menu.

"I think I'm gonna get the cheeseburger," Courtney says decisively and places her menu in front of her.

"So, tell me why you're nervous?" I ask, still thinking about her statement from earlier.

Courtney shrugs her shoulders. "I don't know. Maybe nervous isn't the right word. Maybe I'm worried that you think what happened with us last night was a mistake."

"It was a mistake," I say bluntly.

Courtney's eyes quickly dart up to mine. "Oh, then why are we here? And please don't tell me it's because you think I need you to walk me home."

I placed my menu in front of me and folded my hands on top.

"Honestly, I don't know why I'm here. You and I, as *anything* is wrong, Courtney. For Christ's sake, I'm almost ten years older than you."

"That doesn't matter..." Courtney begins to speak, but I cut her off.

"No, listen to me. I'm almost ten years older than you. I don't live here, so you could lose your job. Do I need to go on? This," I wave my fingers in between us, "is a terrible idea."

"Tell me, Josh, why are you here?"

I inhale a deep breath and exhale slowly before replying to the big eyes staring at me, desperately searching for an answer. I lower my head down for a moment, trying to come up with the best response.

"Honestly, I don't know," I chuckle slightly at the stupidity of my answer. "I like being around you, Courtney. Everything seems lighter around you. I don't know if that makes sense. But you're just you. You're not trying to be someone you're not, and sometimes I feel like I'm surrounded only by people pretending to be someone else solely to get what they want."

Courtney's mouth drops open slightly.

"Holy shit, Josh. I have never heard you say so many words at one time."

I scowl at her comment.

"Don't get me wrong. I like it," Courtney begins to smile at me. This softens my scowl. "I like hearing your unrehearsed thoughts..."

Courtney is interrupted by Olive arriving at our table carrying one Coke and coffee. She sets them down in the middle of the table. Not in front of us, just in the middle.

"We're going to order food as well," I let Olive know before she has a chance to leave. Courtney and I both order the deluxe burger with fries. She opts for gravy on the side, whereas I do not.

Once Olive leaves us alone again, Courtney continues, "As I was saying, I like you, Josh. I do."

"And my age doesn't bother you?" I ask.

"No. Why would it? I'm pretty sure you were as uptight in your twenties as you are now," Courtney grins at me and I release a small laugh.

"Yeah, you're right."

"Besides, I know you aren't as tough as you let on."

"Yeah? How do you know that?"

"Well, it's almost midnight, and you've insisted on walking me home twice now. Most people couldn't be bothered. So, no matter your age, I think you might be one of the good ones, Josh. I would like us to be…friends?"

"Sure, we can be friends, Courtney. But tell me, are you still *friends* with Kai?"

Courtney gives me a sly grin.

"No, not recently. Do you not want me to be *friends* with Kai?"

"The kind of *friends* you were before? No." I shake my head.

"What about you and Isabelle from the other night? Are you two '*friends*?'" Courtney uses air quotes around the word friends.

"No."

"Good," Courtney states as she looks down at her Coke and plays with the blue plastic straw. "I didn't like her."

"Oh?" I egg her on.

"Nah. She's probably high maintenance, anyway." Courtney lets her jealous side shine through. "Enough talk about our other friends. Tell me more about you."

"Like what?"

"Well, you're a lawyer, right? Do you like your work?"

"It's alright."

"That's all you're giving me: it's alright?"

"What do you want me to say?"

"I don't know. Is it your passion? Do you feel like you're making a difference in the world?"

I can't help but laugh at Courtney's youthful optimism.

"No, I don't think I'm making a difference in the world. I think I'm making a bunch of rich people happy when they have legal troubles, and I make them go away."

"And you like that?" Courtney grimaces at my response.

"It doesn't matter if I like it or not. It's my job."

Before Courtney can respond, Olive arrives with our food. This time, she sets a plate down in front of each of us. I notice Courtney's gravy is placed on the side of my plate.

"You have my gravy," Courtney notes as Olive walks away from the table.

"You know what they say? Possession is nine-tenths of the law," I grumble.

"So, are you saying you won't give me my gravy?"

"No, I'm saying that you are going to pay me if you want your gravy."

"What kind of payment?"

I crook my finger and lean my large frame over the table, trying not to drag my clothes through my food. Courtney half stands and reaches her upper torso over the table.

"You are such a..."

Before she has a chance to finish her sentence, I press my lips into hers. It's only been twenty-four hours since I last kissed her, but it feels like it's been too long.

We don't linger long since we are kissing in the most uncomfortable way. But I got what I was looking for, and when we both sit back in our spots, I hand her the gravy dish.

We spend the rest of our meal talking about all sorts of things: our likes and dislikes, where we're from, and so on. I find out Courtney is from a small town named Greensly, which she had mentioned to me before. She is scarce about the details of her family.

"So, you moved here all on your own at twenty? That's pretty brave of you," I note before taking a bite out of my burger, dripping mustard onto the plate below.

"Well, technically, I was nineteen turning twenty when I moved here, but yeah, I did it on my own. Unfortunately, staying in Greensly was no longer an option. I knew if I didn't leave, I would probably end up dying there."

"That's a pretty serious statement."

"Are you implying that I'm being dramatic?" Courtney asks while cocking her one eyebrow. I smirk because I had been implying that.

"Well, I'm curious: what was so bad there that you felt you had to leave?"

"That's a long story, and I think it would be best to save it for another day. Unless you want to unload all your skeletons tonight with me?"

"Hell, no!" I reply quickly.

"Exactly," Courtney laughs while grabbing her glass of Coke and holding it up above the table. "Here's to avoiding depressing conversations and focusing on the positive."

"Hear, hear," I nod along with her sentiment.

"So, to change the subject, do you enjoy being a lawyer?"

"Well, I enjoy the money of being a lawyer," I answer honestly. "The work is what it is."

"Why did you decide to become a lawyer?"

"Because it's what was expected of me. My father and older brother are both lawyers, so naturally, I would be a lawyer, too." I take a sip of my coffee and realize it has gone cold. I look over my shoulder for Olive so I can get a fresh cup.

"What did you want to be when you were younger?" Courtney asks with her eyes shining brightly.

"What do you mean?" I ask.

"Well, I assume you weren't dreaming of being a lawyer when you were a little boy." Her giggle rings in my ears and makes me smile. "Unless you're trying to tell me that you wore suits and carried your lunch box like a briefcase? Did you object when your teacher asked you to colour inside the lines?"

I laugh along with her ridiculous vision.

"No, I suppose you're right. I wasn't dreaming of becoming a lawyer when I was young."

"Damn, because you, as a little kid in his little suit, would have been so freaking adorable."

"What about me in a suit now, not so adorable?"

"Adorable isn't the word I would use to describe the way you look now," Courtney gives me a smirk.

"Oh, and what word would you use?" I flirt back.

Before Courtney can answer my question, Olive returns to our table. We are finished eating by now and she begins to clear away the dirty dishes. When she returns with the bill, I promptly pull out my credit card to pay for the food.

"You don't have to do that," Courtney protests. "You should let me pay since you are walking me home."

"Trust me, you'll pay me back in another way," I say to her, winking as her cheeks turn pink.

When we leave the restaurant, it's well past midnight. We aren't far from Courtney's apartment, and I walk slowly to prolong our time together. We are only a few paces outside the restaurant when I feel Courtney reach over and intertwine her arm with mine. With a tug, she presses my arm tight into her body.

"Sexy," Courtney leans up and whispers in my ear.

"What?" I ask while slowing my steps to a virtual stop.

"Before, when you asked me how I would describe you in a suit now. I would say that you're sexy."

I turn to face her, though keeping our arms locked tight.

"Is that so? That doesn't sound very professional of you, Miss Morgan, checking out your guests while you're on duty."

"Not all the guests, just one," Courtney grins at me. "He's my favourite."

A shiver of excitement courses through my body as I watch her eyes sparkle with vulnerability. I don't look at her for long before I reach up with my free hand and cup her cheek, pulling her towards me. She must've raised herself to her toes because she became closer to me instantly. Our lips touch lightly at first, pressing together with purpose, not haste. Our mouths open slightly to release a rush of warm breath between us before we press together again—this time, there is more desperation.

Standing on the sidewalk in the middle of the night, I feel like I'm getting a first kiss do-over. I can't remember the last time I kissed someone with this much ferocity. There is so much feeling behind it. This is not a kiss with the end goal of sex in mind; this is a kiss of a beginning.

Chapter 9

Courtney

My lips are puffy today. I run my fingers over them slowly as I remember the number of times I kissed Josh last night—there was the kiss over the table at the diner for my gravy; the kiss outside the diner, which was mesmerizing; and there was the kissing, or rather full-out makeout session, on the stoop of my apartment. The tenderness of the earlier kisses vanished as Josh and I became ravenous. Josh had me pressed up against the wall of my building as his mouth and tongue took over while his hands wandered beneath my shirt, grasping at my breasts. I'm not sure if it was the coldness of the winter air or the intense arousal I was experiencing, but my entire body shook.

I recall running the tip of my tongue over his stubbled jaw with beckoning breaths flowing through my lungs. He smelled of a rich, musky aftershave. As I made my way beneath his jaw, I could hear his breath quicken as his pelvis pressed into my stomach. I let my tongue wander over his neck with tiny kisses that followed. His skin tasted salty. I couldn't get enough—I was hooked.

It's been twelve hours since Josh said goodnight on the stoop, declining my invitation to come inside. I'm lying here reliving it over and over. I roll onto my stomach to check the time, the double-sized bed squeaking beneath with every movement. The clock on my single nightstand reads 2:04 p.m. I have just under two hours until I have to be at work. I should get up and shower, but my daydreams keep returning me to Josh.

I turn onto my back, dragging the light blue comforter with me as I go. I tuck myself up into my self-made cocoon once more. I'll give myself fifteen more minutes to reminisce before I get up. I face the window directly above my mattress and close my eyes. I should invest in some thicker curtains, I think to myself. The white sheers are terrible at blocking out sunlight. Since my tiny apartment is less than three hundred square feet, it's the only window and pretty much the only wall my bed could go against. My apartment is basically a rectangle with my bed against the far wall, the kitchen against the opposite wall and a small table with two chairs in between. On the wall adjacent to my bed is a dresser. There is one closet at the front door and a tiny bathroom tucked behind the kitchen wall. There is no large soaker tub for me, only a small stall shower, toilet, and sink. Overall, I love my place. I found it, and I pay for it. Despite the yellowing of the walls and the matted-down carpet on the floor, it's my own.

Six hours later, I sit at the concierge desk, trying to catch my breath. There have been non-stop demands since I arrived. We had a wedding party check into the suites, and the term *bridezilla* comes to mind. I've been busy making reservations for the wedding parties' stag and stagette parties. Not to mention finding tickets for the parents to the newest Broadway show and being the messenger between the happy couple and our events department, I'm exhausted. Unfortunately, I haven't seen Josh enter the lobby amidst all the chaos. I check the time on my computer screen as I look up the rest of our arrivals for the evening, as it's already past eight o'clock. Surely, he should be back from the office by now.

As I scroll through the computer screen, I hardly notice the guest arriving in front of me. The stunning woman, who looks around forty, taps her fingernails impatiently on the counter. Her hair is lying straight and tucks into a perfect bob just above her shoulders. Immediately, I recognize her as the bride's older sister.

"Ms. Perrin," I stand as I greet her. "What can I do for you?"

"It's Mrs. Perrin, and my husband and I would like reservations at Vix for nine," she demands cooly.

"Nine o'clock tonight?" I confirm in shock. "I will definitely try, though that is less than an hour away, and Vix is a very popular restaurant. A last-minute reservation may be difficult."

"Well, it's what we want, and I thought it was your job to make that happen?" She turns her nose upwards with a huff.

"Absolutely, Mrs. Perrin. Please give me a moment, and I'll see what I can do."

I pick up my cell and search for Vix's saved number. I know this is a fruitless act since the chance of getting a last-minute reservation is almost impossible.

Of course, the hostess who answers the phone all but laughs hysterically at my request. As I explain to Mrs. Perrin that a reservation is impossible for this evening, Josh walks up to the desk.

Standing beside Mrs. Perrin, Josh dons athletic wear, like he is heading to the gym, and looks casually gorgeous. He must have come through the lobby earlier when I was preoccupied.

Even Mrs. Perrin takes notice of Josh and immediately softens her scowling face, batting her eyelashes at him.

"I apologize for the interruption, ladies. I couldn't help but overhear that you require a dinner reservation for this evening?" Josh smiles charmingly towards Mrs. Perrin, who all but melts to the floor.

"Yes, but we were not able to get into Vix. Unfortunately, the staff member is not being very helpful," Mrs. Perrin glances in my direction.

"Well, might I suggest Kleins. It's not as well-known as Vix, but the dining experience I had with some colleagues there was fantastic. In fact, it was this wonderful employee who recommended it to me. Isn't that correct, Courtney?"

"Yes, Mr. Hayles," I play along with Josh's blatant lie.

"Trust me, Ms...." Josh trails off.

"Perrin." Mrs. Perrin doesn't bother correcting him regarding her correct title, as she did to me earlier.

"Trust me, Ms. Perrin, you will not be disappointed." Josh produces a warm smile, and Mrs. Perrin blushes before turning back to me.

"Call and make the reservation. You can call my room to confirm," Mrs. Perrin demands.

"Yes, ma'am."

"Good evening, Mr. Hayles," Mrs. Perrin tosses a wink in Josh's direction and presses her hand on his bicep. It's all I can do not to jump over this desk and strangle her.

"Ms. Perrin," Josh nods as she turns to walk away.

Before I can thank Josh for helping me out, he lifts his hand to the desktop and lays down a single white lily. He offers me a small smirk from the corner of his mouth.

"It's a nice night for a walk, perhaps around eleven." Josh turns, walking towards the hotel fitness facility.

My grin widens as Josh walks away, picking up the lily. I run my fingers over the velvety petals, and giddiness fills my chest. I check the time and begin the countdown to the end of my shift.

Chapter 10

Josh

It's been two weeks since I began walking Courtney home every night she works, and it's been phenomenal. We talk and laugh; sometimes, we stop at the diner on our way to her place, and sometimes, we don't. Some nights, we sit on the stairs leading up to her apartment and talk for hours. On other nights, we make out like mad before parting ways. Often, on those nights, Courtney will ask me to come upstairs, to which I reluctantly decline.

In an attempt to be chivalrous and not rush things too fast, I have said no. But God, do I want to go up. Spending the night with Courtney is all I can think of, but I have been resisting it.

I've been living on minimal sleep these days. Between going into the office early to keep up with the demands of this case and staying up late with Courtney, coffee and energy drinks have become my new best friends. On Courtney's days off from the hotel, we text throughout the day until I'm done work. Then, we meet at the little diner near her place for a late supper—that's where I'm headed tonight.

This is Courtney's second day off in a row, and due to my crazy schedule yesterday and client meeting last night, we couldn't meet up. I haven't seen her in almost two days, and I feel like I will crawl out of my skin if I don't see her soon.

Spending the days at work without her is bad enough, but knowing I will see her when I return to the hotel makes my day more bearable—but not seeing her at all? It's torture.

As I round the corner towards the diner, I look up and see her in the distance. We've been fortunate to have had an unusually warm February, but it seems Mother Nature is not quite done with winter yet, despite it already being the beginning of March. Tiny snowflakes are falling from the dark sky. The air is cold, and my ears are burning from the sharp wind.

Courtney's long dark hair blows in the wind despite being held down with a teal-knitted beanie. A black wool coat is wrapped tightly around her body, and her hands are stuffed in its pockets. She's about to pull the door to the diner open when she spots me heading towards her. She lets her hand fall from the silver door handle and briskly walks towards me. I don't have the chance to say hello before her arms fling around my neck. Instinctively, my arms wrap around Courtney's torso. Her face buries itself into the crook of my neck. The coldness of her bare flesh presses onto my warm skin, and it feels sensational.

I push my lips onto her hair, just beside her ear—the smell of her shampoo tingles through my nose. Now, I'm sure it's tangerine.

"You're cold, baby," I whisper to Courtney, and as the words tumble off my lips, I feel a shock through my body. I've never called anyone *baby* before. Before I get too lost in my thoughts, Courtney lifts her face from my neck.

"I've missed you."

"God, I've missed you, too," I reply as I wrap my arms tighter around her back. "Do you want to skip dinner and go to your place?"

"Seriously?" Courtney pulls her head back and looks into my eyes. She seems surprised since I've done nothing but avoid going to her place for the last two weeks.

"Yeah, I don't want to stop touching you, and I don't think Olive will be too happy to serve us with our hands all over each other."

"I don't want to stop, either," Courtney presses a small kiss onto the corner of my mouth. "Let's go before your morals kick in, and you decide to become a gentleman again." Courtney releases my neck from her arms and grabs my hand swiftly with hers.

Before I know it, I'm being dragged through the dark streets as heavier snow begins to fall around us. Minutes later, we are standing in front of Courtney's apartment as she unlocks the front door to the building.

"Okay, but I think I should warn you about my place before we go up there."

"Okay?" I answer hesitantly.

"It's small—like really small. Smaller than your hotel suite. Though, I don't want you to think I'm ashamed of it because I'm not. I worked hard to get this place all by myself and I've made it my own. I just don't want you to feel uncomfortable because I know you're used to a more upscale lifestyle."

"Are you calling me pretentious?" I mumble as we begin to climb the stairs to the floor above. Courtney ignores my question.

The building's inside needs attention as much as its outside. The walls are yellowed, though I assume they used to be white, are cracked and peeling. The brown stairs creak with each step we take, and the air smells faintly of pot.

When we arrive on the second floor, Courtney leads me to the door labelled 203. She unlocks the two locks of the door and pushes it open. Courtney walks in ahead of me and turns on the light located right above us, which illuminates the small area in front of the doorway.

As we move inside and close the door behind us, the smell of pot from the hallway disappears, and my nose is met with a sweet smell of vanilla. Courtney then turns on another light, which lights up the rest of the room—well, actually, it's the rest of the apartment. She was right. It's small—no, it's tiny. It's a tiny studio apartment which I'm guessing is around three hundred square feet, maximum. It's basically an open rectangle with the kitchen at one end and her bed at the other, under the only window in the space.

While it is indeed small, it radiates Courtney. The small table near the kitchen is covered with a bright yellow tablecloth and in the center is a small milk glass vase, holding three bright pink flowers.

The kitchen is basic, with a single stainless-steel sink and a built-in three-foot-tall mini fridge. There are a few light oak cupboards, and the white countertop holds a toaster oven and a single hot plate.

Her bed is small, maybe the size of a double, which is small compared to the California king I've been sleeping on at the hotel—but its light blue cover and puffed pillows look inviting.

"Are you underwhelmed?" Courtney asks as I continue to scan the space. "It's really not so bad…"

Before she can continue to defend her tiny apartment, I stop her by grabbing her arm and pulling her into my chest.

"It's perfect," I tell her, which causes a large grin to erupt on her face.

"I'm glad you like it. Now, let me take your coat."

I realize she's correct, and we're still in our jackets from the cold walk here. I hand her my coat, and she takes it over to closet by the front door and hangs it up with hers.

"The bathroom is through here," Courtney points to a door opposite the closet.

I nod as I decide between pulling out one of two chairs at the table or sitting on the bed. I walk over to the bed because it looks the most inviting. Sitting on the edge of the mattress, I motion with my finger for her to come over to me.

Within an instant, Courtney is in front of me. Now that she has removed her coat, I can see a royal blue knitted sweater, which brings out the blue of her eyes even more so than usual. Her legs are covered in black leggings and thick wool socks cover her feet. I spread my legs apart to have her stand in between them, and her head is towering over mine for a change.

"So, I finally got you in my bed, Mr. Hayles." Courtney places her hands on my shoulders and looks down at me, her dark hair hanging over us.

I run my hands slowly up the backs of her thighs, closer to her perky ass—the same ass I've been staring at for weeks now. As my hands move over her firm cheeks, I can feel myself perk up and harden, remembering that I'm wearing jeans, so my arousal won't be too noticeable.

Courtney leans closer to me and brings her face to mine and darts her tongue quickly over her lips to moisten them. Our lips barely come together before our tongues force into each other's mouths. I raise my hands to Courtney's back and encourage her to follow me as I lie down on her bed. Our lips don't separate as we move into the position, Courtney laying completely over me—she feels so goddamn good on top of me.

Soon, Courtney wiggles her legs up to straddle me, which puts pressure on my hardness, and I can't help but let out a groan. It feels so good. She hears this and grinds herself harder into me, planting tiny kisses on my neck.

"You're teasing me," I growl as she continues to rub herself over me.

"I know," she replies.

"You don't want to play this game, Tiny Bird," I say.

"Are you sure I don't want to play? I might be pretty good at this game, you know. In fact," Courtney grinds down harder onto me as she tosses her hair back and lets out a little moan. "I might just be better than you, Mr. Hayles."

I laugh at her display of confidence. How is this young woman so confident in her sexuality? Her brazen attitude drives me crazy—it takes all my strength not to roll her over and take her so hard that she need not question my abilities again.

"You're pretty sure of yourself," I say as I grab her thighs, which are clung against my torso.

Courtney takes her hands and runs them under the bottom of my T-shirt. She slides them to the bulge of each of my pectorals, teasing my nipples slightly along the way. Her hips are moving in a slow circular motion over my pelvis. If I'm not careful, I'm going to lose it.

In an instant, I flip her over to the other side of the bed and climb on top of her, making sure to keep her legs straddled around my waist. Courtney is small enough in size that the maneuver is easily performed.

Once I'm on top of her, I waste no time pulling her blue sweater up to expose her breasts, which are covered in a light pink bra.

"Bloody hell," I curse the fabric that stands between me and her perky nipples.

Roughly, I grab the lacy material and pull it down harshly to expose the hard bud that I was in search of. In no time, I bring my tongue down to swirl around it. It tastes like an inexplicable euphoria.

I feel Courtney's back pushing upwards in response to my touch. I take the opportunity to pull the clinging shirt further up and over her head and arms. Tossing it aside, I work on the straps of her pink bra, pulling them off her shoulders quickly. I want my prize, and I want it now. Forcefully, I shove the lacy-wired cups down towards her belly, which allows my mouth to return to her perky mounds without any barriers.

I want to devour this woman underneath me despite the sporadic waves of guilt I feel knowing she's so much younger than me. Even if I wanted to dwell in my guilt longer, I'm distracted when Courtney's fingers run through my hair as her body twitches underneath me.

I raise my head and bring my lips back to hers, which are slightly opened as she breathes heavily through her mouth.

"We should stop," I force myself to say.

"Are you kidding me right now? I want you, Josh. I want you so fucking bad," Courtney responds as her heels dig deep into my ass, pushing me harder against her.

"I know, but I haven't earned you yet." I hardly recognize my voice as the words tumble out of my mouth. This is not the type of man I am. When I get a chance to screw, I screw—and then I leave. Here I am talking this beautiful woman out of sleeping with me. What is wrong with me?

"What do you mean you haven't earned it?"

I pull myself further away from her pouty expression and softly push the vagrant strand of hair away from her face.

"Courtney, you don't realize how special you are, do you? I haven't even taken you out on a proper date, and I want to. I want to do everything with you but in due time."

"Oh, no. Did Gentleman Josh return? I was hoping he wouldn't be back for a while." Courtney reaches up and runs her fingers slowly over my jawbone. "Where is bad Josh? I want him to come back."

Ugh, this girl is making it hard to do the right thing.

Before I can think too long, I bring my hand over her tight stomach and inch my fingers into her leggings. The lower I get, the more Courtney opens her legs for me. I find her more ready than I anticipated.

"Okay, I'll stay for a little while longer," I growl as I push a single finger inside of her. Courtney closes her eyes with a slight moan.

"Open your eyes." When she opens to respond to my demand, I continue, "We'll play until you cum, but that's it for tonight."

"But I..."

Courtney's protest is cut short when I insert another finger and press my thumb deeper into her folds.

"Don't argue with me," I hiss as I move my mouth back down to her still-attentive breasts that are begging for my attention.

After a quick nip with my front teeth, I tell her, "Tonight is for you, baby. Don't worry about me, I'll get my turn. I always do."

With that, I get to work on bringing Courtney to the most erotic orgasm I have ever heard.

Chapter 11

Courtney

I'm dying. Well, I'm not literally dying, but I have never orgasmed that hard in my life. We haven't even slept together yet—all of that from just his hand.

I'm still panting hard as Josh kisses me up the side of my neck.

"Oh my God," I finally say, which causes Josh to rumble out a small laugh. "Oh my God."

"I'll take that as my 'thank you,'" Josh mumbles in my ear.

I turn towards him so that we are facing each other.

"I want more," I whisper with a smile.

Josh leans into me with a smirk. "You're a greedy woman, aren't you?"

I bite my lip and nod as his brown eyes devour me.

"Not tonight," Josh replies.

"But I owe you," I argue as I bring my hand over his waist, which is still covered. In fact, he hasn't removed any clothes while I lay here topless.

"Not tonight." Josh kisses the tip of my nose.

I roll over in frustration. This is the first time I've ever had a guy turn me down, and it feels like shit. But I guess Josh isn't like the guys I've been with in the past. Josh isn't a guy at all; he's a man.

"Stop thinking so much and stop pouting," Josh says as he pulls me back into his embrace.

I nuzzle my face into his broad shoulder. Josh smells so good, like spice and cloves. Once my body relaxes into him, Josh continues with his lecture.

"Believe me, Tiny Bird, I have big plans for you. However, if you pout every time you don't get your way, then I will have to punish you." Josh grabs the back of my hair and pulls it until I look straight up into his eyes.

"I don't take kindly to being bossed around, Joshua," I reply defiantly.

"I know you don't, and that's why this will be so much fun." Josh gives me a wink without breaking his stoic face.

"I knew you were an ass from the moment I met you."

"Uh-huh—and that's why you couldn't stay away."

"What? You're the one who insisted on walking me home every night."

"You think I didn't notice you checking me out? That first day when you saw me in my towel, you practically came on the spot."

"Oh, please. I couldn't stand you." My eyes instinctively roll.

"Oh, really?" Josh says sternly as he glares at me.

"Really!" I retort. There's no way I'm backing down now.

We stare at each other so intensely that I can't tell if we are flirting or fighting at this point.

"Can you stand me now?" Josh continues his death stare.

"Hardly," I say without any emotion in return.

Slowly, Josh brings his hand towards his mouth and touches his fingers to the tip of his tongue. "Tough talk from someone I can still taste on my finger."

I stare at him in shock. My heart is pounding fiercely inside my chest. I'm actually speechless.

"Cat got your tongue, Courtney?" Josh slowly pushes my body until I'm lying flat on my back, still topless, which he takes advantage of as his fingers brush over my breast.

"I think I want to taste more," Josh whispers into my ear. "Is that okay with you?"

I can't even speak, so I nod before his mouth claims mine again. However, our kiss is brief before he slides himself down the bed, taking the rest of my clothes with him.

His face disappears between my thighs, and the sharpness of his stubble makes me wince slightly, but only for a moment. The rough stubble is nothing compared to the heat of his tongue, as he claims me with every lick. For the second time tonight, I orgasm harder than I ever have before. By the time I come down from Josh's efforts between my legs, I forget what we were disagreeing about.

Josh kisses his way back up my body. When he reaches my neck, he pulls the blanket from the side of me and covers my naked body before he nuzzles his face into the crook of my shoulder.

"You're the sweetest creature I've ever tasted. You're ruining me, Courtney."

"I was not expecting that," I admit out loud. "I thought you were mad at me?" I laugh at my statement.

Josh laughs in return. "Mad at you? Hell, no. I like the fight in you, Courtney. You keep me in line. I need more of that in my life."

"So, if you need more of that...What does that make me?" I ask.

Josh sits up and cups my cheek with his palm. "Yes, this is a real thing. I know it doesn't make sense. I'm so much older than you, but you make me feel things I didn't think I could feel. You make me..." Josh trails off.

"What?" I ask in a hushed voice.

"I don't know how to describe it. You make me...*feel*," Josh says softly. "I know that doesn't make much sense, but it's true. I didn't think I could feel like this for anyone, but you've got me wrapped tight around your finger, Courtney. You have no idea..."

Ding. The sound of Josh's cell phone startles us both. With a grunt of annoyance, Josh turns away from me and stands up from the bed. I watch as he walks the short distance across my tiny apartment to his jacket hanging in my single closet. He reaches into his pocket and retrieves his phone. He stands still beside the closet and reads the recent text message with a deep scowl.

"Shit," I hear Josh mumble.

"Is everything okay?" I ask while wrapping more of the blanket around my cold body.

Josh shakes his head and walks back over to the bed while tapping furiously on the screen of his phone. He sits back down on the side of the bed before he finishes his text message. When he's done, he sets the phone beside him and looks back in my direction.

"My father and brothers are coming for a few days. They've booked rooms at the hotel. They arrive tomorrow." Josh's shoulders are tense, and his voice has lost all softness that was present only moments ago.

"Is that a bad thing?" I ask.

"They're a pain in the ass. My father, mostly. Also, there's some shit he wants me to do while he's here."

"Oh," I say quietly, unsure how to reply.

"I'll be busy for the next few days."

"Okay."

The atmosphere in my apartment has shifted dramatically since the text message was received. I don't quite understand it. Josh has never opened up about his family much, except that his father seems kind of like an asshole and his brother slept with his girlfriend. I wonder if that brother is coming, too.

"Are all your brothers coming?" I ask.

"Yes." Josh picks up his phone again and begins tapping.

"Are you going to be okay?"

"With what?" Josh doesn't bother looking up from the screen.

"With your brother, who's married to your ex?"

Josh lets out a laugh that is more like a giant breath of air.

"Landry is the least of my problems. My father's the snake in the grass to be wary of."

"Um, do you want to talk about it?"

"No."

Not knowing what else to say, I roll onto my back and stare at the ceiling, waiting for Josh to finish his texting in silence. Josh must sense my discomfort because he slides back onto his side and lays beside me once he finishes with his phone.

"Listen, it's no big deal, Courtney. I'll be busy for a few days, and then things will return to normal, okay?"

"Josh, you don't owe me any explanation."

"Didn't I just tell you you're in my life now? So, yeah, I owe you something. Look, my family is complicated and messed up. I apologize in advance for anything stupid any one of them may say or do in the next few days. I don't envy you having to work while they're there," Josh laughs slightly. "You think I'm a pain in the ass, just wait."

"Josh, no one could be a bigger pain in my ass than you," I quip and smile back at the beautiful man beside me.

Josh grins brightly, making his dark eyes glow.

"I have to go," Josh says and presses a soft kiss on my lips. "I'll text you later, or I'll see you tomorrow afternoon at the hotel."

"Sure," I say softly while trying to hide my disappointment of his departure.

I look in silence as Josh gets up from my bed. He retrieves his jacket from the closet and opens the door. Before he leaves, Josh looks back at me.

"Lock the door behind me," he commands.

"Goodnight, Josh," I reply, ignoring the protective comment.

"Goodnight, Tiny Bird."

Chapter 12

Josh

I rub my sore eyes after staring at my computer screen for the last eight hours. These financial reports are killing me. Line after line, deposit after deposit. Shouldn't I have some young intern to do this work for me?

I'm tired today. Tired and agitated. The thought of my father and brothers arriving this evening ruined my night's sleep. I didn't realize how much I enjoyed my life here in Elmerson without them.

After the few hours I spent with Courtney in her apartment, I almost forgot the outside world existed. It took all the strength I had not to have sex with her last night. Even thinking about her firm body writhing under my touch and the taste of her is getting me hard. I shake Courtney from my thoughts, hoping to calm my erection.

I close the file in front of me and log off my computer. I'm done today. I check the time and see I have at least three hours until my family arrives. That should be enough time to get back to the hotel and have a long workout before they arrive. I need a stress reliever.

When I arrive back at the hotel a short time later, I instantly scan the lobby for Courtney. When I see her helping another guest at the concierge desk, I grunt in annoyance to myself as the man in the terrible brown suit occupies my girl's attention.

As I march past the desk, I know Courtney notices me as her eyes shoot briefly to mine, and the tiniest of smiles crawls across her face. Replying with nothing but a slight nod, I continue to walk straight to the elevators.

When I reach my floor, I immediately notice the table that holds the lilies is bare. No flowers, no vase: nothing. For a moment, I run my fingers across the beige marble tabletop and allow myself to miss the flowers. I love seeing the bright white lilies every time I exit the elevators. For some reason, it makes me feel a love I haven't had in years.

I don't linger long before I continue towards my room. Once inside, I change out of my charcoal gray suit and into my workout clothes. The black basketball shorts and tank top are much more comfortable than the suit.

I'm just about to slip into my running shoes when I hear a rapid knock on my door. For a moment, I freeze, dreading the thought that maybe my father had arrived early.

Pulling the door open, I'm greeted by a much more pleasant sight than my father. It's Courtney, and in her arms are three plush white towels.

"Good evening, Mr. Hayles. I have your towels," Courtney says innocently.

I look at her in confusion since I didn't order any towels, and even if I had, usually housekeeping would bring them up.

"Would you like me to place them on the shelf for you, Mr. Hayles?" Courtney stares at me with her large eyes, waiting for an answer.

"Sure?" I respond hesitantly.

Immediately, Courtney walks past me in my room while I close the door behind me.

"I didn't order any towels," I note as Courtney sets them on my desk.

"I know," she smirks as she turns to face me. "I have exactly fifteen minutes before anyone questions where I am—and I know how tense you are about your family arriving, so I thought, what could I do to help?" Courtney walks over to me and presses her body to mine. With her heels on, her forehead meets my mouth. "Is there anything I can do to help?" she whispers.

I clear my throat and my heart rate increases.

"Well, there are many things you could do, but I don't want you to get into trouble."

"Are you going to tell on me?" Courtney grabs my hand, leads me to my desk, and pulls at the rolling chair before pointing at me to sit.

Courtney leans forward and softly presses her lips to mine when I sit down on the black leather chair.

"I thought about you all night, Josh. Did you think about me?" Courtney's hand lands between my legs and grasps me.

"Of course," I reply with a husky breath. This was no lie—after returning from Courtney's place last night she was all I could think about.

"Good. Now, you're going to sit here like the gentleman that you are, and you're going to let me help you. Is that understood?"

"Are you bossing me around, Tiny Bird?" I growl.

"Never," Courtney says sweetly with a bat of her eyelashes before lowering herself to her knees.

I watch in awe as she moves in rhythm in front of me. I have to remind myself to breathe every few seconds. This might be the sexiest thing I've ever seen.

It's not long, embarrassingly, before I finish with a feral grunt. I'm still trying to regain my breath when Courtney stands before me, tucking everything back in place. She remains silent as she walks towards my washroom, and I hear her fumbling with my bottle of mouthwash.

When she returns to my living room area, I stand and take her into my arms. I kiss her harder than I've ever kissed her before. The taste of mint lingers on her tongue as I press her up against the nearby wall.

"That was amazing," I tell her when we finally pull apart.

"Do you feel better?"

"Yes. You do crazy things to me."

"I make you *feel*, right?" Courtney smiles and presses her hand to my chest, over my heart.

I press my hand over hers, allowing the moment to pass in silence.

"You make me *feel*," I finally reply.

"I have to go back to work now," Courtney mumbles as she presses her lips against my cheek. "Also, your family is arriving soon."

I can't help but groan, "Ugh, don't remind me."

"I'll see you around, Mr. Hayles."

Giving me one last kiss, Courtney turns and leaves my hotel suite.

Chapter 13

Courtney

I'm grinning to myself as I walk towards the elevator after leaving Josh's room. That was completely ridiculous and stupid of me to do to a guest in their room while on duty. It's more than enough to have me fired immediately—and yet, I couldn't help myself. Since he left last night, seeing him again is all I've been able to think about. Watching him come undone in front of me was more than worth the risk.

I feel giddy for the next few hours, recalling the image of Josh in his office chair. However, I'm also anxious. Waiting for the arrival of Josh's family makes me curious. I'm watching closely as guests come and go through the rotating doors.

I do not doubt that I will interact with his family at some point, considering his brothers are staying in gold suites like Josh, and his father reserved a platinum suite on the floor above. I checked their reservation earlier, and they are scheduled to spend three nights here, though I have no expectations of meeting them officially. Since any involvement with a guest is a big no-no, this thing I have with Josh needs to stay under wraps.

While I'm typing away at the computer, updating the guest request log, Milo comes up next to me in a hurry.

"Joshua Hayles' family has arrived. I spotted them getting out of their cars. Trust me, girl, you won't want to miss this. You know how good Josh looks, right? Well, multiply that by four because all these men are worth a second or third look," Milo says quietly as I finish typing my notes. I do not want to miss the Hayles men.

I can't see them while they are at the check-in desk. Two bellhops pass our desk with their luggage carts, so I know they will be walking by shortly.

The sound of formal shoes becomes increasingly louder as a brigade of men emerges. Josh's father must be in front because he is far older than the three men who follow behind. I checked his reservation before he arrived, and I know his name is David — in the notes, it says that he's the mayor of Brighten, a city about four hours away from here.

Josh's father is a tall man with broad shoulders, and his entire aura commands attention. His salt-and-pepper hair is perfectly styled, and not a single strand is out of place. His suit is a classic combination of black pants, jacket, and tie against a crisp white shirt.

Following close behind is an almost spitting image of the older man thirty years earlier. The only difference between the men was their suit colours—Josh's father opted for black, whereas his son's is navy. Josh told me his brothers' names weeks earlier, but I can't be sure who is who. I assume this man is older than Josh. He is also broader than Josh, and his hair is almost black, which matches his dark eyes. A deep scowl lines his forehead, not much different from the scowl line Josh wore all the time when he first arrived here.

Behind these two dominant men are two others. Both are equally handsome but nowhere near as formal. I knew one of them must be Landry, the brother who is now married to Josh's ex-girlfriend. I can't know for sure which one he is, but if I had to guess, I would think he's the taller one in black jeans and an olive-green hoodie. Under the hoodie's collar, I can see black lines of hidden tattoos. A silver ring pierced through his bottom lip, and a couple of earrings in each ear. Despite his tough-looking exterior, there seems to be a sadness in his dark eyes. He looks beautifully broken.

Finally, beside who I assume is Landry, is the youngest looking man of the four. He might be one of the cutest guys my age I have ever seen. I find most guys in their early twenties still haven't grown into their features yet, which is one of the reasons I find Josh so irresistible—he's all man. This younger one seems to have filled out already, and it's quite the sight. His hair is lighter than the other men, even lighter than Josh's chestnut brown hair. His eyes are a soft hazel, and he bears a single dimple on his left cheek. Unlike the other men, he looks relaxed and not so serious.

Milo and I are both standing in awe as the men move out of sight and enter the elevators.

"Holy shit, did that family hit the jackpot of the gene pool or what?" Milo says as he answers the phone, which has just started ringing.

I don't have time to bask in their looks because soon, there is another guest in need of assistance in front of me.

Milo and I run for the next couple of hours since the hotel is at ninety percent occupancy right now. Every department is swamped. As such, I'm not surprised when the kitchen calls to ask for assistance in an in-room service request. One server from the restaurant is preparing to take the food up on her own—as it turns out, the large order is going to a platinum suite, and she's a new employee, so we are helping out.

Milo is assisting a high-profile guest, a national news reporter, with itinerary scheduling. The guest and Milo have been slouched over the computer for almost an hour. I tell Milo that I'm headed up to the suites for meal service and have my phone if he needs me. Barely looking up from the screen, Milo gives me a quick wave before I head to the kitchen.

The kitchen is hot and humid when I arrive through the swinging doors. The smell of garlic is heavy in the air, and the entire space buzzes with voices and bodies.

"Behind!" I hear one person shout, followed by, "Who's on the vegetable station?"

As I weave through the servers, I spot Kai over a flaming grill. When he catches my eye, he throws me a quick wink. It's been weeks since we hung out.

"Well, if it isn't Ms. Mason. I forgot that you work here," Kai yells in my direction.

"Yeah, Court. Where have you been?" Steve asks from the dish pit.

"I'm a busy lady, boys. Very much in demand," I laugh as I find the carts prepped with the guest's food.

Immediately, I check the bill and see that this is going to the Hayles room, 1501. Butterflies tickle my insides, realizing that we are serving Josh's father and that there is a good chance Josh will be in that suite as well. I haven't seen Josh since our afternoon encounter in his room, and the memory of it causes my already hot body to heat up even more.

"Courtney, I'm so glad you're helping me," a high-pitched voice speaks from behind me. I turn to see Ellie, the server I'm here to help.

Ellie has been working here for about three months, and while she's very competent, she lacks confidence—something you need when dealing with demanding guests. Ellie is a tiny girl, standing around five feet, with long red hair that is twisted into a tight bun. Dressed in a standard servers' uniform, Ellie has on black dress pants and a white blouse.

"Of course, I'm happy to help. Now, let's review the order before we head up to be sure we have everything."

Ellie and I double-check everything to ensure we are well prepared before taking the carts and head to the back elevator. The closer we get to the top floor, the more nervous I become.

When Ellie knocks on the door of David Hayles' room, I take a deep breath and straighten my posture. I'm somewhere between excited and terrified. When the door opens, we are greeted by the friendly smile of the youngest-looking Hayles brother. Now that he is closer, I can't help but notice how his smile radiates kindness.

"Please, come in," the dimpled man says while holding the door open.

Ellie wheels her cart in first while I follow closely behind. The platinum suites are more like an apartment than a hotel room. They have a separate dining area and living room. Both rooms are draped in royal blue, ivory, and gold. I catch a glance into the living room before wheeling through the doorway of the dining room. I see Josh's brothers sitting in front of the TV, though there's no sign of Josh. I can't help but feel disappointed. I was hoping to see him tonight, even if it was from a distance.

Ellie and I begin taking the trays of food off the carts, placing them on the dining table. Dishware and silverware are already supplied to the suites and are in the cupboards along the back wall, but I need to know what kind of placement David Hayles wants for the table set up and food service. I'm usually not intimidated by guests, but given the circumstances, I have to keep my legs from shaking while I walk.

Looking around the living room, I see the cute young brother, and the one I'm sure is Landry, sitting on the large, white leather sofa. Both brothers are looking down at their phones and don't even notice when I enter the room.

At the far end of the living room, the older brother sits in a dark gray chair and is furiously typing on the MacBook in his lap. That deep scowl line from earlier is still intact.

"Excuse me, Mr. Hayles?" I ask quietly while approaching the other gray chair on the opposite side of the room.

David Hayles turns his head slightly when I approach him. His dark eyes look at me over the black-rimmed reading glasses perched on his face.

"Yes," he replies stoically.

"How would you like your table set?" I ask, still in my hushed voice.

Turning his body, David Hayles removes his glasses and looks at me from head to toe.

"Would you be so kind as to bring us the charcuterie board and the sparkling water here to start?" He asks pleasantly with a smirk.

"Of course, sir," I reply and retreat immediately to the dining room.

Minutes later, I return with a platter filled with meat, cheese, olives, and crackers. Ellie follows behind me with two bottles of freshly opened Perrier water. As I gently set the board in the center of the coffee table, I notice the two younger brothers looking around me at the TV. There appears to be a basketball game that they are eager to watch.

I try to move quickly, as does Ellie since we seem to be more in the way than anything. In a hurried motion, Ellie sets one of the bottles of water too close to the table's edge, causing it to tip backwards and land on the carpeted floor. Fizzing bubbles appear at my feet as the bottle drains. The commotion causes everyone in the room to take notice. Quickly, I bend down to pick up the green bottle and immediately begin apologizing.

"Mr. Hayles, I'm so sorry. We'll have this cleaned up immediately." I turn to Ellie. "Ellie, please go back to the restaurant and retrieve another bottle of water. Perhaps a bottle of complementary wine, as well. I'll stay here and clean this up."

Ellie swiftly walks towards the door to complete the tasks while I go back to the dining room to retrieve some dish towels to soak up the water. When I return to the room, all the men have continued their business as though I'm not even there. While on my hands and knees soaking up the spilled water, I heard a familiar voice yelling from the attached bedroom.

"For Christ's sake, Wiggins!"

It's Josh's voice, no doubt about it. Immediately, my pulse quickens. My thoughts are interrupted when I hear the youngest brother yell in response to Josh's outburst.

"Josh, if you'd just come in here and watch a real team play instead of the Warriors, you might enjoy the game."

I realize Josh has been here the entire time, just in the other room. I allow a tiny smirk to appear on my face.

"Would you boys be quiet?" David scolds the room. "Josh, come here and tell me about your date with Ms. Clarke."

Suddenly, my interest is piqued. I remembered Isabelle Clarke, who was here with Josh weeks ago—the red-headed woman whose coat I took to Josh's room.

"There's nothing to tell. I'm not interested," I hear Josh's voice boom from the other side of the wall.

"Josh, please. Her uncle is the mayor of Elmerson. I'm sure there is something you found intriguing?"

"Yeah, ask him about her head skills," the oldest brother's voice behind me rumbles. His comment makes me freeze.

Remembering where I am and what I'm doing, I continue to dab at the carpet, though most of it has been soaked up.

"Shut up, Isaac. Dad, here's the thing," Josh's voice is becoming increasingly louder, which tells me he must be walking this way from the other room. "I'm not interested in Isabelle. In fact, I'm not interested in anyone, so please stop. Isaac was right, Isabelle was great on her knees, not the best I've had since I arrived here, but good enough. That's the only type of relationship I am interested in. I don't care if she's some mayor's niece. After the shit show of my last relationship..."

I can't help but shoot a glance toward Landry on the couch, who notices the sudden movement, and our eyes lock.

"The last thing I want is to deal with some needy chick's feelings. Besides, they'll probably just end up fucking your brother, anyway." Josh's words tear through my chest. I can't believe he's speaking like this. He sounds nothing like the man I was with last night, nor the one from mere hours ago when *I* was on my knees in front of him.

Knowing Josh is now in the same room with me, I begin to panic. There's no way I can get out of here without him seeing me. I'm also furious. I feel like I don't know this man at all, the man I've spent the last few weeks talking with, laughing with, being intimate with.

"Joshua, please," David's command interrupts my thoughts. "There's a lady present. Mind yourself."

Everyone looks in my direction, forcing me to stand and make myself known.

"I'm sorry. I'll get out of your way." My eyes immediately dart to Josh, who is staring at me, dumbfounded.

As quick as our eyes meet, he looks away and clears his throat.

"My apologies, Courtney. That was rude and uncalled for," Josh replies to appease his father, no doubt.

"Mr. Hayles," I look at Josh's father. "I think the carpet should be fine now. However, if you require more cleaning, I can send housekeeping up here right away."

"No, that's fine. In fact, you can go now, too. We can take care of the food ourselves."

"Of course, please feel free to contact the front desk or concierge if you require anything else. Ellie should be back here in a few moments with your fresh water," I quickly look at the Hayles brothers, who are all staring at me. "Have a good evening, gentlemen."

With my arms full of wet towels, I lower my head and walk straight out of the room. I can't get out of there fast enough. Once I'm in the hallway, I take a quick look around to make sure I'm alone. I momentarily lean back on the wall when I see no one else. My eyes are beginning to sting with rage-filled tears. What was I thinking? I can't believe Josh sold the nice guy act so well. I'm reminded of my first impression of him, realizing my initial assessment was correct.

I only give myself a minute to reflect on what happened before pushing off the wall. It's not like this is the first time I've had to deal with a manipulative jerk. I take a deep breath and hold my head high as I walk to the nearest housekeeping closet to dispose of the wet towels.

After I exit the closet, I take a deep breath and remind myself to keep my professionalism in check. I look at my watch to see how much longer I have left in my shift—I'm so ready for this night to be over.

Chapter 14

Josh

The look on Courtney's face when she stood up after I said that asshole remark about only wanting women on their knees… ugh, I feel like a piece of shit. I mean, I wasn't talking about her. She must know that, right? It's just easier with men like my father to be crude for them to shut up. Surely, she gets that.

It was all I could do not to run after her when she left the suite. I need to talk to her, but I have to play it cool. I can't have my family finding out about Courtney and me for several reasons: one, because my father will have a fit and ruin everything; two, because I don't want to deal with any of their opinions; and three, Courtney could get fired.

Immediately, I check the time on my phone. It's almost nine o'clock, which means Courtney still has a couple of hours left of work. I'll have to wait until she gets off work at eleven. Until then, I'll sit with my father and brothers, acting like nothing's bothering me.

Time drags on as I wait for eleven p.m. to arrive. I left my father's suite around ten, declaring I was tired and going to bed. I change out of my dress clothes into a pair of black track pants and a gray hoodie. I toss on my ball cap and head down to exit the hotel.

While leaning against the brick wall, I marvel at how warm the weather is today compared to yesterday when it was snowing while Courtney and I were walking to her apartment. Can that really be only last night that I was with her, listening to her moans while I tasted her flesh?

Finally, after waiting ten minutes, the side door swings open, and my beautiful Courtney steps out. As usual, she has changed out of her work clothes. Now, she is wearing jeans with her knee-high winter boots. Her black wool coat is left open, and an emerald green shirt peeks out from underneath.

"Hey," I greet her when she turns in my direction.

"What are you doing here, Josh?" Courtney asks, sliding her hands into her pockets.

"What do you mean? I'm walking you home."

Courtney rolls her eyes. "I think I'll be fine on my own."

"Courtney, come on." I cross my arms over my chest.

"Come on *what*, Josh?" She mimics my stance by crossing her arms in the same way.

"I think you're overreacting."

"Seriously? Do you know how humiliating that was? How insulting?" Courtney asks in disbelief.

"I wasn't talking about you. You know that."

"Do I know that, Josh? How would I know that? Because what you were describing sounded a lot like what you have with me? Oh, and what about Isabelle? You've had both of us on our knees, Josh, so what more could you want?"

"Is that what this is about, Isabelle and me?"

"No, Josh. This is about you being an asshole. It's like that guy I was with last night doesn't even exist. Even right now, everything about you screams pompous jerk. The way you're standing, the way you're looking at me like I'm being ridiculous for having this reaction—ugh, the arrogance is nauseating."

"I don't do drama, Courtney," I growl at her in annoyance as I watch her arms fling up in frustration.

"Great, then go inside. I never asked you to come out here and walk me home. You can go; I'll be fine," Courtney replies.

"Is that what you want? For me to go back inside?" I can't help but glare in her direction. God, she's infuriating. Courtney says nothing but glares back at me.

I don't want to go back inside, but I also don't want to be dealing with this. I realize at this point that I've never actually apologized to Courtney for what I said.

"Courtney, I'm sorry you were bothered by what I said, but that's how I speak sometimes, especially around my family. Do you know how often my father is on my case about dating a certain type of woman?"

"No, I don't know, Josh, because you don't talk to me about your family."

"And you don't talk to me about yours," I retort.

"Then I guess this should be easy to walk away from," Courtney says to my surprise.

"Is that what you want?"

"What I want is to go home," Courtney begins to walk towards the street.

"Well, I'm still walking with you. It's not safe," I tell her sternly.

"I've been doing this for over a year, Josh. Believe me, I don't need you to save me. I'm fine without you."

Courtney turns her back to me and walks away. I'm torn between following her or going back into the hotel. I watch her without moving until she leaves my sight before going back inside. It's probably better this way; I can't stand the drama. Maybe it's my fault for getting involved with someone so young. Again, I remind myself as I head towards the elevators that this is for the best. It's the best thing for me, Courtney was making me act out of character, act weak and vulnerable. That is not the man I am, nor is it the man I want to be. I reaffirm to myself; this is the best thing for me. Though, I can't figure out why my stomach is rolling with nausea, and my heart is having pangs of remorse. I ride the lift up to the fourteenth floor reminding myself that I'm stronger than my sadness— I am stronger than what I *feel.*

Chapter 15

Courtney

I don't know how I managed it, but I was able to avoid Josh all day yesterday. After our confrontation the night before last, I did everything I could to avoid all the Hayles men — amazingly, it worked. From what I could tell, they were out of the hotel for most of the day and evening, so avoiding Josh was easy.

I'm hoping today will be another day without their presence. I'm still angry with Josh, and since it's clear he's not feeling bad about any of this, I guess it's time to forget about it. When I left work last night, he wasn't outside waiting for me, which, I hate to admit, somewhat disappointed me. I know I told him not to walk me home, but honestly, I'm missing him. Ugh, why did he have to be such a jerk?

It's early in my shift, and I'm standing at my concierge desk when I hear men's dress shoes walking towards me. I look up to see David Hayles headed in my direction. I quickly look behind me to see if Milo is around to relieve me, but he is nowhere to be seen. David is dressed in a formal black tuxedo. I must admit, he is a rather handsome man, despite his awfully cold demeanour.

As David approaches, I plaster on my best fake smile and greet him accordingly.

"Hello, Mr. Hayles. How are you today, sir?"

David Hayles sets a large manilla envelope on the marble countertop in front of me.

"I need you to deliver this promptly to my son's room." He looks at me sternly and his voice offers no niceties.

I swallow hard, "Yes, sir. Which son, though?" I ask, hoping it's not Josh's room.

"Landry's room. It's imperative that he receives this right away. He will be requiring it before tonight's mayoral event."

"Yes, sir," I reply with relief when hearing Landry's name instead of Josh's. I take the envelope and ensure that I will personally deliver it immediately.

As David is walking away, the phone rings beside me. I'm trying to listen closely as the guest asks about local nightclubs until I see Josh's oldest brother walk through the lobby in a similar tuxedo to David's. With his black hair and piercing dark blue eyes, he radiates dominance. I try to confirm with the guest what they have requested. I lose focus moments later when I see Josh passing through after his brother and father. Like the other two, Josh is in a black and white tuxedo. His chestnut brown hair and whisky-brown eyes leave me speechless. A small smattering of stubble covers his sharp jawline. I stare for an inappropriately long time. He looks like no other man I've seen before, and I almost forget I'm angry with him. *Almost.*

A sideways glance from Josh shoots in my direction, and we make eye contact. Neither of us gives an ounce of emotion. As quickly as he looked my way, Josh turns his head back towards his brother and father. Together, the three walk towards the exit and disappear from my sight.

After I finish on the phone, I grab the envelope David wants delivered to Landry's room. After changing the desk phone to be forwarded to my cell, I head up to the fourteenth floor.

I wonder where the other two brothers are during the elevator ride, knowing there's an important function tonight. Obviously, they aren't going with Josh. I hope Landry isn't in his room when I arrive and that I can drop off the envelope quickly.

When I arrive at Landry's room, I knock and wait. After a moment of hearing no sound behind the door, I knock again for good measure before swiping my master key. I walk to the desk to place the envelope when I enter the room. Looking around the room, I notice Landry is a lot messier than Josh, with clothes tossed around and several beer bottles scattered throughout.

As I turn to leave, my nose catches the smell of marijuana floating through the air. Looking back towards the open balcony door, I see the silhouette of a man leaning against the railing.

"Excuse me, Mr. Hayles," I speak loudly so he can hear me.

Slowly, Landry turns around to face me through the doorway. I can see the joint pressed between his fingers now. He's dressed in formal attire, the same black and white tuxedo as his brothers. His dark hair is combed back.

"I left an envelope for you from your father on your desk."

"Courtney, right?" Landry replies, ignoring my statement about the envelope.

"Yes," I remain standing beside the desk.

"Come out here for a second," Landry requests before turning back toward the city lights.

I hesitate for a moment before walking towards the balcony. My black heels click against the concrete of the balcony floor as I pass through the large glass door.

"What can I do for you?" I ask as I stand beside Landry, hoping the smell of pot does not get on my clothes.

"I'm just wondering how long you and Josh have been...whatever it is you are doing?"

"Excuse me?" I ask in shock. "I'm not sure what you're talking about."

Landry lifts the corner of his mouth and exposes a lopsided smile. "Come on, Courtney, you can tell me. I saw the way you looked at him the other day when he made a complete ass out of himself. That wasn't a look of being in an awkward place. That was the look of hurt. Well, hurt and then anger. Not to mention that since that moment, he has been a complete dick to be around—even more so than usual, I mean."

Landry takes another hit from his joint. I remain silent beside him, trying to figure out how to respond while my fingers fidget on the edge of my blazer.

"Also," Landry continues, "You know about me. I could tell you knew what Josh was talking about when he mentioned his brother and ex-girlfriend. You knew he was talking about me. So, unless that's the type of information you require at check-in, I'm assuming he must have told you."

"Yes," I whisper in a hushed voice. "Please don't say anything. I could get into so much trouble if anyone found out," I plead.

Landry begins to laugh. "I'm not going to rat you out, but I am curious about you two. You're nothing like the women Josh usually dates."

"Because I'm young?" I can't help but ask.

"Well, that, and you don't seem like an uptight bitch."

I can't help but grin.

"Right? Have you met Isabelle?" I wince after the wildly unprofessional words fall out of my mouth.

Landry roars with laughter, "I have, actually. I'm sorry that you had to, also."

I relax my stance and lean against the railing more informally. I like Landry despite knowing what he did to Josh.

"Anyway, I'm thinking you and Josh are fighting since he's being an asshole to everyone. I'm sure it's because of his stupid comments. The thing you have to know about Josh is that he's very guarded. He has this hard exterior that he thinks he has to have on all the time, especially around our father. He thinks he has something to prove. Before I messed everything up, he was pretty good to me. He helped me out more times than he should have. Underneath all his macho bullshit and stubbornness, Josh is actually kind of a softy." Landry stops to take the final drag off his joint before dropping it into an empty beer bottle. "Don't you dare tell him I told you that," Landry's voice creaks as he holds his inhale.

"Well, thanks for the advice, but it's not needed. Josh and I aren't anything anymore. It was some reckless thing that is more than over," I assure Landry while looking at the twinkling of the city lights and feel a lull of sadness.

"Are you sure about that, Courtney? Because I see you looking out over the city lights the same way I have been for the last hour," Landry's eyes scan over the thousands of streetlights in front of us. "Wondering which fucking light is hers."

I realize Landry isn't talking about Josh and me anymore.

"Who is she?"

Landry shakes his head but doesn't take his eyes off the skyline.

"She's gone."

We stand together in silence for an extended moment.

"If there's any chance this thing between you and Josh is something, give him another chance, Courtney. If it's real, fight for it. You don't want to screw up something like that."

"Did you screw up something like that, Landry?" I ask, though I already know the truth.

Landry shakes his head as we turn simultaneously towards one another.

"I destroyed it."

The phone in my blazer pocket buzzes, breaking my gaze with Landry's dark eyes. I retrieve it to read a message from Milo asking where I am.

"I have to go," I say while slipping my phone back into my pocket. "Are you going to be okay?" I ask Landry before I leave.

"Peachy keen," Landry says while turning his back.

I step back inside the suite from the balcony but stop in time for one more question.

"What's her name?" I twist my neck back slightly.

Landry doesn't turn around; he only drops his head slightly.

"Her name is *Cricket*."

I leave feeling even more confused about my situation with Josh than before. I'm still annoyed with him, there's no doubt, but now I'm wondering if there is something more there. I think about the moment we had a few days ago when our hands were placed over each other's chest, and Josh whispered, "*You make me feel.*" Did that statement mean more? Is there something between us worth fighting for?

***

Thank goodness for the anniversary party happening in one of the banquet rooms tonight. The joyful atmosphere helped the rest of my shift go by quickly, although I was run off my feet all evening. Between the party and the arrival of the Scottish tourists, I hardly had time to stop and eat—which, honestly, was fine with me.

After my conversation with Landry, my stomach's been in knots the entire night. Any spare moment I had was flooded with thoughts of Josh. I tried not to let myself become too sensitive when thinking of him. For all I knew, he was off at his posh party with swanky Isabelle. They could drink their stupid expensive champagne, laugh about their stupid money, and sneak off somewhere for Isabelle to give him another sloppy bj. Okay, maybe I was bothered by Josh's admission of what he and Isabelle had done together a few weeks ago.

None of this matters, I think to myself as I walk home in the dark. I debated stopping to pick up food on the way home, but ultimately decided that a bowl of Lucky Charms would suffice. My feet are killing me as the ice and salt crunch underneath my boots.

When I approach my apartment building, there is a silhouette sitting on the concrete stairs. As I get closer, I can see it is Josh. Still in his black tuxedo, his tie is undone and draped carelessly around his neck. His head is resting against the railing. His eyes are closed, and his hair is disheveled, though he still looks amazing. He must have heard my footsteps approaching because he sits up straight and looks at me.

"What are you doing here, Josh?" I ask in a monotone voice.

Rubbing the spot of his head that was pressed against the iron rails, Josh clears his throat. "Christ, it took you long enough."

As Josh begins to stand up, I notice a slight sway in his legs.

"Josh, how much have you had to drink?"

"A little bit," Josh smirks at me and I try to resist the urge to smirk back.

"Let me call you an Uber," I say and pull my phone from my pocket.

"No, wait. Courtney," Josh walks down the stairs until he's standing beside me. "I wanted to see you." His fingers intertwine with mine. "Are you done being mad at me?"

"I don't know, Josh. Are you done being an asshole?" I reply. Though he's cute as hell right now, I'm still not letting him off the hook.

"Why are you being so stubborn?" Josh growls.

"*I'm* being stubborn? Are you kidding me, Josh? You're not only the most stubborn man I've ever met, but you might be the most arrogant, too. If you're here looking for a booty call, you'd be better off hanging out on Isabelle's stoop," I shout up at him as he glares back at me.

"Careful, Tiny Bird."

We stare at each other intensely, neither willing to give an inch.

Finally, after a minute or so, I give up.

"Ugh, come on," I say as I walk up the stairs to my apartment. Josh follows behind, though not too close.

As I unlock the deadbolt to my place, I feel Josh's hand rest on the small of my back.

"This is not going to be a booty call," I remind him as I let us inside.

We walk in, and both remove our jackets. While I'm in a pink sweatshirt and grey yoga pants, Josh is still in a white dress shirt and black dress pants.

After I wash up, I walk to my tiny kitchen to retrieve the box of Lucky Charms and milk. As I reach for a bowl, I turn to Josh, who's now sitting on my bed.

"Do you want some?"

"Lucky Charms?" Josh eyes the box with a hint of disgust.

"Yes," I reply. "Don't act like you're too good for Lucky Charms."

He doesn't respond, so I continue preparing a single serving. Once finished, I sit at the table and eat my very late supper.

I hear a sigh from the bed before I see Josh stand up and walk to the counter, where I left out the cereal and milk. A moment later, he sits across from me after fixing himself a bowl. We eat in silence, only the clanging spoons and crunching to fill the air.

After the late-night snack is complete, we remain at the table, and I watch as Josh shifts awkwardly in his chair.

"Courtney, look, I'm bad at this. I have no idea what I'm doing."

"I'm bad at this, too," I say with a sigh.

Josh gives me a devilish grin before pushing his chair away from the table, but he doesn't stand up. Instead, he crooks his finger, signaling for me to come over to him. I scowl in return, though my body stands and walks over to him. Reaching up, Josh grabs the back of my neck and pulls me towards him until our foreheads meet.

"I'm sorry," he whispers. "I'm so very sorry, Courtney. I didn't mean what I said. It was disrespectful. You being hurt and angry, ugh, it broke me a little."

"Thank you, Josh," I reply as I look into his glossy eyes. Their softness begins to melt my anger away. I'm reminded of the Josh who was here the other night with me.

"Do you want to stay, or do you want me to call you an Uber?"

"I think I'd like to stay."

"To sleep," I confirm.

Josh agrees, "Yes, to sleep."

I press a tiny kiss to his lips before pulling away and walking to my dresser to get my pajamas. I take out my sleep shorts and tank top.

Josh stands and unbuttons his shirt before lying it across the back of the dining chair. When he begins to undo his pants, I stop him.

"What are you doing?"

"Courtney, I'm not going to sleep in my clothes."

Josh removes his pants and socks, standing before me only in black Calvin Klein briefs. On top of his toned brown chest is a thin layer of chest hair—I'm reminded on the first time I saw him in only a towel weeks earlier. All the other guys I've seen this close have been younger, less filled out, and less manly. Tingles move throughout my body.

"You're staring," Josh states as he carefully folds his pants and sets them on the chair seat.

"Well, you're practically naked!" I exclaim.

I quickly shift out of my clothes and into my baby blue boxer shorts and white tank top. Unlike Josh, who neatly puts his clothes aside, mine are left carelessly in a mess on the floor.

After all, it's my apartment. Before crawling into bed, I brush my teeth and wash my face. Taking a moment alone in my bathroom, I try to calm myself with a few deep breaths.

When I re-emerge, I turn the lights off on the way. There's a faint glow coming from the one window that gives me enough light to see where I'm going. As I slide under the covers, the heat from Josh's body tickles my skin. Since my bed is only a double, it's impossible not to touch one another, especially with Josh being as large as he is.

Turning onto my side away from him, I'm instantly engulfed by his large arms, which are pulling me tight into his body. The faint smell of alcohol still lingers off him as I feel his lips press softly against my shoulder.

"Sweet dreams, Tiny Bird," Josh mumbles into my skin. Within seconds, I hear faint snoring coming from the man behind me.

I lay there for a while longer as I bask in the warmth of his arms. I think Landry might have been right, I do feel something. I'm not sure what it is, but it feels like something I don't want to let go of; something I would risk everything for. It isn't long before sleep lulls over me and I find a certain solace I have longed for for in the last few years.

Chapter 16

Josh

I wake up with a searing pain in my left leg. Before I can open my eyes, I remember that I'm crunched up in Courtney's small bed. I try my best to straighten out without moving too much so I don't wake her. I can finally shift my body from my side to my back, and the relief is immediate after being wrapped around Courtney for hours. Though I will rightfully admit, the pain is worth it.

Courtney lets out a tiny groan as she rolls her body over to her other side. Now, she's facing me. I listen carefully to see if she's awake or not. I don't think she is.

The light from the window allows me to see her slightly. With lips parted, she breathes steadily. Though stretching out on my back feels a thousand times better, my arms want to hold her again. I roll onto my side in her direction and scoop up her sleeping body, pressing her into me. Her face nuzzles tightly against my neck, pressing our chests together. The squish of her breast against me almost awakens my inner beast, though I keep myself in check, and eventually, I drift off to sleep again.

I don't know how long I'm asleep this time before I'm woken again, since it's still dark in the room. However, tiny kisses are being dropped along my neck as I feel Courtney's hand drag across my bare back. That beast I tamed before awakens with full alertness.

"You're playing with fire, Tiny Bird," I rumble into the dark as I become harder with every touch of her lips.

"Mmm, I like fire," Courtney replies as the tip of her tongue darts out, swiping across the skin under my jaw.

We're still lying facing each other with our bodies pressed together. Courtney's leg lifts over my hip and presses my waist to grind into hers.

"I thought you said this wasn't going to be a booty call," I mumble against the top of her head.

"I meant I wasn't going to be your booty call. I have no problem making you mine," she replies as her hand runs up my back, causing my skin to tingle.

Without hesitation, I grab a fistful of her long hair. I pull down hard to force her face up to mine. As her chin is tilted upwards towards my face, I can see a bit of light reflecting from her widened eyes. They're full of lust and needy desire—and who am I to turn down a woman in need? Especially since we've waited so long already. I'm sick of being a gentleman, sick of trying to be a nobleman. I'm ready to take every ounce of this woman.

"Are you ready for me?" I growl while staring back into her eyes.

"I've been ready for you for weeks. So, I think the real question is, are you ready for me?" A smirk crawls across Courtney's lips.

"You're such a goddamn brat."

"Mmm," Courtney hums as she closes the gap between our lips. "Perhaps," as she presses our lips together.

Our lips don't remain closed for long before our tongues break free and absorb one another. Courtney still has her leg draped over my hip as she moves against my body. My frustration grows as every part of me wants to press into her. In no time, I push my body against hers, using my weight and size difference to my advantage, and easily flip her over onto her back. I rest my weight on my elbows so as not to squish her too hard. Instantly, I feel Courtney spread her legs to allow my hips to grind against hers. Our lips do not separate, not even for a moment.

I shift my weight to my left side to free my right elbow and allow for exploration down the side of Courtney's body. She's so soft. I allow my fingers to make their way under her thin tank top, wasting no time before cupping her breast. This causes a moan to rise from Courtney's throat.

"You like that?" I ask with a raspy voice. Although the only response I get is another gasp and moan. I squeeze a bit harder before my thumb and finger trap her hardened nipple and roll it around.

Courtney's hips lift into my groin as her legs wrap tightly around my ass.

"I want more," Courtney mumbles.

Reaching down, I grab both her wrists and drag them up, holding them firmly above her head.

"More?" I reply by pushing hard into her mound.

"*More!*" Courtney cries.

I release her wrists from my grasp, but not before I warn her not to move her arms. I sit myself up on my knees, with her legs still draped around each side of my thighs. Harshly, I pull up her tank top until both her breasts are exposed. The material is bunched up on her sternum, and maybe it's uncomfortable, but

I don't care as I palm both her tits harshly. Courtney doesn't seem to mind as she arches her back, forcing herself into my grasp. When I replace my hands with my mouth, I suck on one and then the other.

"You have thirty seconds to get your clothes off. I assume you have a condom," I warn.

"Yes," Courtney replies breathlessly because my fingers are pumping inside her.

"Get it," I demand as I remove my hand from her shorts and lean back on my knees so she can get out from underneath me. As I watch her slide her tank top over her head and wiggle out of her shorts and panties, I remove my own briefs. Once I'm free of the black material, I can't help but palm myself.

Courtney reaches over to her nightstand and pulls out a foil package. Sitting up on her knees in front of me, she watches me touching myself before handing over the condom.

"No," I tell her. "You put it on."

I catch a slight eye roll from Courtney in response to my bossiness, but she does what I say without complaint. The second the condom is secured over me, I can't wait a moment longer. I reach over and grab Courtney's ribs and lift her over to me.

The instant I feel her body engulf mine, a wave of euphoria floods my entire body. Never in my entire sex life have I felt this instant high.

We're moulded together perfectly as her slight body moves over mine. My hands are holding her ass. Her arms are wrapped around my shoulders. Tiny whimpers escape Courtney's lips when I bring our mouths together.

"Can you handle more, baby?" I ask into Courtney's mouth.

Courtney's eyes meet mine for a second before replying, "I'm counting on it."

I brace my hands around her back before I lift her just enough to free my legs but not enough to leave her body. Placing Courtney onto her back, we're now laying on the bed horizontally. Courtney's head hangs slightly over the edge of the mattress, exposing her soft white neck. My hand anchors itself onto it as I continuously pump into her. When I realize how hard my fingers are pressed into her skin, I slide my hand down to her collarbone.

"Put it back," Courtney groans.

"If I do, I'm gonna leave marks," I grunt.

Courtney raises her head enough for her eyes to meet mine. They're darker than I've ever seen them before. "Then mark me."

God, at this rate, I'm not going to last much longer. This woman is unbelievable.

Courtney's moans increase steadily. The vibrations from her throat tingle against my palm. Her legs press tight against my ass, pushing me in further until she arches her back as high as she can with my arm still holding her down by her neck. When her body's contractions, along with her breath gasping voice, catches me off guard, I can no longer control my own release.

It takes us both a minute to catch our breaths. Courtney's head is still flopped over the edge of the bed. I can hear her breathing through her small apartment.

Finally, I lift myself off her sweat-stricken body and walk straight to the bathroom to dispose of the condom and do a quick wash-up. When I walk back into the only room, Courtney is up from the bed, too. Back into her shorts and tank top, with her long hair pulled back into a ponytail, she's standing at the kitchen sink, filling a glass of water. A dim light over the kitchen sink is on.

"Do you want one?" She offers.

I walk over to her, still naked but not caring.

"Just wait," I say when I stop in front of her. "Put down the glass."

I grab her empty hand when the glass is set carefully on the countertop.

"Come here," I demand and pull her into my embrace. I kiss her softly on her puffy lips before looking at her neck. "You have finger marks."

Courtney giggles, "Oops."

"I feel bad. Are you okay?"

"I'm better than okay. I've been marked by *the* Joshua Hayles. I don't know if you know this, but I've heard he's a big deal."

"Hmm, is that so? Well, you know what it means to be marked by me, don't you? You're at my complete mercy, Tiny Bird," I move my lips to her ear and whisper.

"Are you gonna get all tough and macho on me now? Caveman-style?"

Courtney's sassiness is driving me crazy. I reach to the top of her head and grab a fistful of her long dark hair. "If you deserve to be dragged around by your hair, then yes."

Courtney's blue eyes sparkle at me, coated in mischief. "You know, you act all tough, but I think underneath it you're just a big ol' buttercup."

I can't help but crack a smile. "Did you call me a buttercup?" I let go of my fistful of hair.

"Oh, I think I'm onto something, Buttercup."

"You're not calling me Buttercup," I growl as I reach down and pick up Courtney by the back of her thighs. Instinctively, her legs wrap around my waist as her arms cling to my shoulders.

I carry her a few steps over to the wall, and I press her back up firmly against it. Her body flinches when the cool surface touches her bare skin.

"You better be careful, Buttercup. I don't want you to pull a muscle."

"Stop talking," I warn as I bite into the flesh of her shoulder.

"You said that to me the first night I met you."

"I meant it then, too." I press her harder into the wall as I feel the blood rushing down towards my groin.

"You're getting hard again, Buttercup. I think you must like your new nickname."

"God, you're infuriating."

"You love it," Courtney says in a hushed tone.

I really do.

Chapter 17

Courtney

I wake up to the sound of Josh moving around my apartment. I can hear the rattle of a belt buckle before I even open my eyes.

"Why are you up so early?" I grumble as I pull a pillow over my face to shield myself from the brightness of the window's glow.

"Because I have to meet my father and brothers for breakfast before they leave today. First, I need to return to my room to shower and change out of this suit." Josh pulls the pillow off my face and nuzzles his nose into my bare neck. "But I'd rather stay here."

Josh is fully dressed in the tux he wore last night on my doorstep, minus the tie.

"I'd rather you stay here, too."

"Do you work later?" Josh asks as he plants kisses up my neck and behind my ear.

"No, today's my day off."

"What are you going to do all day?"

"I have a ton of schoolwork to catch up on. Groceries and laundry, too. What about you? What are you doing after breakfast?"

"I have to head into the office and work on some stuff. I fell behind the last couple of days."

"Was it because you were heartbroken over me?"

"It was because my family was in town. My blue balls were because of you," Josh growls as he turns the soft kisses into forceful nibbles against my skin, and his fingers press hard against my ribs.

The tickles make me squirm and laugh.

"Stop it!" I shout.

"Well, don't be such a brat," Josh mumbles and moves his mouth onto mine, giving me a firm kiss which ends far too quickly. "I'll text you later," Josh stands up from my bed, causing an empty imprint beside me.

"Okay," I begrudgingly agree.

Minutes later, I'm left alone in my place, feeling a slight ache in my chest, which is stupid because I'm usually tougher than this. I never felt this anytime Kai left me the morning after we hooked up, and I definitely didn't feel it anytime I was with Dylan—not that he ever left me alone long enough to miss him. Nope, this is a new feeling for me.

Debating whether I should go back to sleep for a while or get started on my day, I finally drag myself out of bed and start working on my schoolwork. The dread of knowing I'm behind in some classes is gnawing at me. After I took a shower to get last night's sex sweat off me, I put on a pair of comfy, dark green fleece pants and an oversized sweatshirt. Then, I make myself a strong pot of coffee in my French press and get to work.

Four hours, three cups of coffee, and two bowls of Lucky Charms later, I'm finally at ease, knowing I have no more assignments hanging over my head. I silently vow to myself not to get this far behind again.

Now that the burden is gone, I decide to treat myself to a nap. It's only the early afternoon, and I still have lots of time to get groceries and do my cleaning and laundry. Josh hasn't texted me yet, and I'm trying to pretend I haven't checked my phone multiple times.

It doesn't take long to feel the lull of sleep despite the sunshine flooding my apartment with golden light. I pull my comforter over my head and drift off soundly. That is until I'm awoken to the sound of fast knocking on my front door.

"Ms. Courtney, let me in," Liv's voice calls from the other side of the door.

I stumble out of bed and open the door to see my best friend standing in her work uniform, holding two cups of coffee.

"I thought I would stop by for a visit before I head to work," Liv announces as she pushes past me without being formally invited in. "Were you sleeping?"

"Yes," I grumble as I pull a chair out from my table and sit. "Thank you for the coffee." I open the lid of the red cup and allow the steam to drift over my face. It smells fantastic, like vanilla and cream.

"How's the day off going?" Liv asks as she takes a seat across from me.

"Good, I finally got caught up on my schoolwork. I was so far behind."

"How could you be that far behind? You don't even come out with us these days. You always go straight home after work."

Liv is right; I never go out with my co-workers anymore. Even when I'm asked after a shift, I make up some excuse to ditch to meet up with the tall, brooding man waiting to walk me home in the alley.

I debate whether I should tell Liv about Josh or not. I know I could get into trouble at work because of my relationship with him, but I'm not worried about Liv telling my secret. I might be a little worried about her judging me for being with a man so much older than me.

"I don't know, I've just been busy," I shrug.

"You're not upset that Kai's been seeing Maya, are you?"

"Maya from the front desk? I didn't even know that." I think about it for a second before I respond, "No, it doesn't bother me."

"So, what have you been busy with?"

"Okay, if I tell you, you have to promise not to tell anyone."

Liv's large blue eyes widen at the promise of juicy information, and she eagerly nods.

"I've been seeing someone, but no one can know."

"Why? Is he married or something?"

"What? No! He's, um, a guest."

"Really? Who?"

"Josh Hayles," I admit as I avert my eyes down to my coffee, which is partially gone.

"Josh Hayles? The hot lawyer from the suites? Oh my God, are you serious?" Liv's voice squeaks a little bit higher with each question.

"Yes," I confirm with an uncontainable grin.

"Ah, I'm so freaking jealous," Liv squeals, causing me to burst out laughing.

"You're not mad at me for sneaking around with a guest?"

"No! Not when the guest is as fine as he is."

"And you don't think the age difference is strange?"

"How old is he exactly?" Liv asks quizzically.

"Thirty-one," I mutter before taking a drink of my coffee.

"Pssh, that's not a big deal. It's not even ten years. Give me all the details of how it started. No, wait, first tell me about the sex."

I can't help but let out a groan as my memories flood with images of Josh from the night before. "Hands down, the best I've ever had. He's nothing like Kai or Dylan. He is all man, and he knows exactly what he's doing."

"Ugh, now I'm really jealous."

"But seriously, Liv, you can't tell anyone!"

"I swear on your sex life that I won't tell a soul," Liv smirks and places a hand over her heart. We both erupt in laughter.

Liv stays for another half hour before she leaves for work. I promise to fill her in more tomorrow.

I realize it's now after three p.m., and I still haven't heard from Josh, though I'm trying not to dwell on it for too long. I gather my laundry and take it down to the machine in the basement. When my wash is going, I begin cleaning my apartment. I strip my bed and replace the sheets with clean ones—but not before I take a quick sniff of the pillow Josh used last night. His lingering scent makes my heartbeat quicken for a moment.

I shake the romantic euphoria from my mind and get back to work. Cleaning my apartment doesn't take long, but the running to and from the basement for laundry has the time passing quickly. Before I know it, the sun is beginning to set. I realize that I still have to go out and get groceries. Luckily, there's a store only a few blocks away. After I pulled my last load of laundry from the dryer, I bundled up to walk to the store, and there was still no text from Josh.

When I return from shopping, I check my phone. It's now after seven p.m., and I'm beginning to lose hope and getting a little annoyed. I put my food away before flopping onto my now-clean bed with a pout. I turn on my well-loved DVD of *Friends*, opting to watch *The One with the Routine* because it never fails to make me laugh.

By the time Monica and Ross finish their dance, there is a knock on my door for the second time today. I pause my show and trudge over to the door. I open it to find Josh leaning against the frame, dressed in grey sweatpants and a black hoodie.

"You didn't text me," I say, forgoing a formal greeting.

"Can I come in?" Josh smirks sheepishly.

"I don't know. I've had a pretty busy day." I cross my arms and block the doorway.

"Me, too." Josh mimics my stance by crossing his own arms.

We stand in silence before Josh rolls his eyes and retrieves his phone from his pocket. After he taps away on the screen, I hear my phone, which is lying on the kitchen table, notify me of a new text message.

"Now, can I come in?" Josh asks as he shoves his phone back into his pocket.

A smile creeps over my face as I move out of the way, allowing his large frame to pass by. I close the door behind him, locking it.

Josh removes his hoodie and tosses it over one of the kitchen chairs, leaving him in a blue T-shirt. He walks over to my bed and sits down.

"You better check that text message," Josh grumbles.

"Fine, fine," I say nonchalantly while sauntering to my phone. I casually pick it up and read the waiting message.

Josh: Get your ass over to the bed. Now!

I look up to see his brown eyes staring at me with hunger. I set my phone back on the table and slowly walk over to the bed. When I reach the bed, Josh has spread his legs wide so I can stand in between his thighs. Placing my hands onto his shoulders, I feel his hands run up the back of my legs.

"I missed you today," Josh comments as he buries his face into my chest. "Work was boring, and the hotel is not the same without you. Brenda never comes up to my room and offers me a blowjob."

"I should hope not!" I grab Josh's brown hair and thrust his head up towards mine.

"Aw, baby. Such a temper on you." Josh moves his hands under my oversized sweatshirt and undoes my bra with one hand while sliding his fingers under the loosened cup. "Maybe I should put you to bed for the night."

I toss my head back and groan slightly as Josh's fingers work my nipples, tugging at them with enough force to make them ache.

"Do you need to go to bed, Tiny Bird?"

"No," I whimper as I still hold onto his thick hair.

"Are you sure about that?"

"No, I'm not sure," I groan as Josh works his fingers feverishly under my sweater.

"I'll tell you what, first we'll order some take-out and lay in bed the rest of the evening watching *Friends*." Josh stops to gesture at the TV, paused at an image of Chandler holding an old shoe. "Then, I will put you to bed properly."

"And what's the proper way?" I ask as I drop my head down to his neck and press into his warm flesh.

"One that will cause you to get very little sleep tonight," Josh mumbles as I move my lips to his earlobe and nibble softly.

"Hmm, I like that idea. However, I'm not that hungry right now, and *Friends* can wait for a few minutes."

"Well, if you can wait to eat, I can definitely wait, too," Josh quickly stands up and swoops me into his arms long enough to place me on the bed underneath him. "You're really something else, you know that, Tiny Bird?" Josh says as he runs his fingers over my cheek and down my neck. "I never knew it could feel like this."

Josh didn't need to say anything more because I knew exactly what he was talking about. The pull between us, the feelings that shouldn't have come on this quickly, and the fear that it might be all taken away.

"I know exactly what you mean, Josh. It's hard to put it into words, but..." I pause, trying to articulate exactly what I want to say. "I feel..."

Josh echoes my response, which is the same one he gave me only a short time ago. "I *feel*, too."

We say no more and let our lips devour each other, expressing all the things our words are failing to do. When trying to describe the indescribable, sometimes only passion will do.

Chapter 18

Josh

"Are you hungry?" I ask Courtney as she's draped over my chest with her long dark hair covering my bare shoulder.

"Yes! I'm starving. We should order pizza."

"What kind of pizza do you like?" I ask, grabbing my phone off the night table beside the bed.

"Pretty much anything, but nothing with pineapple."

"What's wrong with pineapple?" I question not because I particularly like pineapple on my pizza but because Courtney sounds thoroughly disgusted by the idea.

"Are you kidding me? Everything is wrong with pineapple on pizza. My ex-fiancée would always get it, even when he knew I hated it, and then, he would get grumpy when I picked it off."

I lift my head, startled after the words "my ex-fiancée" tumble out of Courtney's mouth.

"Hold on, did you say ex-fiancée?"

Courtney's body tenses on top of mine before she lifts herself up to a seated position.

"Yes," she says meekly.

"You were engaged? How is that possible? You're barely old enough to drink, let alone almost get married?"

Courtney bites her lip softly as her eyes dart around the room.

"It was before I moved here," she responds, still speaking quietly.

"Please explain to me how you were engaged once upon a time, and you are only twenty-two."

"Josh, it's a long story. You don't want to hear it."

"Try me," I counter.

Courtney looks uneasily at me as her eyes begin to gloss over. I sit up to meet her face-to-face, softly touching the tip of her chin to offer her comfort.

"You don't have to talk about it if you don't want to. I get it. But if you do, I'm a great listener."

"No, I do want to tell you, but I don't want you to judge me."

"Unless you slept with your ex's brother, I absolutely will not judge you." My joke causes Courtney to smirk.

"No, I didn't sleep with his brother. I did leave him the day before the wedding, which was a pretty shitty thing to do."

"Come here, baby." I offer my open arms to Courtney, who leans into them immediately. "Let's order our pizza, and then you can tell me your runaway bride story."

Minutes later, I have ordered a large chicken Caesar pizza, which will arrive in about thirty minutes, according to the app.

"Okay, but if I have to tell you about Dylan, then you have to tell me about your ex-girlfriend-slash-sister-in-law," Courtney negotiates.

"I've already told you that story."

"No, I want the details. I can already tell she's a piece of work, but I want to know how she got two of the best-looking men I've ever seen to fall for her tricks."

"Fine, but you go first."

"Okay. I've known Dylan for most of my life. He was my brother, Adam's best friend, so he was always around. Though, we didn't become a couple until after the accident."

"Accident?" I ask with a furrowed brow.

"Yeah. Dylan, Adam, and I were all in a car accident together when I was sixteen. They were eighteen."

"What happened?"

"It was late one night after a party, and we were driving home. The weather was terrible, wet snow and high winds. Adam was driving. We hit a white-out spot, and he over-corrected his steering. That's when we slid into an oncoming truck," Courtney's voice trembles.

"Oh my God. Was everyone okay?"

Courtney sits in silence. Her heavy breaths fill the space as tears drip down her cheeks.

"No," Courtney shakes her head. "Adam was killed instantly."

The admission causes Courtney to break down into a full-out sob. Her body vibrates against mine as I tighten my grip around her. Rubbing my hand over her hair, I try to comfort her as best as I can, though I honestly don't know where to begin.

"I'm so sorry, sweetheart," I whisper into her hair.

"It's okay. I'm okay," Courtney says, wiping her dampened cheeks. "It was years ago."

"But still, you must miss him. Was it him...the lilies?" Courtney nods as a teardrop falls from her chin. "Were you close?"

"Yes, he was my best friend. He always sided with me when my mom would lecture me on being a 'proper Christian girl.' My parents were very strict growing up."

"What happened after he died?"

"My dad became bitter and angry. He hardly spoke to anyone and would spend all his time working on something or another in the garage. My mom threw herself into church even more—praying night and day for Adam's soul and for me to find my way to God."

"And did you?"

"No. I found my way to Dylan. It was like he was the only person who truly understood how I was feeling since he'd lost his best friend, too. Plus, he was there that night."

"You and Dylan were both uninjured?"

"I was okay for the most part, cuts and bruises mostly. Dylan had a broken wrist and a few cracked ribs, but compared to Adam, yeah, I'd say we were fine. After the accident, Dylan and I spent more and more time together. We mourned Adam together. He had his own place, and I went there a lot, mostly to get away from my parents. Dylan and I had always gotten along well growing up, though I'd never considered a romantic relationship with him. Eventually, after the accident, we just kind of fell into it." Courtney begins to laugh slightly. "My mother was thrilled since Dylan's grandparents were elders at her church."

"So, you were with Dylan for a long time?" I ask softly.

Courtney wipes her dampened cheeks.

"Almost five years before I left. We dated for the rest of my high school years while he apprenticed in auto-mechanics. After I graduated, I really wanted to go to college, but my mother thought it was a waste of money since I would be married and have kids in no time, anyway. Dylan agreed with her. So, I got engaged and moved in with Dylan. My mother wasn't thrilled with us living together before marriage, but she reluctantly agreed to it since it was with Dylan.

"I worked in housekeeping at a small motel. Dylan hated that since we didn't need the money—between his apprenticeship earnings and an insurance payout he'd received from the accident, we were okay. But I had to do something besides sit around our apartment all day and wait for him to get home. So, I started saving my money. At the time, I told myself it would be my rainy-day fund, but now when I look back on it, I think I knew subconsciously that I would need this money to escape one day."

"Escape from who? Dylan? Did he hurt you?" My soft voice disappears completely as anger begins to form in my stomach.

"No, not physically. As time went on, Dylan became clingier. He always told me that he was scared he would lose me, too. Soon, he didn't hang out with anyone but me, and he hated it when I worked. He even hated me going out with the ladies' group at the church once a month. He wanted me all to himself."

"And your parents didn't care?" I grimace at her admission.

"Care? Oh, no. They thought it was great that I had someone wanting to take care of me. My mom thought it was sweet how attentive he was towards me."

"What made you decide to leave finally?"

"Well, the wedding was only a few days away and I was terrified to go through with it—and I was terrified not to go through with it. I felt trapped. I went over to my parents' house to drop off my veil that I had just picked up. My mom wasn't home, but my dad was. He asked me to come talk to him before I left. When I found him out in the garage, working on an old space heater, he immediately stopped working, which never happened. I always had to wait for him to finish tinkering with whatever he was working on. When he turned to me, I could feel his concern coming off his body. It was strange because I had never seen my dad like this before. He sternly asked me if this was what I wanted, to marry Dylan and live here for the rest of my life. Naturally, I said yes because that's what I had been conditioned to say to anyone who asked me. Then, he said something that changed my life." Courtney pauses to take a breath. I give her the moment in silence while gently rubbing her leg. Her tears have subsided, though her body is still slightly shaking.

Courtney clears her throat before she starts speaking again.

"He said to me: *When your brother died, a part of me died with him. The pain of losing him was like nothing I'd ever felt. But when I look at you, Courtney, into your eyes, I feel that pain again. Your light has faded, my girl. I worry that this life here won't kill you physically, but it might kill your spirit. There's a big world out there. I want you to find it. Find it for Adam, and find it for yourself.*

"And then he turned around and kept working on his heater like nothing happened. I spent the next few days planning my departure. I knew if my mom or Dylan found out, they would talk me out of it. The day before the wedding, I packed a single duffle bag, left Dylan a letter, and hopped on the bus."

"And you came here?"

"Yep."

"You are so brave, Courtney," I say as I pull her face towards mine, pressing my lips firmly to hers.

I'm amazed at how a young woman could go through all that, the loss of her brother, her crazy mother, and her controlling fiancé, and be strong enough to make it this far on her own.

"You are one of the most unbelievable people I've ever met," I mumble against her mouth.

Courtney begins to laugh. "I doubt that. I'm just a girl who left her fiancé, disappointed her mother, and now lives in a dumpy studio apartment."

"Don't do that. Don't talk down on the stuff you've done. You are amazing. Do you hear me, my Tiny Bird? You…"

Courtney cuts me off before I can continue my thought by pressing her hand to my chest. "I make you feel?"

"God, if you only knew what you make me *feel.*"

"You make me *feel* too, Josh." Courtney leans forward to kiss me again, but this time, our kiss is deep.

When we pull apart, we start at each other. Her wide eyes, still glossy from the tears, have me in a trace of sorts. Every part of me wants to say what I feel and not just say that I *feel.* I can feel the words beckoning to come out, but before they can, the sound of the apartment buzzard breaks my spell. The pizza is here.

"Do you want to eat this on the bed or at the table?" I ask after I tend to the delivery driver and now stand with the warm box in my hand.

"Bed," Courtney replies, already reaching for the box. "I'm so hungry."

We sit in silence on top of the bed and the cardboard box is place between us as we both stuff our faces.

"This is so good," I comment between bites.

"I told you," Courtney smirks with a mouth full of crust. "Okay, it's your turn."

"My turn for what?"

"Oh, no you don't, Mr. Hayles. You owe me one sappy story, so out with it. Tell me how your brother stole your girlfriend."

"Well, first of all, he didn't steal her. As far as I understand it, she approached him."

"He didn't say no, though."

"No, but knowing Landry, he probably didn't know what he was saying at the time. Either way, as much as I would love to tell your sadistic side that this event shattered my world and broke my heart, I have to disappoint you. Losing Lindsay was nothing to me. Actually, it might have been more of a relief than anything."

"And losing Landry?"

"Landry has made my heart hurt for almost his entire life. This was just the final puncture that stopped its beating." Courtney's eyes stared at me widely, shocked. "What?" I ask.

"Josh, that was so...I don't know, sensitive and poetic—and kind of beautiful. I didn't know you had it in you."

"I can be sensitive," I laugh slightly. "It's probably the only thing I got from my mother—and believe me, my father hated that about me growing up."

"Tell me about your mother."

I shrug my shoulders. "Not much to say. She died when I was five, so I don't remember her too well."

"I'm sorry," Courtney reaches over and rubs my arm. "But you remembered that she was sensitive, right? Probably kind, too?"

"Yes, she was. Before she died, we spent almost every day together. I remember her taking me to a lot of gardens and museums. We'd spend hours walking around parks and eating ice cream. It was always just the two of us. We played silly games like watching for butterflies, and the one who spotted the most won. She loved nature, birds, and flowers, and of course, you know that lilies were her favourite."

"How did your mom die, if you don't mind me asking?"

"Cancer. She was diagnosed with ovarian cancer, but it was too late; it was already spreading to other organs. She died about a year after her diagnosis. After that, my father became miserable, even more so than before. He hired a nanny to do most of the caregiving for Isaac and me. We hardly saw him growing up unless it was to keep up his family-man persona."

"How old were you when your dad had your younger brothers?" Courtney asks as she bites through her second piece of pizza.

"I was ten when Landry was born and twelve when Rob was born. Their mom was nice enough. I don't know, I didn't really have much to do with her. I just know one day she was there and the next she was gone, but left the boys behind."

"What about Isaac? How did he handle your mother's death?"

"Isaac's been moulded to be exactly like my dad. From a young age, he was told not to show emotion, not to cry, basically not to be a pussy. So, after Mom died, I think that was even more reinforced in him since Dad was all we had left. He always tried so hard; hell, he still tries to please our father like his praise is priceless." I stop to lick pizza grease off my fingers before continuing. "Believe me, Isaac has issues of his own to deal with. Underneath his tough exterior, something is slowly killing him from the inside. I see it happening before my own eyes, and I feel like there's nothing I can do to stop it."

"Kind of like Landry?"

"Yes, like Landry. I'm not saying Rob and I are perfect by any means, but those other two brothers, they have demons inside them that I don't totally understand."

"What about you? What are your demons lurking around inside?" Courtney smirks with one eyebrow cocked and tosses her half-eaten slice back into the box.

Before answering her, I lift the pizza box off the bed and toss it onto the floor beside us.

"It would seem I have an unhealthy attraction to someone much too young for me." I reach for Courtney's arm and pull her towards me until she has positioned herself on my lap. "Someone who has their entire life in front of them and doesn't need the likes of me weighing them down. Yet, I don't really care because I want that someone more than I've wanted anyone before in my life."

"Well, you should know that someone feels the same about you and doesn't really give a shit about the age difference or what anyone thinks about it. However, one thing I am worried about is what we will do when it comes time for you to leave Elmerson." I feel Courtney's entire body tense up as she releases her statement. "I'm sorry to bring that up right now, I don't want to be a downer, but I do think about it."

"I know," I admit. "I think about it, too."

"How long do you think you have left on your case?"

"A few weeks, for sure. Then, after that, I don't know what will happen. I'm technically still employed by my father's law firm in Brighten. Plus, I have a condo there."

"So, it only makes sense that you would go back there. I get it." Courtney's voice is meek and quiet.

"Hey, hey now, Tiny Bird, you don't need to worry. We'll figure something out."

"You know, I don't know why you insist on calling me Tiny Bird when you clearly have the bluebird in your heart."

"What are you talking about?"

"You know the old Charles Bukowski poem, *There's a bluebird in my heart, but I'm too tough for him.* That's you."

"I don't think I've ever heard it before."

"What?" Courtney sits up in shock. "You have to listen to this poem, Josh." Courtney hops off the bed in one swoop to retrieve her phone from the kitchen counter.

By the time she gets back to bed, she has loaded her YouTube app and is frantically typing away.

"Okay, ready?"

I nod as she crawls back onto my lap while holding the phone, pressing play on the loaded video. The deep voice echoes as the words fill the air around us. The story of a man who acts tough on the outside but has a bluebird in his heart causes my heart to beat rapidly. I have flashes of memories of my mother, who used to call me Baby Blue J; my father, who moulded me to be as tough as nails; and now images of Courtney, who saw through it all to remind me of the bluebird I have inside of me.

With my eyes closed as the poem ends, I wrap my arms around her tighter than before. I dare not open my eyes for the fear of the moisture that threatens to fall. We sit in silence, neither of us saying a word for a few minutes.

"My mother used to call me Baby Blue J," I finally say out loud. "I've never mentioned that to anyone before."

"Really?" Courtney sits up again so we are face to face. Placing her palm onto my cheek she moves in closer to me. "Then I will keep it close to my heart."

"I want to be in your heart, too." I shake off the embarrassment that I probably sound more like a child than a grown man.

"Believe me, Bluebird, you're in my heart. In fact, you might be its keeper," Courtney whispers.

"Good, because I want it to be mine. Because I feel..." Courtney opens her mouth to speak, assuming I'm through with my thoughts—I stop her by placing a single finger over her lips. "Because I feel *love.*"

I remove my finger from her gaping lips and slide my hand around the back of her neck. I pull her towards me and firmly press my lips to hers. Her hands sit on my shoulders as we continue to kiss with eager lips. My brain is scrambling with excitement and panic. Did I use the word *love*? Never have I said that to a woman before, my mother excluded. I can't explain what's happening to me—happening inside of me. I'm so tired of being angry, of being lonely. Somehow, Courtney has filled voids within me that I didn't even know could be filled. I feel different around her. I feel like, maybe, just maybe, I can be a man worthy of receiving love from a woman like her. I can be the man my mother always wanted me to become; I can be the man *I've* always wanted to become.

Chapter 19

Courtney

Two weeks later, Josh hasn't said the L-word to me again, and I'm trying not to freak out. I mean, in all fairness, I haven't said it to him either. Josh and I have spent all our free time together, and I must admit that despite not saying it, I'm feeling its effects.

I was surprised when Josh asked me to fly to Brighten with him this weekend. Although I usually work on the weekends, I begged and pleaded with my co-workers to switch shifts. Luckily, they agreed and didn't ask too many questions.

Josh needed to return to Brighten for an important meeting with his father's law firm, which is also Josh's firm, when he's not working on side cases like in Elmerson. The flight to Brighten from Elmerson is quick, only forty-five minutes. Waiting for our luggage and the Uber took longer than the flight itself.

Finally, we are on our way to Josh's condo, and I'm both excited and nervous. With our hands locked together in the back seat of the Uber, I distract myself by watching the city lights outside the window.

"You seem tense," Josh's voice breaks the silence.

Turning to meet his large, brown eyes, I shrug. "Maybe a little bit. It's weird to be here in your real life—where you live, where your family lives. Do you think I will see any of your brothers or your father while we're here?"

"I hadn't planned on you seeing any of them, but if you would like to, it could be arranged."

"Do you think they will have a problem with me? I mean, with the age difference and all?"

"I don't give a shit what they think," Josh scowls in my direction. "I want you here, and I want you with me. That's all that matters."

"That's a nice thought, Josh, but we have to be realistic. Some people are going to have a problem with us. I can see your father being upset."

"My father's always upset. You don't have to worry about any of them; I'll take care of them." Josh lifts his hand and tucks my hair behind my ear. "I meant what I said about the love thing," Josh's voice softens.

"Yeah, and what's that?" I whisper in return as my heartbeat quickens. I can feel Josh's warm lips touch the edge of my earlobe.

"About feeling love for you, Tiny Bird. I've never said this to anyone else before, but I do love you."

My heart is beating rapidly as I struggle for a full breath. My eyes moisten, though it's not sad tears they are filling with, it's something else. I turn my face to nuzzle back into his.

"I love you," I reply with honesty. I haven't spoken those words to anyone since Dylan, though saying them to him and saying them to Josh feels like I'm speaking in different languages.

"Is that so?" Josh brings his lips to meet mine.

"Uh-huh," I mumble against his lips.

"So, then, we have nothing to worry about. Anyone who has a problem with us can go to hell."

Josh continues to kiss my lips softly until the Uber slows down before coming to a stop in front of a large silver building. Josh exits the car before holding his hand back to help me out of the car and into the night's air. Feeling the warm spring breeze against my cheek, I look up at the exuberantly large building.

"This is where you live?" I ask in amazement as Josh approaches me with our rolling luggage behind him. "It makes my little building seem like trash."

"No, my love, your place is perfect because it's where you are," Josh corrects me.

"Joshua Hayles, don't tell me you're becoming a mush?"

"Perhaps, but don't tell anyone," Josh says with a smirk.

"Your secret's safe with me, Bluebird," I reply while taking my suitcase from his grip.

Josh lets out a slight huff of air, "Well, I must admit that Bluebird is better than Buttercup."

As we walk through the glass doors of the building, I'm taken aback by the large black and chrome-coloured chandelier that towers over the foyer. It's beautiful, though I can't help but cringe slightly as my rubber-soled shoes squeak on the shiny tiled floor. Luckily, Josh is dressed as casually as I am, in dark denim jeans, a black jacket, and Nikes that squeak when he walks, as well.

We enter the elevator at the end of the large entryway, and Josh's finger presses the number seventeen, lighting it immediately. Moments later, our silent ride has ended. Unlocking the door to his condo quickly, Josh walks through the black door just far enough to hold it open as I follow with my luggage in tow.

The light overhead turns on, revealing an entryway bigger than my entire apartment. The walls are light gray with black moulding at the top and bottom. After removing our shoes, I follow Josh through the space that leads into a large, open kitchen. It has stainless steel appliances and a black, marble-topped island that is completely bare except for one bowl in the center, holding an assortment of fresh fruits.

"How is it possible you even have fresh fruit here when you haven't been here in weeks?"

"Martha, my housekeeper, got them for me. I also asked her to stock the fridge for us and grab a few other things," Josh tosses a wink in my direction. "Which we'll get to in a second, but first, let's get our luggage to our room and then I'll give you a tour."

"Our room? Don't you mean your room?"

"First, you're not sleeping in a guest room, obviously. Second, I want you to think of everything here as yours." Josh's body leans against the island.

"Oh? I can think of that giant TV over there as mine?" I ask while gesturing to the large screen on the wall of the living room, separated from the kitchen only by a fireplace.

"Of course," Josh says as he pulls me closer and lifts me onto the island in front of him.

"So even if you're watching the NBA playoffs and I want to turn to, oh, I don't know, let's say, HGTV, you'd be okay with that?"

"I said that it was yours, too. I didn't say I would be okay with you turning off my basketball," Josh growls as he moves his body in between my legs and begins to nibble on my neck.

Running my fingers through his brown hair, I ask, "What if I want to seduce you during a basketball game? Would that be okay?"

"What do you think half-time is for?"

"Half-time? That's all the time you're giving me?"

"Tiny Bird, are you becoming needy already? I just got you home, and you're already trying to get your way. I should warn you about what happens in my house to needy women."

"Mmm, what's that, Bluebird?"

"They get taken to bed early."

Josh lifts me from the counter in one quick swoop, causing my legs to wrap tightly around his waist. I hold onto his large shoulders as he marches us down the dark hallway to the door at the end of the hall. Josh doesn't stop to turn on the lights, so all I can see is the green glow from a clock on a small table. I don't even get a chance to read the time before I feel my body tossed onto a plush bed. The blanket feels cool against my bare arms. Instantly, my body is covered with Josh's. His lips take mine fiercely as he pins my hands to the bed above my head.

Josh stops kissing me only long enough to mumble, "You have no idea how happy I am to have you in my bed."

"Tell me, are you planning to fuck me or make gentle love now that you've turned to mush?" I tease him.

"Why do I have to choose? I'm going to fuck you like I love you," his growling words cause an eruption of goosebumps over my entire body as his hands release my wrists and slide down the length of my arms.

Keeping my arms over my head, Josh quickly removes my clothing and his own before his body is back over mine. Our bare skin melts together as we kiss and nibble, lick, and taste, all while whispering sweet nothings of complete intimacy. A euphoria I've never felt before between myself and a lover—and we hadn't even gotten to the sex yet.

Without warning, Josh suddenly braces his arms around my back while flipping me over so that we are both kneeling on the bed. His firm chest is pressed tightly against my back as our knees intertwine. I can feel his hardness pressing up against my opening as his one hand holds me close under my arm and over my chest while the other is braced around my neck. I use one hand to anchor myself steady on his knee as I reach behind and greedily grab onto his thick hair. I can hear Josh's panting against my ear as he begins to thrust himself inside of me.

"I want you to be mine, Tiny Bird."

"I am yours, baby," I reply between unsteady breaths.

"I mean forever. I want this with you forever. I want you in my bed every night."

"Maybe I should make you beg me?" I tighten my grip on his hair.

"You think you're in a position to make me beg?"

"I think I'm in a position to make you do anything I want."

"We'll see about that," Josh says with a grunt. He thrusts his body forward, causing me to lose my balance and fall onto all fours. Josh towers behind me. Looking over my shoulder, only the clock's glow illuminates Josh's outline.

"This is how you beg?" I ask with sass.

"No, baby," I feel his hand run over the smoothness of my backside. "I don't beg for what I want; I demand it."

Suddenly, Josh's gentle touch turns into searing pain as the sound of his hand slapping against my skin echoes throughout the room. I can't help but let out a light whimper.

"Josh," I manage to say as I push myself back towards him wanting more. "Of course, I'm yours forever. You're too goddamn stubborn not to get your way."

I can hear the smile on Josh's face when he replies, "Well, not quite the compliance I was looking for, but good enough," Josh pushes himself into me with unforgiving force.

After the final peak of intensity, first with me and then with him, we lower ourselves onto the bed and pull the blanket around us like a burrito.

"I meant what I said," I say as I nuzzle into his shoulder. "About this being forever."

"Good, because either way, I'm not letting you go. You make me feel more like myself than I have in years, maybe my entire life. As sappy as this probably sounds, it's kind of like you've saved me," Josh mutters and pulls me in tighter.

"Saved you from what?" I wonder out loud.

"Myself. If you wouldn't have come into my world, then I think I probably would have ended up exactly like my father. Now, I feel like maybe I will end up exactly like the man I wanted to be."

"What kind of man is that?"

"A kind and worthy man, the type of man you deserve."

"You know, you're actually pretty sweet for a stubborn bull."

"You make me sweet, Tiny Bird."

"And you make me happy, Bluebird."

Chapter 20

Josh

After our impromptu sex, Courtney and I drag ourselves to shower, which takes longer than it should because I can't seem to keep my hands off her. After the shower, we both get into comfy clothes since we have no plans to leave my place for the rest of the night.

I watch Courtney curled up on my black leather couch under a beige blanket, playing on her phone. I'm supposed to be getting us wine from the kitchen while we wait for our Thai food to arrive, but I've gotten distracted.

Everything about this moment seems right. It's not only the ambiance of the city lights through the large windows nor the flickering of the fireplace. It's mostly because of the woman sitting on my couch, as if it's the only place she belongs, smiling at some silly TikTok video playing on her screen. Perfection is the only word that comes to my mind. I am stupefied that I, Joshua Hayles, am having these feelings. I don't allow myself to dwell on this too long since I still have wine to deliver to—dare I say, the love of my life. For a moment, I hardly recognize myself and these thoughts of love.

When I arrive at the couch with two glasses of wine in hand, Courtney immediately lifts the blanket high, allowing me to sit down before replacing it over us both. Sipping on our wine, we sit quietly in our contentment.

"I was thinking," I break our silence. "I want you to come to dinner at my father's house tomorrow night. I want to introduce you as my girlfriend."

"Are you serious? Do you think that's a good idea?" Courtney replies in shock after coughing on her wine.

"I think it's a fantastic idea. Honestly, I want everyone to know about us. I'm rather proud of us."

Chewing on her bottom lip, Courtney asks hesitantly, "What about your father? And my job? What if somehow from work finds out?"

"First of all, I don't care what my father thinks. Second of all, I would rather move out of the hotel and get my own place somewhere else than hide being with you anymore."

Courtney grins, "You could move in with me."

"Into your tiny apartment?" I can't help but laugh at the notion. "How long do you think it would be until we killed each other?"

"Um, I would give us a week—but, hey, It would be a fun week, wouldn't it?"

"It would be the best, Tiny Bird." I reach over and grab her free hand with mine. "Honestly though, I don't know how much longer the case in Elmerson is going to be."

"Then what's going to happen?"

I take a deep breath, knowing this topic would come up again, eventually.

"Well, then I will have to move back here—and I would like you to move back with me."

"What about my job? My apartment? My schooling? I have a plan, Josh," Courtney fires off the questions in a panicked tone.

"I know you do, but couldn't you do all that from here? Brighten has some fancy hotels, and your school is online, anyway. Also, if you were here, you wouldn't need that tiny apartment. You would have this one…with me."

"This is a lot to process, Josh. I always thought I would do this alone, and I didn't need anyone's help. I didn't need to be rescued like my mom or Dylan thought I did."

"I'm not trying to save you, Courtney. I'm trying to create a life with you." I can feel frustration building in my chest. Why is she so stubborn all the time?

"I get that, Josh, but you have to understand that this is a big deal for me."

"I do know that," I mutter with an eye roll.

"So, are you saying you'd move to Elmerson for me? Quit the law firm and give up your place here in Brighten?"

"Courtney, you know it's not that simple. First off, that job at the law firm isn't just any firm, it's my father's. If my suspicions are correct, he is making Isaac and I full partners tomorrow since he has officially left the firm when he became mayor. We knew this would come, eventually.

"Second, this isn't just some apartment I rent, this is a condo that I own. All this stuff in this place, I own. The two cars parked downstairs in the parking garage, I own them, too. So, no, it's not the same for me to move to Elmerson as for you to move to Brighten."

"God, you can be such an ass sometimes, Hayles," Courtney grits her teeth in anger. "Is all this supposed to impress me? The fact that you own all this and make more money should have me kneeling at your feet and doing whatever you say? Maybe that's how the women you've dated before have acted, but I'm not that kind of woman, Josh. Honestly, I'm a little offended that you are expecting me to be."

Courtney's voice is now raised as I feel myself getting angrier by the second. Standing up from the couch, I set my wine glass on the side table before turning back to her. With a reddened face, Courtney remains stoically on the couch.

"You know what, forget about it. I was wrong to assume you might want to come here with me. For the record, I didn't expect you to want to come here because I had the job or the condo; I expected you to want to come here with me because you said you loved me. Perhaps we have different expectations of what comes with that." I turn away from her and march out of the room. "I'm going to do some work. The food should be here soon. I've already paid for it. I hope that's okay with you." I regretted the last statement the moment it left my mouth, but there was no way my pride would let me turn back to apologize. Not yet, anyway.

I walk down the hallway and turn into the first door on my right, my office, slamming it behind me. Immediately going straight to the bar cart next to the two large oak bookshelves, I pour myself a generous glass of scotch. I sit down behind my large black desk, setting the glass on top of a pile of papers to ensure no ring mark will be left behind. I rub my hands over my face and take a deep breath, trying to figure out if I am being unreasonable or if Courtney is being her typical implacable self.

A few more gulps of scotch and the glass drains, and my anger dissipates. I realize this is our first night together at home, and we're already fighting. I shake my head and decide to be the bigger person and apologize. However, when I open the door to my office, I find Courtney pacing in circles in front of it. She notices my presence as I lean on the doorframe with my arms crossed, and she stops walking immediately.

"I suck at this love thing," Courtney says without looking up from her fidgeting fingers.

"Yeah," I sigh. "So do I."

"What are we going to do?" Courtney looks up as her wide and glossy blue eyes meet mine.

"Well, first, you'll come over here, Tiny Bird." I open my arms towards her, and within seconds, she has tucked herself inside them. "Second, you need to understand that I feel like I've waited for you my entire life and the thought of not being with you every second, let alone not being in the same city as you, scares me. I don't like it, and I don't want it."

I hear a small sniffle as Courtney shakes her head into my chest.

"I don't want that, either," she agrees.

"I think we should leave it on the back burner for now and enjoy our weekend together."

"Okay," Courtney says, pulling back to look at me. "I'm sorry for being so stubborn and defensive."

I laugh, "Trust me, I know how you feel. Sometimes, I feel like I'm dating the female version of myself. What did you call me earlier, bull-headed?"

"We're quite the pair. Two assholes in a pod," Courtney jokes.

"Speak for yourself," I scoff.

Pushing herself onto her toes to reach her lips to mine, Courtney presses a kiss against my mouth.

"Tell me I'm your forever," she mumbles with her lips still on mine.

"You're my forever, Tiny Bird. As long as you want this old Bluebird, he's yours, too."

Chapter 21

Courtney

Despite the little blip in our evening last night, my time here in Brighten has been great. Josh made me a wonderful breakfast in bed: eggs, toast, fruit, and coffee. After we ate in bed together, I offered him a thank-you in his preferred way before he headed off to a meeting with his father.

Josh told me he would be gone for a few hours and offered me the keys to one of his cars. Since I'm not familiar with the city of Brighten, I opted to stay at the condo for the morning. My first order of business is to take a long bubble bath in his giant two-person jetted tub. The separate shower on the other side of the suite is the same one we showered in last night, and I've been eyeing up this tub ever since.

In preparation for our arrival, Josh had his housekeeper stock up his bathroom with bubble bath, salts, oils, and anything else you might want for some pampering. As I soak myself with bubbles sitting as high as my chin, I feel like a princess.

I take this time alone to reflect on the argument Josh and I had last night. I didn't want to admit this to him, or even to myself, if I'm honest, but when he suggested that I move here with him, I got scared. The fear of being reliant on him, or anybody, again is paralyzing. I never want to be in the same situation I was in with Dylan. The control and resentment, ugh, never again. I don't want to be at anyone's mercy with the stifling feelings of guilt and shame. I promised myself that I would never do that again. But what do I do now? A great man, a man I love, wants to be with me and create a life together. Of course, it makes sense that I would move to be with him versus him moving to be with me. He has a better job, a better home, a better…well life. But still, I feel resistance inside of me. What about all that I have been working for? What about my dreams of finishing school and becoming a hotel manager at a five-star property, maybe somewhere foreign? How can I give all that up for Josh? Is it selfish of me to not want to give that up?

Dunking my head under the water, I try to silence my thoughts until my lungs give out. When I rise up, panting for breath, it's all I can do not to let my mind go back into overdrive.

After I wash my hair and get out of the tub, I check the time and see that it's already past noon. I wonder how much longer Josh will be at his meeting. I was going to wait until he returned to eat lunch, but I'm feeling too hungry to wait. After helping myself to the food in his fridge, I eat silently at the large island alone.

I try to picture myself living here with him and what my life would look like. I can see us cooking meals together in his kitchen and watching movies in his living room—I want that, I really do. So, why does my heart pound so erratically at the thought of giving up my life in Elmerson?

After eating some of the leftover Thai food from last night, I don't know what to do with myself. I suppose I could watch TV or something, but I know I won't be able to concentrate on anything right now. Instead, I grab my phone and look up hotels in Brighten. Like most cities, there are accommodations ranging from downright nasty to extravagant. I noticed that one hotel called The Whitestone is located only a few blocks from Josh's downtown condo. The pictures of the property are stunning, and it has a five-star rating. I change out of my loungewear and walk down to the hotel to look around. While some women would prefer shopping as their therapy, luxury hotels are mine.

An hour later, and with still no word from Josh, I find myself walking through the Whitestone lobby. It's stunning. While The Valemont is an old building with an antique architectural design, The Whitestone is new and modern. Everything shines pristinely. Bright, white floors sparkle, while the large windows are draped in dark teal and silver fabrics. The chrome chandelier overhead glows with the same teal-coloured glass over each bulb. The furniture is also white, and I wonder how on earth they manage to keep it looking so clean. A fireplace in the center of the lobby is a cylinder that stretches up to the top of the tall ceiling. Even the front desk is made of white marble. The front desk attendants are dressed entirely in black except for a teal scarf for the women and a teal tie for the men. The space smells of a combination of fresh apples and cinnamon. Of course, my eyes land on a perfect display of bright red apples in the center of a nearby table—clever.

Slowly, I wander through the lobby, lost in my thoughts, which are cut off when I'm approached by a beautiful blonde woman in a crisp black, wide-legged suit. Her pointed-toe heels peek out from the hem of her pants. A simple strand of pearls wraps around her neck, which is mostly covered by a high white collar. Suddenly, I feel underdressed in my black linen pants and red pea coat.

"Is there something I can help you with?" The woman speaks to me with a smile, and I immediately notice her name tag reads *Nancy, General Manager.*

"Oh, I'm sorry. I was just looking around. I'm not a guest or anything; I hope that's okay. I really wanted to look at your beautiful hotel."

"Absolutely. Are you a resident of Brighten, then?"

"No, I'm from Elmerson. I'm staying at a friend's place a few blocks away. I work as a concierge at The Valemont, so naturally, when I noticed this hotel was walking distance from me, I couldn't resist."

"Well, isn't that fabulous? I've stayed at The Valemont in Elmerson. It's a lovely property."

"Thank you. I enjoy it there, but I do have one question for you if you don't mind me asking?" I ask with a bright grin.

"Of course," Nancy smiles in return.

"You aren't hiring by any chance? I have been thinking about moving to Brighten and I am curious about the job market."

"Well, we aren't hiring a concierge at the moment, but we may have a couple of positions in other departments. Are you open to working elsewhere?"

"Yes, I could be. Honestly, my ultimate goal is to be a GM one day, like yourself. I'm currently working on getting my degree in hotel management."

"Well, that's fantastic. I'm sorry I didn't catch your name."

"Courtney Mason," I reply, extending my hand to which Nancy shakes promptly.

"I'm Nancy Lamont. Why don't you take my card, Courtney," Nancy reaches into her blazer pocket and retrieves a glossy black business card. "And if you decide to move here, please call me and we'll figure something out."

"Wow, thank you. This means so much to me," I beam.

"You remind me of myself at your age. Not everyone gets the love of hospitality, but once you're bitten by it, there's no turning back."

"You're right! Thank you so much for this," I say, holding up the card. "I have a feeling you'll be hearing from me."

"I look forward to it, Courtney," Nancy smiles again before turning away and greeting some other nearby guests.

I feel like I'm dreaming as I place Nancy's business card into my coat pocket. It's as if the universe wants me to move here to be with Josh. Is that what's happening, or am I looking for any reason to move here to be with him?

I walk a little lighter as I move through the streets of downtown Brighten. I imagine living here, walking to work at the hotel, and coming home to Josh. It all seems too good to be true.

When I arrive back at Josh's condo, I'm even more happy when I see him leaning against the island when I come through the doorway.

"I was getting worried about you," Josh says as he sets down the glass of water he's holding.

Still dressed from his meeting with his father, Josh is in a navy suit and tie. However, his blazer is removed and tossed over the back of the tall chair beside him. His tie has been tugged loose.

After I remove my shoes and jacket, I skip over to him and instantly wrap my arms around his neck. My euphoria is still high.

"You don't have to worry about me, I was having a great time," I grin.

"I tried to call you, but you must have turned your phone off," Josh notes as he wraps his arms around my waist.

"Actually, it died earlier, so I left it here to charge."

Josh furrows his eyebrows at me.

"What?" I nuzzle into his neck knowing he is irritated with me, but also knowing I can turn him to mush as I plant tiny kisses along his jawline. "I have some exciting news, but first, I want you to tell me about your meeting with your father."

"My father exhausts me. He's so demanding all the time," Josh sighs.

"Let's sit in the living room, and you can tell me all about it." I let go of his neck and tug at his arm to follow me.

We settle on the couch, with my legs swung over his lap and my head on his shoulder. Josh lets out another sigh.

"You know this meeting was to implement Isaac and me as full partners into the firm, right?"

Nodding in agreement, I run my fingers over his thick neck.

"Well, the contract that was drawn up is riddled with conditions. That's why the meeting took so long; Isaac and I had to fight all morning with our father. And not just conditions on us, but also conditions that would affect any spouse and children."

My back tightens with the thought of Josh's last statement. Not that Josh and I have ever discussed marriage, let alone children; I can't help but feel a twinge of nerves rattle through my body, considering how quickly our relationship has moved thus far.

"It's nothing you have to worry about, Tiny Bird," Josh's voice has softened. "I won't rush you into anything, so please don't get scared. That being said, I know that there is a very good chance that you will be my future…everything, I will make sure you are always protected."

"Who says I'm scared?" I sit up enough to move my body over top of his so my legs are now straddling his waist. "I'm not scared of a future with you."

"Well, I thought since you've already been engaged and almost married these things would be completely off-limits for a long time."

"No, you're right. I'm in no rush for that stuff, but at the same time, I'm very much in a rush to be your…what did you call me? Your everything? I mean, with an offer like that from Joshua Hayles on the table, how could a girl possibly refuse?"

Josh leans forward and cups my cheeks into his large hands. Our eyes lock onto each other, saying everything we need to say without the necessity of words.

"I do adore you," Josh speaks first.

"And I adore you," I reply. "Do you want to tell me more about your meeting?"

"Absolutely not. Not while I have the most beautiful woman in the world in my arms. Discussing anything beyond how much I want to give her everything or how many dirty things I want to do to her is completely out of the question. Besides, we still have to go to my father's house for supper. Let's not ruin the freedom we have for the rest of the afternoon."

Josh moves his mouth to mine, and eventually, it goes down my neck. As his tongue runs over my flesh, I think about telling him about my meeting with Nancy from The Whitestone, but I don't want to interrupt this moment. With his mouth kissing my skin and his hands, which have a firm grip on my backside, I decide to tell him later. We have plenty of time.

Chapter 22

Josh

We arrive at my father's house a little after seven p.m. I use the term 'house' loosely since it's a grotesquely large building for one man. The outdoor lights illuminate the two-storey building like a museum. A stone staircase leads to the front door. I glance over at Courtney, staring at the structure with her mouth agape.

"This is where you grew up? Geez, no wonder you're so high maintenance," she offers me a sideways glance and smirks.

"Trust me, this place has nothing on your apartment in Elmerson."

"Aw, are you missing my humble abode, Josh? Is it the bed size or the endless supply of Lucky Charms?" Courtney's giggling fills the car as I turn into a parking spot.

I can't help but notice more cars than usual for an intimate family supper. Immediately, I know that my father has turned this into a pompous evening to parade in front of a large crowd.

"Courtney, I have to apologize, but I think there are going to be more people here than I expected. Are you going to be okay? I don't want you to feel uncomfortable."

Turning towards me with her eyes glowing, Courtney smiles at me.

"You know I deal with rich people for a living, right? Trust me, I can handle snotty small talk."

"Okay, sweetheart. You know, I have a feeling I'm not going to want you out of my sight tonight," I reach up and brush a strand of hair off her face. "Did I mention how beautiful you look?"

"Only a few times since we left your place," Courtney winks.

Getting out of the car, I offer Courtney my hand, which she takes with ease. I wasn't lying about how stunning she looked this evening. Wearing a form-fitted, knee-length black dress with a slight flare, the skirt flows softly with each step she takes. She has a pair of black heels on, and her hair is up in what I was told is called a *French Twist*. I received an earful about messing it up before we left my place when I tried to push her against the wall of the elevator and cover her in kisses. When we reach the top of the stairs, I stop her before entering the house.

"I apologize in advance for anything stupid my father might say this evening, and my brothers and—"

"Josh, stop worrying. It's going to be fine," Courtney leans up and presses her lips to my stubbled cheek. "Remember, I love you, and I've got you," she whispers into my ear before pulling away.

I don't know how Courtney is so confident about how this evening will go, but I love her for it.

When we enter through the doors, Jean, my father's long-time housekeeper, immediately greeted us. The tiny woman with white hair, which I have only ever seen in a bun on top of her head, offers a welcoming smile to both Courtney and me.

"Joshua, how wonderful to see you," Jean says while offering me a quick embrace. "And you brought a date, how lovely."

"Jean, it's nice to see you, too. This is Courtney."

"It's nice to meet you, Jean." Courtney offers her bright smile.

"Let me take your coats. Everyone is currently in the living room. Dinner will be ready in thirty minutes."

As Jean leaves with our jackets, I watch Courtney take in her surroundings. Walking slowly through the foyer of my father's house, the sound of Courtney's heels clicking against the dark brown and beige ceramic tiles.

"Wow," she mutters in amazement as her eyes look to the large staircase and the crystal chandelier. "It's like a hotel."

Slowly, Courtney makes her way to the large side table, which is topped with a crystal vase of white lilies, as always.

"Here are your lilies, Josh. It really is like the hotel," Courtney laughs softly as her fingers touch one of the petals.

I walk up behind her, wrapping my arms around her waist.

"It's the only reminder of my mother that my father keeps around here."

"That's kind of sweet."

I have no reply except to grunt slightly at the notion of my father being sweet. Before we can say anything more, we are interrupted by the booming voice of my brother, Isaac.

"It's about time you showed up. I was getting tired of talking to Dad's friends on my own." Playfully slapping my back, Isaac asks, "Also, I'm wondering why a woman this lovely is here with you?"

Courtney and I turn to face my brother, who stands taller than me by a couple of inches. His black hair is combed back, and like me, he wears a light layer of stubble on his face. Permanent scowl lines are indented between his brows. Dressed in a black suit and tie, my brother looks like anything but the warm and fuzzy type.

"Isaac, this is my girlfriend, Courtney."

Offering her hand to Isaac, his large palm engulfs Courtney's as they shake.

"Courtney, you look familiar."

"You probably would recognize me better if I were on the floor, cleaning up spilt water," Courtney laughs as she reminds Isaac of their brief encounter in Elmerson a few weeks ago.

"Yes, of course, from the hotel. Well, can I offer you two a drink?"

"Why don't I get the drinks?" Courtney offers with ease. "Just point me in the direction of the bar."

"You don't have to do that," I say.

"Please, I want to. It will give you a chance to tell your brother how smitten you are with me," Courtney gives me a sly smile.

After giving her our requests and pointing her into the living room, Isaac and I are left alone in the foyer.

"Okay, let me have it," I cross my arms and turn towards my brother who is undoubtedly waiting to give me his two cents.

"She's young, Josh," Isaac comments while sliding his hands into his pockets.

Running my fingers through my hair, I nod, "I know, but it's not like that."

"Not like what?"

"I'm not just fooling around with her. It's more than that."

"Enlighten me," Isaac scoffs.

"It's hard to explain. She makes me feel, I don't know, lighter or something. When I'm with her, I feel less angry. I feel free."

Isaac stares at me with his deep blue eyes, and for a moment, I see a flash of sadness before he clears his throat, bringing him back from the memories I know he will never speak of.

"And she doesn't mind that you're an old man?" Isaacs's attempt at humour is his way of changing the topic.

"No, I don't think so," I smirk.

"Are you happy?"

"Yes."

"Good, that's all I want. Now, let's go find your girl before one of your brothers sleeps with her," Isaac pats me on my shoulder.

"Piss off," I growl as I punch my big brother in the arm hard enough to make him wince.

Before entering the living room, buzzing with the voices of my father's guests, Isaac and I offer each other a quick smile and a nod of mutual, albeit always unspoken, love for each other.

We locate Courtney quickly, still at the bar, making small talk with my father's assistant, Claire. Upon our arrival at the two women, Courtney hands over our drinks with an apology.

"I'm sorry. I got distracted."

I lean over and press a half kiss onto Claire's cheek, "Nice to see you, Claire."

"Joshua, I'm happy to see you have found yourself such a lovely woman," Claire gestures at Courtney, who beams with pride. "Better than that last one you brought around. Speaking of which, they should be here soon," Claire presses her tiny red lips together.

"Landry and Lindsay?" I ask, though I already know the answer.

"Uh-huh. Your father wanted all his sons here tonight. Steph Grant from the *National Times* is here, as well." Claire says. That explains why my father has made this supper a bigger deal than it should be.

"I should have known," I mumble, raising the glass of scotch to my lips.

"There's always an angle with him," Isaac grumbles beside me.

"Alright, boys, that's enough," Claire scowls at us. "I'm going to find your father now, but you two be on your best behaviour. It's a big night for him."

Claire marches off in search of my father. At that moment, I witness Landry and Lindsay making their way into the living room. I'm surprised to see them here tonight since they live in Reddington now. However, I know that if my father requested their attendance, then the hour drive would have to be made, no matter what. That's how it has always been with my father, his wish is always his sons' command.

In a long red dress, Lindsay's baby bump is on full display. With her arm tucked into Landry's, who is dressed in a black suit minus the tie, the couple makes their way over to Lindsay's parents, who are schmoozing with another old, stuffy couple.

"Is that her?" Courtney's voice interrupts my thoughts. "She's beautiful."

Isaac grunts, "Wait until you speak to her. That opinion will change."

The three of us are distracted by the couple across the room when my father arrives beside us.

"Did you two settle everything after I left the meeting today?" My father's dominant voice takes over. Isaac and I only nod in response.

"Good. Claire informed me that you are aware that Steph Grant is here tonight, so I don't want any drama from either of you. Is that understood? Also, if you see your brother acting out of line, you must stop it immediately." Of course, he is referring to Landry. You can hear the disdain in my father's voice anytime he speaks of him.

I take the break in the conversation to introduce Courtney to my father, though truthfully, I'd rather not. My father politely greets her, though I can feel his disapproval rolling off his body in waves. I'm not sure if it's her age that he disapproves of or the fact that she doesn't qualify in his social ranking system, but what I do know is that I will be hearing about this later. I'm already dreading that conversation.

I do everything in my power to steer clear of Landry and Lindsay, yet we end up seated across from them at the large dining table a short while later. My father has his more important guests seated near him—by more important guests, I'm referring to the people he can get the most from to serve his own purpose.

This leaves his family at the other end of the table. With Isaac placed at the foot of the table, Courtney is on his left, while Lindsay is on his right. Landry and I are directly across from each other and beside our respective dates. Rob is on the other side of Landry, as always. I don't know if my father does things like this on purpose. I'd like to think that perhaps it is at the ignorance of his staff that we are seated like this, though I wouldn't put it past my father's sadistic nature to also have a hand in this. Courtney remains confident, with her posture strong and her head up, even though Lindsay is staring daggers in her direction. Landry breaks the thick silence once we are seated and served our first course—creamed asparagus soup.

"Courtney, it's lovely to see you again," Landry says warmly to Courtney.

"You as well, Landry," Courtney replies.

Landry offers her a kind smirk, which is returned with a bright smile from Courtney. I don't know the details of the conversation they had weeks ago in the hotel, but it was significant enough that there seems to be a mutual respect.

"You two have met before?" Lindsay interrupts their greeting with a sharp turn of her head to Landry, which causes her blonde hair to whip harshly past her shoulder.

"Yes, Courtney works in the hotel I stayed at when visiting Elmerson."

"I see," Lindsay shifts her eyes to Courtney, passing my cold stare. "And that's where you two met as well, I presume?"

Knowing that she is referring to Courtney and me, I answer on Courtney's behalf to stop Lindsay before she begins an interrogation.

"Yes, as a matter of fact, it is where we met," I say matter-of-factly.

"Now you two are dating? Seems a bit strange," Lindsay snorts.

"How so?" Courtney cuts back into the conversation, placing her spoon to the side to wait for Lindsay's analysis. Meanwhile, Isaac and Rob both watch with interest, no doubt laughing to themselves at the exchange.

"Well, first of all, one might question your professionalism when dating a guest. Second, no offence, of course, but you seem very young. Too young to be in a relationship with a man in his thirties."

"Lindsay," Landry's voice finally pipes up as he warns his wife to stop. Lindsay, however, doesn't even flinch at Landry's harsh tone.

"What? All I'm saying is that I don't quite understand the situation here, so please share it with us. We're all family here," Lindsay says snidely.

"Well, not that I feel the need to give you the details you are asking for," Courtney begins, "but I'll do so anyway. You see, it's very simple, Lindsay. I was a single woman, and Josh was a single man. We wanted to be together, so we were together. There is nothing complicated about it. We are together because this is what we want. Age doesn't matter, and our vocations do not either. What matters is that we have mutual respect and love for each other." Courtney reaches for her glass of white wine and raises it to her lips. "And, of course, we are faithful to each other—siblings included."

As Courtney takes a long sip of her wine, Isaac cannot resist bursting into laughter as Lindsay leans back in her seat with a look of disdain in her eyes. She begins to rub her swollen belly.

"Some things are serendipitous, don't you think, Landry?" Lindsay looks over to her husband, whose smile doesn't reach his eyes. The short smile ends when Landry lifts his glass of scotch and drinks what's remaining in one gulp.

The awkward conversation is interrupted by the tapping of silverware on a crystal glass at the other end of the table. All attention turns to my father, who expresses his regard for his guests and continues about something I mostly tune out. I reach over and grab a hold of Courtney's hand, which is resting on her lap. She meets my eyes and offers me a slight smirk and wink.

After my father finished his short speech, the serving staff brought out the main course, and we all enjoyed it without any further drama from Lindsay. Rather, Rob and Isaac continue their non-stop bickering about sports, a welcomed distraction.

Two hours later, after saying goodbye to the last of his guests, my father makes his way back into the living room, where Courtney and I sit closely on the couch. Rob and Isaac are each sitting on chairs across from us. Luckily, Lindsay and Landry left immediately after supper, as Lindsay was complaining about not feeling well and demanded Landry take her home.

"Well," my father says as he pulls his necktie loose before walking towards the bar for a drink. "Overall, that evening was a success. Commissioner Phillips seemed satisfied with my efforts to work on the request to increase his budget. Hmpf, it's never going to happen, but for now, he's off my back."

My father is talking loud enough for us to hear, though I'm unsure if he's talking to us or simply boasting to himself. Either way, our input is not required. Walking over to the group, my father stands in between Isaac and Rob's chairs, staring directly at Courtney and me.

"Joshua, before you leave, I want to see you upstairs in my office. Isaac and Rob, keep Ms. Mason company for a few moments." Neither request comes out even remotely close to a question.

"I'll be okay," Courtney nudges my knee with hers before I release a deep sigh and stand to follow my father to his office.

I don't know the exact details of where this meeting will head, but if I were a betting man, I would wage that I will not leave the room in a pleasant mood. If the slight pit in my stomach indicates anything, it tells me that this will not be unlike all the other times my father uses everything in his arsenal to make me fall in line. Or, as Courtney might describe it, his ability to silence my bluebird—again.

***

I followed my father to his office located on the second floor of the house. Neither of us speaks as we walk together down the dimly lit hallway to the second door on the right. Upon entering the office, my father walks towards his large oak desk before placing his hands on the top and hanging his head forward. I only allow myself to take a few steps from the door, not wanting to encourage a long, drawn-out discussion.

"Joshua, tell me what you are thinking of accomplishing by bringing that young woman here?" My father asks without lifting his head and I cross my arms in defence.

"I don't know what you are talking about. I brought Courtney here as my date because she's my girlfriend," I reply.

"For Christ's sake, Joshua," My father looks up with anger. "What the hell is the matter with you? A girl like that is not someone you bring to an important family dinner, and she sure as hell is not someone you call your girlfriend. You're thirty-two years old, when are you going to start acting like it?"

"Look, I don't know what you want from me. I found someone who makes me happy, doesn't that mean anything to you?"

"This life is not about finding happiness. It's about being successful, and unfortunately, my success depends too much on your success and reputation. In fact, to make sure you remember how good this life can be, I'm offering you more of it. I was going to make you and Isaac equal partners, but I don't have to. I can give you more. More money, more power, you can be the boss of it all, Joshua. All you have to do is find a woman from a better family. One who will make sure you remember where your priorities lie, it's that simple."

"You mean someone like Lindsay," I scowl.

My father stands up straight and walks towards me.

"Lindsay was the perfect match for you until your brother screwed that up. At least now I have him settled down and I have less to worry about. I never thought I would have to worry so much about you, however."

"Settle him down? Dad, Landry is miserable! Don't you see that?"

"Landry is fine. Lindsay is good for him."

"You're unbelievable." I toss my arms up. "You don't care about any of our happiness, do you? We're your children, not your pawns. Besides, I would never do that to Isaac, undermine him. I can't believe you would do that to him."

"Ugh, don't even get me started about Isaac. Actually, when I think of it, every single one of my sons have been a disappointment to me. How is it possible that a man with four sons can't even have one grateful one? I have given you everything. You owe it to me to do as I say, and I am saying you need to get rid of that girl. If you don't, you will not like the consequences."

"So, now you're threatening me?" I scoff.

"I'm telling you how it's going to be. If you don't come to your senses, I will not hand you over the law firm. How about that? I'll give you nothing," my father seethes.

"You know what? Maybe I don't want anything from you. Maybe I would rather spend my life with nothing; as long as I have Courtney, I don't need anything else."

My father begins to laugh in my face before his eyes turn cold.

"You and your romantic bullshit; you're as bad as Landry. It's such a shame, Josh. All your mother ever wanted for you is to have a good life, find a suitable partner, and have a beautiful family. If she were alive today and would have seen who you have brought home as your partner, well, dare I say, she would be just as disappointed in you as I am."

"Do not bring Mom into this," I warn as I can feel my face turning red as my hands clench closed.

"Yes, you always were the biggest mama's boy, weren't you? Listen to me closely, Joshua, figure your shit out and remember your place in this family. I will not tell you again. Now get out of my sight, and take that hotel clerk with you."

Chapter 23

Courtney

Josh was up in his father's office for almost a half hour. During that time, Isaac and Rob entertained me with stories about Josh's childhood. My favourite one was the story of teenage Josh and Isaac, talking the much younger Landry and Rob into watching *A Nightmare on Elm Street* late one night. Since Isaac and Josh knew they would get into trouble for letting their younger brothers watch the scary movie, they had to have week-long sleepovers with the brothers so their parents wouldn't find out about the resulting nightmares. Rob said that he and Landry insisted that the four of them sleep in the same bed to ensure their safety from Freddy Kruger, and Josh would tell them stories until they fell asleep. Though Isaac rolled his eyes, saying they were "a bunch of wimps," I saw a tiny smirk come and go from his lips when Rob said it was one of his favourite memories.

When Josh finally appears in the doorway of the living room, his tie is completely removed, and his top shirt button is undone. His eyes look dark beneath the deep wrinkle in between his eyebrows. When our eyes meet, no smile appears on his face.

"Are you ready?" Josh asks in a monotone voice.

"Sure," I reply while standing up from the couch. I bid my farewell to Isaac and Rob before leaving the living room. I don't see David again that night.

It isn't until we pull out of the driveway of Josh's father's house that I finally decide to speak.

"Is everything alright?"

"Yes," is all Josh offers for a response, his eyes never leaving the dark road ahead.

We don't speak again for the rest of the trip home. Once we enter the quiet condo, Josh only stops briefly to remove his blazer and tosses it over the back of the high-backed island chair. Then, he walks swiftly to the fridge and removes a bottle of vodka from the freezer.

"Do you want one?" he asks me but doesn't look in my direction.

"No, thank you," I reply, still uncertain how to read the situation.

Josh's cold and distant demeanour is troubling and I'm not sure of my best course of action. Since I have no idea what was said in his meeting with his father, I can only assume it wasn't pleasant.

After I turn down the drink offer, I tell Josh that I'm going to get ready for bed.

"I'm going to stay up for a bit," Josh replies and walks into the living room, plopping on the couch while turning on the TV.

I head down the dark hallway towards the master bedroom, removing my tight heels before flopping onto the king-sized bed. I lay there for at least a half hour, lost in thoughts about what caused Josh to shut down. His behaviour is off—this is not my Josh, but I know he's in there somewhere.

I decided right then to do what I could to help Josh rather than let him wallow. Before returning to the living room, I draw a hot bath with a ridiculous number of bubbles threatening to spill over the edge. Walking quietly into the kitchen as Josh stares at the TV screen stoically with his drink still in hand, I continue my mission. He doesn't notice me as I rummage through his kitchen cabinets, searching for candles. Finally, I find a few deep in the back of the one drawer—unburned and still covered in plastic, brittle with age.

I take the candles and leave them lit in the bathroom before finally taking off my dress. I help myself to Josh's charcoal grey housecoat and make my way back into the living room. I am standing directly in front of Josh before he notices my arrival.

"Hey," his voice is softer than before. His eyes, however, look tired and defeated as the flicker of TV light dances across his dull brown irises. "Is everything okay?"

I reach my hand towards him and leave it hanging until he reaches back and grabs mine in return.

With a slight tug of his hand, I say, "Come."

"Nah, I think I'm going to stay up a little while longer."

"Come," I say again, not abandoning my position that easily.

Letting out a sigh, Josh stands and lets me lead him slowly down the hallway toward his bedroom. When we arrive in the bedroom, we don't bother to stop, but rather, I lead him directly into his master bathroom, where the bubble bath and soft candlelight await.

"Courtney, look, I..." Josh begins to speak before I reach up and press a single finger against his lips, allowing the sound of "shh" to exit mine.

A flash of relief crosses Josh's eyes as I undo each button on his dress shirt. After I finish and remove it in silence, I work on the rest of his clothes until he is completely nude. I remove the robe I'm wearing and toss it to the side, landing in a pile near Josh's discarded clothes. Again, I grab his hand before I step into the warm water, and urge him to follow me. When we are seated, I sit with my back against the cool wall of the tub and pull Josh into my embrace, pressing his back into my chest. A small amount of water and bubbles slosh over the edge of the tub, and I can hear it hit the floor, yet neither of us are concerned.

Sitting in silence, I run my wet hands through his dry hair, dampening it with each pass. Josh's body relaxes with each minute that passes as we let ourselves be in the moment and be together. Obviously, I'm dying to know what was said between him and his father, but I know this is what he needs right now. It's a delicate balance for him to fight whatever battle inside but also to know he is not alone.

Minutes pass by, and our bubbles slowly disappear. Josh reaches up with his right foot and uses his toes to turn the hot water tap slightly. After letting the temperature of the water increase, Josh uses his foot again to turn off the running water. He shifts back into position with our legs entangled and his arms resting over the top of my bare knees.

"He wants me to leave you," Josh's voice fills the silence that has encapsulated us up to this point.

"I assumed as much," I reply without a shred of surprise. From what I have been told about David and the short encounters I've had with him, he would never accept us.

"I told him no, obviously."

"But…"

"Well, at first, he tried to bribe me—offering more privileges at the firm over Isaac and more money, too. I would never do that to Isaac, anyway. After that, he tried to scare me into it, telling me all he could take away from me if he wanted to. I dared him to try. And then…" Josh's words trail off, and I remain silent until he's ready to continue. "Then he turned vicious. He started telling me things like how I'm a failure of a son, how the only thing he and my mother ever wanted was for me to be successful and marry someone who deserved to carry on the family name. He said if my mother were still alive, she would be so disappointed in me and that it would break her heart to see me making the choices I've made."

"You know that's not true, right? I mean, I never knew your mother, but I think she would be so proud of the man that you are. You are kind, charming, and fearless. You are all things that people aspire to be, and so few become them," I encourage Josh, though my heart aches for him.

"Well, I don't know about that, but I know you're right about my mom. I don't think she would be disappointed in me. As for my dad, well, I don't think I care if he's disappointed in me. Still, though, it's hard to hear, even at my age. It's stupid, really, to be in search of some sort of approval from your parents when they will never be able to give it without a catch. I doubt I will ever become the man my father thinks I should be," Josh sighs with defeat.

"Well, I'm grateful for that. I love the man that you are. On the outside, you come off as tough and detached, but once you get past that layer, you are such a gentle soul. I love that I get to witness that part of you because I have the feeling that very few people do. Let me tell you, this man that I'm holding onto right now is just about perfection in my eyes. Now, don't let that go to your head, you're still stubborn beyond repair." I poke Josh's ribs with the tip of my finger. "And sometimes," I continue with a whisper, "If I listen close enough, I can hear that bluebird sing."

Josh shakes his head, "You and your damn bird analogies."

"Was everything with your dad the reason you were so quiet afterwards?"

"Yes and no. Leaving you isn't an option; I get that more than anything. However, I debated leaving this life—the firm, my father, this city. Honestly, though, I don't know if I can leave Isaac like that, with the entire firm on his shoulders. It's something we've always dreamed about doing together, partners at a law firm—maybe trying to expand our clientele and take on cases that mean more to us, not just bringing in rich clients."

"What kind of law are you interested in?"

"I've always had an interest in environmental law, but being that I've only ever practiced at my father's firm or with this outsourced firm, I've never had a chance to pursue it."

"How did you end up with the law firm in Elmerson, anyway?"

"Dad owed Richard McKay a favour, and he asked for me to come work on a couple of cases. I thought once I finished up with Boulder Crest, I could return to the firm here with Isaac, and we could begin moving forward now that Dad is no longer an active partner."

"And you were thinking about leaving all that behind for me?" I ask with disbelief.

"Of course."

"Josh, that's insane. You can't leave now, not when you're about to get what you've been waiting for."

"None of that matters if I don't have you, Courtney, not anymore." Josh runs his hand down the length of my submerged leg.

"Listen, I've been thinking too, and I think I should look into getting a position at The Whitestone."

"The hotel down the street?" Josh asks with confusion.

"Yes. I never got the chance to tell you, but I had a very interesting morning." I then tell Josh about my encounter with Nancy and our discussion regarding employment at the hotel.

"Court, that sounds fantastic, but you should think about it a bit more. Don't get me wrong, I want you here with me, but I also want you to do what you want."

"I understand what you're saying, Josh, and I appreciate it. It's just that the thought of not being with you every day kills me. Not to mention the thought of leaving you here with that father of yours, well, I won't have it."

"And you say I'm stubborn, Tiny Bird?"

"Absolutely, you're stubborn."

"That's rich coming from the queen of stubbornness," Josh says while rolling over so we are face to face. This causes more water to cascade over the edge of the tub.

After pressing a tiny kiss on my lips, Josh remarks, "I'm cold now."

"Me, too," I agree.

After getting out of the tub, with beads of water running down his skin, Josh grabs the fluffy white towel hanging on a nearby hook. He doesn't use it to dry off but rather holds it open toward me, offering an invitation to be cocooned—an invitation I accept without hesitation.

A half-hour later, we are bundled up under Josh's large comforter, speaking casually about where we think the future will take us. I've never experienced a closeness like this with another living soul. It's a combination of terrifying and exhilarating. I feel as if our bond is growing with every minute we spend together, and I want to know everything about this man. I realize that living without him would never be an option.

"Josh," I whisper during a lull in our conversation. "Tell me a secret."

"What kind of secret?"

"Something you've never told anyone else."

Josh remains quiet as he searches for the perfect confession.

"The night before the BAR exam, I bought myself a one-way ticket to London. I sat in the airport for three hours before the flight, daring myself to get on and never look back. All I had was my passport and wallet, but I didn't care. I felt like I was suffocating in the life I was living. Throughout university, I partied like there was no tomorrow to escape the realities of what I was becoming."

"You mean becoming a lawyer?" I ask.

"No, I mean I was becoming my father. I had watched him destroy Isaac and break everything in him that was pure. I watched the light in Isaac die and reignite into something darker inside him until he became almost unrecognizable. I watched it and did nothing. I knew that my father would do that to me eventually if I didn't get out of here. From a young age, both Isaac and I had certain expectations placed upon us, and if we didn't live up to them, my father would ensure we would be punished until we did or until we died."

"And you didn't get on the place, did you?" I ask, but already know the answer.

"Of course not. How could I? I suppose I took the cowardly way out, taking the walk-in life that was built for me instead of going out to find out what I was made of."

"I don't think you are your father. You're nothing like him." I try to reassure Josh with a soft brush of my hand over his stubbled jaw.

"Aren't I, though? Haven't I defended horrible people because they had the money to pay for it? Haven't I slept with women I didn't care about because they inflated my ego, or fit into the mould of who I was supposed to be with? Haven't I treated people like garbage when I thought they weren't in the same class as me? Courtney, I have done all these things!" Josh takes in a few deep breaths before he continues in his confession. "But I believe I'm changing. I can feel the shift inside me; it's like some divine reformation making me a better person, and I think it's because of you."

I can't help but let out a disbelieving chuckle, "I hardly think this is my doing, Josh."

"But it is you, Tiny Bird. You make me feel…"

"I love it when you say I make you *feel*," I interrupt.

"But it's more than just *feel*, it's something I've never felt before, and in turn, it makes me want to do better."

"And what's that?"

"You make me feel s*een*."

Chapter 24

Courtney

It's been three weeks since Josh and I left Brighten after our quick trip to meet with his family. I'm rapidly walking in the bright April sunshine. There is no doubt that spring has sprung in Elmerson as the birds chirp their songs without reservations. The buds of flowers are beginning to show their hidden colours. Perhaps it's because I'm in love, but I swear, the petals are brighter than they have ever been before.

Love, what a crazy thing it can do to a person. It's because of love that I'm on my way home from my last shift at The Valemont. I should be feeling more melancholy, considering I was saying goodbye to a job and coworkers I adore, yet I'm walking with an extra skip in my step.

I was surprised when I saw my last scheduled shift was during the day, for a change. My boss had scheduled that shift on purpose since it wasn't a real work shift anyway. My wonderful friends and coworkers threw me a going-away party for the second half of my shift. Although there is a slight ache in my heart for leaving my job, and as of tomorrow, my first apartment, I know something is even better waiting for me.

Josh left Elmerson two weeks ago when his case with the Boulder Crest finished earlier than expected. I guess the jury didn't need much time deliberating. Josh had done a fantastic job defending his client. However, that meant Josh had to return to Brighten ahead of me to help Isaac with the partnership transition at their father's firm. As it turned out, all of David Hayles' threats were meaningless. Josh did not give in to any of his father's demands, and David is still handing the firm over to him and Isaac. I guess he's more bark than bite.

Josh told me some of the ideas he and Isaac had regarding the future of the firm and the types of cases they would like to work on. I am wholeheartedly excited for them to pave their own way as lawyers and hopefully no longer be under their father's thumb.

My thoughts are interrupted when my phone vibrates in my back pocket. I know it's Josh calling before I even look at my screen.

"Hi, handsome," I answer with a wide smile.

"Hey, Tiny Bird. Did you know that in less than twenty-four hours, you will be here and held hostage in my bed for at least the next forty-eight hours?"

"Sounds like you miss me," I laugh.

"You have no idea."

"I miss you, too."

"Don't forget, the movers are coming tomorrow morning at eight," Josh reminds me. I can't help but roll my eyes, though my smile is still intact.

"Yes, I remember. The movers are here at eight. My flight is at three, and I will be there by four."

"And?" Josh asks for more.

"And I will be your hostage for forty-eight hours after I arrive in Brighten, so I shouldn't make any plans," I giggle as I recall a previous conversation.

"And?" Josh asks again.

"And I love you," I say without an eye roll this time.

"I love you, Tiny Bird. So much. I can't wait to get you here."

"Me neither…" My last word is cut short after a beep rings in my ear. The sound tells me that I only have ten percent of battery left. "My phone's about to die, but I'll call you back when I get home in five minutes."

"I'm about to head into a meeting and supper with Isaac. Call me later this evening, around seven."

"Sounds good. Love you, my guy."

"Love you, my girl."

I hang up reluctantly from Josh's call and continue my swift steps down the street towards my apartment. My packing is already complete. I only have a small stack of boxes to take with me, and I hardly need movers, yet Josh wouldn't hear it any other way. I wouldn't need any of my furniture, and it turns out that a young tenant like me is taking over my apartment on their own for the first time. They are more than happy to take the apartment furnished.

As I round the last corner towards my building, I notice a man sitting on the concrete stoop. It doesn't take long for the familiar sandy blond hair and lanky build to bring forth the memory of my first love, Dylan. My stomach flops, and my heartbeat quickens. Once he sees me walking towards him, Dylan stands straight up and descends the few steps in front of him to meet me on the sidewalk.

"What are you doing here?" Is the only greeting I can conjure up, letting shock take over all sense of proper etiquette.

"Your mom sent me," Dylan nervously mumbles, running his fingers through his wavy hair. "Your dad is in the hospital."

"What?" I screech as my shock quickly becomes distressed. "What happened?"

"He had a stroke or something like that. They think he will be okay, but your mom wanted me to come and get you."

"Why didn't she call me?" I ask in a panic.

"I think she was worried you would try to come down on your own and didn't want you to drive while upset, so she sent me," Dylan offers a half smile.

"Okay, I..." My mind races a million miles a minute as I process everything. "I need to run upstairs and grab a few things. Then we can go."

I quickly run up the stairs and let myself into my building with Dylan following close behind. When we enter my apartment, I immediately grab my backpack and throw in the few clothes I had left unpacked—clothes I had planned to wear tomorrow during my move to Brighten.

As I frantically grab my toiletries from the bathroom, I hear Dylan ask, "Are you moving or something?" Obviously, he is asking because of the pile of cardboard boxes labelled and sealed for the movers tomorrow.

"Yes," I answer without an explanation, knowing that between him and Mother, I will be explaining myself and my actions this past year in great detail later.

After I throw my toothbrush into my backpack, I grab my phone charger, remembering my phone is about to die.

"Do you have a USB port in your truck?"

"Nah, it's an '04," Dylan laughs slightly as I toss my charger into the bag, knowing I will have to wait until I get back to Greensly before I can charge my phone.

I quickly check my phone's battery, which is now at four percent, and use the last bit of charge to text Josh a brief explanation of what is happening. I know he is in a meeting right now, and the text will be left unread until it is over, however long that may be.

As I zip up my bag, signalling to Dylan that I'm ready to go, he takes the bag from my hand to carry. I follow closely behind him, locking the door as I leave and rush down the stairs behind Dylan—trying not to think about walking back into a world I swore I would never re-enter, let alone with my ex-fiancé at the wheel.

Chapter 25

Josh

I never thought that meeting would end. Thank goodness my father wasn't in attendance, now that he has officially stepped down from the firm. However, his original partner, Lance, is still very much involved in the practice and wanted to hear everything Isaac and I have planned as partners. Then, he wanted to inform us that everything we suggested was completely useless. Tomorrow, we meet with the entire staff and begin a new orientation now that Isaac and I are partners.

Tugging at my tie with enough force that it doesn't only loosen but undoes its knot completely, I return to the solitude of my office. When I sit behind my desk, I immediately fish around the inside pocket of my blazer to find my silenced cell phone. The first notification was sent over three hours ago from Courtney.

After reading her brief text, I frantically dial her number. The phone rings at least six times before her hushed voice finally picks up.

"Josh?"

"Baby, are you okay? I just got your message."

"Hey, I'm fine. I'm at the hospital, that's why I'm whispering. My dad had a stroke."

"Is he going to be okay?"

"They think so. He's very lucky. My mom's a wreck, though."

"I can imagine. Give me a few hours, and I'll be on my way."

"Oh no, you can't do that. You're doing your transitioning stuff at the firm this week. You can't leave Isaac with that. You need to be there."

I pinch the bridge of my nose in frustration, knowing she is right but feeling awful for not being there for her, too.

"I need to be there for you, you're more important," I state matter-of-factly.

"I'll be fine, but I think I need to spend some time here with my mom, at least until my dad is released from the hospital. I've already called Liv, and she is going to meet the movers tomorrow at my place, so my stuff will still be sent to your condo."

"Our condo," I correct her.

"Right, our condo," Courtney agrees but with little enthusiasm.

"You're the only thing I want here."

"I know, me, too."

We sit in silence for a moment before Courtney speaks again.

"Listen, my mom is walking toward me right now. I'll call you later once I'm at home," Courtney mutters quickly.

I don't know why, but how she refers to her old place as home but not my condo here in Brighten unsettles my stomach.

"Of course. Call me when you can. Don't worry about the time."

"I love you, Bluebird," Courtney whispers through my earpiece.

"I love you, Tiny Bird," I reply before the sound of three sharp beeps notifies me that the call has ended.

I hang up with a heavy feeling in the depths of my stomach. I feel powerless for one of the first times in my life. I can usually take control of most things that come my way, but this…I feel stuck. I want to be there for Courtney, but I have commitments here. Also, I can't help but feel that she doesn't want me there. I'm probably being paranoid, and I scoff at myself for even having this inkling. However, something keeps nudging me towards this single conclusion.

I decided to end my evening early and drown my sorrows in a few heavy-poured glasses of top-shelf whiskey—always a sure bet to lull me into a deep sleep. I turn my phone on the loudest possible setting to ensure I don't miss Courtney's call later, as she promised.

***

I awake the next morning with a throbbing headache, a reminder that I drank way too much. Immediately, I check my phone, silently cursing myself for missing Courtney's call last night. The chastising thoughts are replaced promptly with frustration, as there are no missed calls on my phone.

Chapter 26

Courtney

It was late by the time I got back to my parents' house last night, and even later by the time I convinced my mom to go to bed. Although Josh told me to call him no matter the time, I didn't. I would like to say it was solely because it was late, but part of me also knew I avoided calling him for other reasons.

Aside from the one night we had weeks ago when I told him about Adam and the accident and my engagement to Dylan, I had avoided telling him anything since. Honestly, it had felt so nice to keep my world with Josh completely separate from my world in Greensly. Part of me fears that if I combine the two, neither will be the same.

I never meant to abandon my parents forever, but I needed a long break from them—some time on my own to figure out what I wanted from life. However, when Dylan turned up literally on my doorstep to tell me about my father's stroke, I was immediately thrust back into this life with little warning. I wasn't ready for Josh to see it.

When I pull myself out of bed after a terrible few hours of sleep, I sit quietly on my childhood bed with its peach-coloured flower print. The pilling of the polyester fabric is rough on my fingertips.

Everything about this place is old. My parents are not wealthy people, nor could I say that they are considered middle-class. We were, and always had been, poor. The three-bedroom house is nothing more than one floor with a kitchen, a living room, one bathroom, and a short hallway leading to three bedrooms: my parents' room, my room, and Adam's old room. If it's anything like it was when I left, the room remains untouched since the day he died.

A picture of Dylan giving me a piggyback from three years ago is hanging on the wallpapered wall beside my bed. It mocks me and reminds me of where I came from. I know I took that picture down long ago; my mom must have put it back up. I can hear her in the kitchen, probably fussing about breakfast. Before letting her know I'm up, I grab my phone. There are no notifications from Josh, which doesn't surprise me since I was supposed to call him. There is a missed text from Dylan asking me when I wanted to go to the hospital as if I couldn't get there alone. I'm already regretting the fact that I gave him my new number.

I try my luck and call Josh, though I'm sure he will be at the office already. Of course, the call goes straight to his voicemail. I left him a brief message apologizing for not calling him last night, telling him to call me when he's free, though I know he has a busy day ahead.

Once I finish with my message to Josh, I go to the kitchen, where my mom is hunched over a frying pan full of eggs. The coffee pot is still mostly full, so I pour myself a generous cup and refill my mom's, which is on the counter beside the stove.

"Good morning, Mom. How did you sleep?" I ask as I put the pot back on the burner and retreat to the kitchen table on the other side of the u-shaped counter.

"Not well," my mom notes while flipping the scrambled eggs. "But I'm so happy that you are home now. You've been gone too long, Courtney Ann." My mom always uses my middle name when referencing me.

"I've been really busy the last year,"I reply with a hint of defensiveness tickling the back of my throat.

"I know, spreading your wings and all, but I think it's time you stay home now. With your father sick, we are going to need you here. You've had your so-called independence for long enough; it's time you start thinking about your family and those who care about you."

Fourteen hours, that's how long it took for my mom to begin with her guilt trip. I'm not surprised by it, though I am surprised that it took this long for her to say something.

"Mom, please don't start," I plead as I raise my coffee mug to my lips. "I told you when I left that I needed time and space to figure out my life."

"Yes, and we gave that to you, but now it's time to come home."

"Mom, I have a life in Elmerson now, but that's only the beginning. I have other plans and dreams."

"Oh, nonsense. One day, you will need to grow up, my girl. Honest to goodness, if your father's stroke doesn't get you to finally do that…well, then, I don't know what will."

Rubbing my hands over my frustrated face, I clench my teeth together. The doorbell rings before I can explain to my mom that I am not staying here forever.

"I'll get it," I say, using it as an excuse to leave the conversation.

When I open the door, I'm greeted by Dylan, awkwardly holding a teal casserole dish. His dirty blonde hair is brushed back, possibly still wet from a morning shower, and he's wearing an orange T-shirt and blue jeans. I see now that he has aged in the last year. His eyes have tiny wrinkles that were never there before.

"My mom sent this over," he mumbles as he pushes the dish into my hand, offering a shy grin.

"What are you doing here?"

"Your mom asked me to take you to the hospital this morning. Didn't you get my text?"

I clench my jaw so I don't lose my temper, and allow Dylan to follow me to the kitchen, where I place the dish of what looks to be meatballs into the fridge.

"Good morning, Glenda," Dylan says while walking over to my mom and pressing a soft kiss on her cheek.

"Oh, my sweet boy, I'm so glad you are here." My mom moons over Dylan's arrival the same way she has done since we lost Adam.

After their greetings, my mom offers Dylan a cup of coffee, which he accepts freely before sitting beside me at the table. For a moment, I think he has intentionally moved his chair closer to me before he sits down.

"Why is Dylan taking me to the hospital this morning?" I ask my mom. "Are you not coming, too?"

"Of course I am, Courtney Ann, don't be silly. You know I have to stop at the church on the way and light a candle for your father. I know better than to ask you to join me."

My memory slips briefly back to the fight I had with my mother not long after Adam died—I told her I had no interest in going to a church to pray to a God that took someone like Adam so easily, with no questions asked. Her 'almighty' took him, and we were supposed to pray in gratitude and praise him with songs. No, thank you.

"Fine," I reply without making eye contact with either my mom or Dylan, who are both looking at me. "I'll be ready in fifteen minutes, and then we can go," I say to Dylan after finishing the small amount of coffee in the bottom of my cup.

"You should eat something before you go," my mother adds.

"I'm not hungry," I declare, despite the rumbling in my stomach. I leave it at that and march down the hallway back to my old room to get ready to leave.

Twenty minutes later, I'm back in Dylan's old truck, heading towards the hospital. We have barely spoken to each other despite being together yesterday in this same truck for over an hour. So, I'm taken by surprise when his voice booms through the cab.

"You know, you should be nicer to your mom. She's been through a lot."

"Please don't tell me how I should or should not behave," I wince at his demand, suddenly feeling like I've been thrust three years into the past.

"You know, since you decided to up and leave all of us last year, we've all been hurting. Your mom feels like she's lost two children, your dad hardly speaks to anyone anymore, and, well… I've missed you more than anything."

Dylan's admission shocks me as I turn to meet his hazel eyes briefly before they glance back at the road.

"Dylan, I…"

"No, you don't need to say anything. I know I screwed up. I should have treated you better, and I'm sorry." Despite his apology being a year and a half too late, a small tug pulls at my heart as my old self and her resentfulness soften the tiniest bit.

"What's his name?" Dylan asks without looking away from the road.

"Whose name?"

"The guy you're moving for. You didn't think I missed all the moving boxes in your apartment, did you?"

"What makes you think there's a guy?"

Dylan side-eyes me with raised eyebrows.

"Joshua Hayles," I finally admit, as the roll of the *s* lingers on my tongue long enough to make me smirk.

We don't speak again until we arrive at the hospital. Dylan drops me off at the front door and tells me he will get us coffee and bagels from down the street before coming up. I'm grateful for the food and a moment alone with my dad before Dylan or my mother joined us.

When I enter my father's hospital room, he is partially propped up with two thick pillows. A light blue blanket covers his body, which I used to think was indestructible. Today, it looks more fragile than I've ever seen.

My father turns his head slightly when I enter the room, and I can see the smile he is trying to produce, although his left side remains mostly still.

"Hi, Dad," I whisper as I approach the chair beside the hospital bed, the same chair my mother occupied all day yesterday.

"Hi, Courtney-bear," my dad's voice mumbles so inaudibly that if I hadn't heard him call me by the endearing name a million times before, I wouldn't have known what he was saying.

"Do you need anything?" I ask, deciding only to give him yes or no questions so he doesn't have to speak too much.

"No," falls from his lips.

Looking around the drab room, I can feel tears forming in my eyes. I don't know how to process all that is happening. I feel torn between two lives—the one in Greensly where there are roots, and the one with Josh that makes me want to fly.

Reaching over and clutching my father's hand, I allow a few teardrops to fall down my face. My father gives my hand a gentle squeeze before his eyes close. Once I'm certain he is sleeping, I let my sobbing take over.

Chapter 27

Courtney

It isn't until a week later that my mother finally corners me in the family room. It's late in the evening, long after visiting hours. This is the first night that my aunt Norma hasn't been here hovering over us.

My mother walks slowly into the small living room, which has only a sofa, a single rocking chair and an oval coffee table. The sofa's pattern of dusty rose flowers gives away its nineties manufacturing date. There's a small TV in front of all the furniture, which I know would be airing baseball if my father was home right now. This thought causes tears to flood my eyes, and I try to blink them away before my mother notices.

"He's going to be okay, honey." My mother sits beside me, obviously noticing my poorly hidden emotions.

"I know," I reply while swiftly wiping the tears from my eyes.

"It's nice having you home again."

I nod only but don't speak since I haven't decided I share the same sentiment.

"I hope this is for good, Courtney Ann. We've all missed having you here so much, especially Dylan."

"Mom, don't start."

"I understand why you left. I really do. Young people sometimes need space to find their way and figure out who they are, but eventually, it's time to come home again—and we need you home again. Especially now, with your father needing more care with the physical therapy that's to come."

"He doesn't need me here for that."

"No, but I do. I can't do this without you, and I would like to think, after losing Adam and now with your father's health, that you would finally set your selfish wants aside to help your family."

"Mom, please…" I trail off when the panic and tears spring into my eyes. "I can't. I have plans."

"Is this about the boyfriend?"

"How did you know?"

"Dylan told me."

I roll my eyes. "Of course, he did."

"He's too old for you," my mother's comment comes out coldly.

"How do you know that?"

"Dylan told me he looked him up on Google; a thirty-something-year-old lawyer from Brighten?"

"Ugh, I'm going to kill Dylan."

"Don't take this out on Dylan. He's only trying to protect you. But this man, the lawyer, he had no business messing around with a twenty-two-year-old girl. Men like that aren't looking to settle down."

"Mom, you don't know what you're talking about." I stand up to leave and abruptly end the conversation. I'm furious with Dylan, and I intend on telling him exactly how much the next time I see him.

I stomp down the short hallway to my old bedroom, still radiating with anger. The buzzing of my phone on the dresser breaks my attention. I see Josh's name pop up, and I debate answering it when I'm this upset. However, my temptation gets the best of me, and I answer, trying to hide my anger.

"Hey, Josh."

"Am I calling at a bad time?"

"No, I just—It's been a long day," I say while flopping myself onto my bed.

Josh clears his voice before proceeding. "I wanted to check on you. I'm worried about you."

Between my mom, Dylan, and Josh's worry over me, I'm beginning to feel like a docile little mouse who can't take care of herself. I hate this feeling.

"I wish people would stop telling me that," I growl into the phone, and it comes out harsher than I intended.

"Well, what am I supposed to think when I don't know what's going on with you, how you are doing, or what I can do to help?" Josh's voice has become deeper and sterner.

"Oh my God, Josh. I don't need your help, alright? I'm not a child. I need everyone to leave me alone while I figure my shit out!"

"Courtney, stop being so stubborn. I'm not treating you like a child. I'm treating you like my partner, which I thought you were."

"Of course I am."

"Are you sure? Because you have hardly talked to me lately and you don't want me to come there. What am I supposed to think?"

"Not everything is about you, Josh," I hiss into the phone.

"Now you *are* acting like a child."

We both remain silent, stewing in our own fury.

"Courtney, what do you want from me?"

"Nothing, Josh. I want nothing from you."

"So, that's it then. I'm just supposed to sit here in Brighten and wait for you to eventually come home if that's what you decide to do. Or maybe you're thinking that your little life in Greensly isn't so bad after all. Toss all your dreams and goals to the wayside so that you can live a simple little life where your mom and Dylan can dictate your every move."

"Josh, stop it!" I cry into the phone.

I hear Josh take a deep breath on the other end of the line.

"Courtney, I'm going to ask you one more time. Do you want me to come there?"

"I don't know."

"Then, I suppose I should let you go until you figure it out."

Chapter 28

Josh

My mood has been less than stellar the last few days, ever since I abruptly ended my phone conversation with Courtney. I'm not sure where things stand between us right now. I'm angry with her as much as I'm angry with myself. Perhaps I pushed her too hard and was too much of a dick, considering her dad is in the hospital. Also, from the little she's told me about her mom and ex-fiancé, I'm worried they will get to her and make her forget her dreams once again—and if I'm really honest with myself, they'll make her forget me, too. God, when did I become such a pussy?

The thoughts burn in my brain as I run along the pathway of Pebblestone Park. Choosing to hit this trail early in the morning, I take what enjoyment I can from the solitude. I've been running the same pathway for years; I could probably run it with my eyes closed. It weaves through the forest that surrounds the lake. The city maintains the pathways meticulously throughout the warmer months, so I am surprised when my ankle gives way to a pothole. The twist of my foot causes my body to tumble to the side. When my knee hits the pavement, my skin instantly burns from its tearing away from my kneecap.

"GODDAMN IT!" I curse out loud when my body finally stops at the edge of the path. Fury rises inside me as the pain of my knee and ankle try to outdo each other.

"Fuck!" I curse again while punching my knuckles into the grassy ground beside me, connecting with a hidden rock.

At this point, I can't help but laugh with disgust. Sitting all alone on a vacant pathway, bleeding because of my own stupidity, and knowing that the real pain I'm experiencing is in the dark corner of my heart, it's all too much to bear. The pain grows every day that Courtney and I don't speak, but I'm beginning to realize the very real possibility that she might not be coming back.

I sit in self-pity for a minute as the blood continues to trickle down my leg. It makes its way between my brown leg hairs and soaks into my sock. My knuckle isn't bleeding as much as it is throbbing. My frustration and self-loathing are interrupted by the whistle of a bird from a nearby tree. I look up to see the bright wings of a blue jay and its beady black eyes perched smugly on a branch overhead.

Instantly, I can hear Courtney's voice reciting the words of the Charles Bukowski poem, and I'm reminded of what I had and what I don't have anymore. I add that stupid little bluebird to the list of things I'm currently despising, though still leaving myself at the very top of the list.

I'm able to limp along the rest of the path back to the parking lot where I left my car. As I approach the edge of the beach, I feel a cool breeze of lake air. Looking towards the water, I see a man sitting alone on the sand. with his knees pulled loosely towards his chest and his arms draped around them. As I get closer, the outline begins to take a familiar shape; it's my brother, Landry.

I debate whether I should approach him or not. Landry is by far one of my least favourite people these days. However, I wonder why he is here this early in the morning in a city he doesn't live in. When my curiosity gets the best of me, I turn off the path and onto the sand. The instability of the sandy surface puts more strain on my pulsating ankle.

Landry doesn't notice me as I approach until I am beside him. He looks up at me with red-rimmed eyes. He's either high, or he's been crying, or both.

His eyes scan over me with little emotion, but he scowls when he sees my bloodied leg.

"What the hell happened to you?"

Before responding, I sit beside him on a cool patch of sand.

"I could ask you the same thing." Landry continues to stare at me, still waiting for a response. "I tripped while I was jogging."

Landry turns away and looks back at the water. "You should clean it really well, so it doesn't get infected."

"Thanks for the tip," I sarcastically reply, and I almost feel a hint of guilt. "What are you doing here?"

"At the beach or in Brighten?"

"Both, I guess."

"I just dropped Lindsay off at her parents' house. She's going to stay with them for a bit."

"Trouble in paradise?" I scoff.

Landry remains silent for a moment and doesn't remove his eyes from the water. Hell, he barely even bothers to blink. Finally, with a slight hitch in his voice, he reveals the reason for his current state.

"We lost the baby."

Guilt instantly takes over as my stomach begins to flip with remorse and sadness. "Shit, man, I'm so sorry."

We sit silently together, with only the sound of crashing waves around us. Eventually, Landry reaches into his back pocket and produces a single joint and lighter. Usually, I would berate him for his drug use, but today I stay silent. The skunky smell burns my nostrils instantly. After taking a few hits, Landry offers the joint to me, to which I wave my hand in refusal.

"Do you want to talk about it?" I mumble to my estranged brother.

"Nah," Landry says with a sharp inhale of smoke.

"Well, for what it's worth, I really am sorry. I mean that, Landry."

Landry turns his dark blue eyes in my direction; they are glossy with tears. He nods in acknowledgement.

"So, now what?" I ask.

"Well, I suppose I should go see Dad before heading back to Reddington. I still have classes to finish up. I have no idea how long Lindsay plans to stay with her parents."

"Makes sense," I comment.

Landry stubs out his cherry on the sand beside him.

"How's Courtney, by the way?"

I exhale deeply and run my fingers through my hair.

"Honestly, I don't know. We haven't spoken in a while."

"What's going on?"

"Well, her dad had a stroke. He's going to be okay, but she went home to see him and hasn't come back. I don't know if she wants to come back, to be honest."

"But Rob told me you two were going to move in together?"

"We were supposed to, but the last time I spoke with her on the phone, she didn't know what she wanted."

"So, go see her."

"She doesn't want me there."

"So?" Landry retorts.

"*So*, I'm not going somewhere I'm not wanted," I growl in return.

"Do you love her? I mean, like, *really* love her?"

"What do you mean, *really* love her?"

"I mean, the thought of living without her makes you sick to your stomach. That not having her there with you, day after day, makes you question the point of living. That nights without her aren't only unbearable, but also useless because even if you do sleep, she's just going to invade your dreams, anyway. That's what kind of *love* I mean."

I sit still for a moment, internally agreeing with every scenario Landry described.

"Yes," I finally admit.

"Then you have to fight for her, Josh. You have to fight until you die because on the other side, it isn't even death; it's only a muted existence. An existence that isn't without its pain but isn't with much else. I mean, you're there physically, but you're not really there—because she's not with you." Landry's eyes begin to gloss over with tears again.

My heart is beating heavily because I know my brother is right. I also know this so-called "muted existence" he describes is the one he endures now. Though he is not completely blameless for his current situation, I can't help feeling his sorrow. Landry has always been his own worst enemy, but in this moment, he is my redeemer.

"You're right," I say. "I need to fight for her—for us. She is everything to me, Landry."

"Then stop wasting your time with me and go figure your shit out."

Before I stand, I ask, "Are you going to be okay?"

Landry shrugs his shoulders. "Ah, you know me."

"Call me if you need anything," I say as a sort of peace offering.

"Thanks, man."

Before turning to walk away, I ask Landry one more question.

"You never did say why you were out here on this beach, of all places?"

"It's where I find the most peace."

"How come?"

"Because it's the only thing I have left."

I feel a slight sense of confusion with Landry's statement, but leave it at that. Some logic is only understood by the heartbroken soul that creates it.

I hobble back to the parking lot, leaving Landry alone on the beach again. After I get into the blisteringly warm car, I text Rob, telling him to keep an eye on Landry. After hitting send on my text, I drive straight home to clean up and start arranging travel so I can get myself to Greensly—back to my Tiny Bird.

Chapter 29

Courtney

I sit quietly, watching my father's machines beep in a constant rhythm. My fight last week with Josh still weighs heavily on my mind. We haven't spoken to each other since that night. I'm sure he's waiting for me to call first since he said to let him know when I figured out what I want—but I still feel just as lost as I did last week, so I haven't called.

This morning, I'm trying to ignore the impending headache at the back of my skull. I feel as though I have two different lives happening. First, of course, is this life in Greensly, the one I've been doing everything to forget. Maybe not forget, but rather run from. Run from the church, my mom, Dylan, my dead brother; run from it all. So, I ran. I ran, and I ran, and I ran—and then I found Josh.

Somehow, I'm back at the starting line. The race was for nothing, and Josh felt like a pitstop on my way back to where I had come from.

After a few more minutes of silence, my father begins to rustle around on his bed. I watch as his eyes flutter open. It's a minute, maybe more, before he sees me sitting in the dark beside his bed. His smile is slight.

"What are you still doing here, Courtney-bear?" My father asks with a noticeable slur in his voice.

"What do you mean? I came to see you, Dad."

"I mean, here in Greensly."

"I wanted to be here for you and mom."

"You should go. If you don't go…If you don't go now, you may never go. Trust me."

"Dad, I'm fine. If I stay here or go somewhere else, I'll be okay. But for right now, I want to help take care of you." I reach over to his hand, laying on the beige sheet, and take it in mine.

"Courtney, listen to me," my father is practically breathless now. "There is nothing worse than living a life trapped by circumstances that you yourself have created."

"Dad, what are you saying?"

My father closes his eyes softly.

"There's a great big world out there, and I want you to be a part of it. I want you to see everything you've ever dreamed of seeing. I want you to find a love that drives both of you to the brink of madness. I want you to be free."

I sit in shock for a moment because I have never heard my father speak this way before. Besides the fact that he has always been a man of few words, I have never heard him speak of love and madness, of dreams and being free.

"Dad, I don't know what to say. I'm so conflicted about what to do. I want to do all those things you said, but I also want Mom to be okay. I feel like if I leave now that I will be abandoning her again, and I don't know if she will ever forgive me if I do."

"Your mother hasn't always been so set in her ways. After we lost Adam, she changed, and rightfully so. But you shouldn't suffer at the hands of her fear and bitterness. That's not fair to you."

"What about you, Dad?"

"Aw, don't you worry about me. Your mom will take care of me."

"No, I mean you lost him, too; and by the sounds of it, you lost some of your dreams along the way."

"Courtney-bear, sometimes your life doesn't go the way you think it should have, but there comes a time when you have to accept it for what it is and find happiness regardless. But you, my sweet girl, have so much time to make mistakes, go wild, and find your happiness. Do it for me and do it for Adam since he never got that chance. Do it for yourself. Now, I won't say anything more about the subject, and whatever you choose, I will respect it. You know my thoughts on the situation, but the decision must be yours."

The hospital door creaks open, and my mother enters the room, putting an abrupt end to our conversation. Mom informs us that the doctor told her Dad would be able to come home tomorrow. It is such a relief to hear. They are hoping that with a new assortment of medications and lifestyle changes, Dad will be able to make a full recovery.

I excuse myself from the room shortly after my mother's arrival. After the drastically opposing conversations I've had with my parents in the last day, I need some time to think. When I walk through the sliding hospital doors, the warm sun hits my face with blinding force. Taking a deep breath of fresh air, I know exactly where I need to be right now. Somewhere I can reflect in peace about everything my parents said to me. I need to see my brother. I need Adam.

Chapter 30

Josh

Of all the people I could imagine myself taking advice from, Landry would have been the last. Yet somehow, sitting with him on the beach has left me with his words of living a muted existence on constant replay in the back of my mind. I know Courtney is the one; I feel this more deeply than I've ever felt anything before. I feel like my truest self when we're together, and I believe she does, too.

Maybe I should respect her wishes to stay home. However, I know how stubborn Courtney can be. Almost as stubborn as I am, marching through the airport in Elmerson and heading straight to the car rental kiosk.

Greensly is too small to have an airport, but since it's only an hour or so drive from Elmerson, I figured my best bet was to rent a car and drive the remainder of the trip. I didn't bother telling Courtney I was coming since I already knew what she would say. I'm worried about her. I'm worried that things are worse than she's letting on. I think back to the night at my place when she held me fiercely in the tub, comforting me in a way only she seemed to know how. I want to be able to do that for her if she lets me. Truth be told, something in the pit of my stomach tells me that I'm not so sure she will.

It's late afternoon by the time my black, rented Lexus sedan pulls into Greensly. A local gas station on the edge of town tells me just how small of a town it is. A sign notes two things that large city businesses don't abide by anymore: the first is that the gas station and the attached Gram's Café are closed on Sundays, and the second is to have a "blessed" day. Bizarre.

Considering there are only a handful of streets with businesses and the rest of the town is made up of houses, I can find the Mason residence easily since I had Liv retrieve the address from the hotel employee records. Inappropriate? Possibly, but sometimes you do what you have to do.

I pull up to the small white house with forest green shutters and notice that despite the house being small and probably from the nineteen-thirties, it's still in good condition. It's better than some of the neighbouring houses, for sure. A large weeping birch tree stands in the yard, whose leaves are starting to pop out of their buds.

While walking up the concrete path towards the front door of the house, my heart is starting to beat faster with each step I take. I'm nervous—I don't know how Courtney will react when she sees me. Hopefully, it's a combination of shock and relief. I also don't know what her family will say when they meet me for the first time and see that I'm noticeably older than Courtney. Courtney has shared very little information about her family, so I feel like I'm entering this entire situation blindly.

I approach the small white veranda and press the red doorbell button. I can hear soft chimes on the other side of the wooden door with a half-circle window at the top. I wait patiently for several minutes until resigning to the fact that no one is home. Not knowing exactly what to do next, I sit down on the top step of the porch. I retrieve my phone from the inside of my navy suit jacket. Since my decision to come here was somewhat spontaneous, I didn't even bother to change after leaving the office for the airport. With my phone in my hand, I debate whether I should call Courtney or wait for her to come home. I assume that she is at the hospital right now, and I don't want to bother her there. I decide to hunker down on the veranda step and wait for her to come home.

I'm not there long before the heat gets the better of me, and I remove my jacket and tie and roll up the sleeves of my white dress shirt. A few times, people have walked past the house with dogs on leashes. Kids on bikes also race past, and their laughter is still heard long after they leave my sight. I wonder how long I will have to wait for Courtney to arrive home. It's not that I mind waiting for her, but I'm anxious to see her and to wrap my arms around her. Strangely, I feel homesick for her. I never knew one could feel this way about a person rather than a place, but it turns out the feelings are indeed transferable.

Sitting in full sunlight now and wishing I had a bottle of water with me, I'm finally greeted by a car turning into the small driveway beside the house. I stand up in relief, hoping that Courtney is finally here. My relief is quickly replaced with disappointment when an older woman exits the car alone. There's no doubt in my mind that she is Courtney's mother, with the same long dark brown, almost black, hair. However, there is a mix of white throughout the long braid that runs down her back. The woman stops abruptly on the lawn when she notices me on her stoop.

"Can I help you?" Her voice is cold and impatient.

"You must be Mrs. Mason," I say while stepping down from the porch. "I'm Joshua Hayles, a friend of Courtney's." I extend my hand, though it is not taken.

"So, you're the lawyer. What can I do for you, Mr. Hayles?" Courtney's mother looks at my waiting hand but does not move. I drop my hand after a moment of it being unreceived.

"I was waiting for Courtney to arrive home. I assumed she was at the hospital."

"I just came from the hospital, and no, she's not there. I don't know where she is right now, but I can tell her you stopped by," Mrs. Mason says with annoyance.

"I was hoping to wait here for her if you don't mind."

"Actually, Mr. Hayles, I do mind, and let me tell you why."

Courtney's mother crosses her arms over her chest before releasing a fury of angry words in my direction.

"Tell me, what business does a thirty-something-year-old man have chasing down a twenty-two-year-old girl? Perhaps it was her naivety that made her an easy target for you, but I can assure you that you will not be able to fool me. I know exactly who you are."

"Please, do tell me, Mrs. Mason. Exactly who do you think I am?" I grit through my teeth as my anger begins to rise.

"You are an entitled and pompous man who thinks he can get whatever he wants from whoever he wants. When someone like you sets his sights on someone like my daughter, I know exactly his intentions."

"Which are?"

"Perhaps using a young woman makes you feel young again, or maybe you enjoy the thrill. We both know this is nothing more than a quick fling for you, and I would appreciate you leaving Courtney alone before her head gets even more confused than it already is. You've led her to believe this is a real relationship, but let's be honest with each other, this is nothing more than a fun time. Eventually, you will settle down with someone more suited to your age, and my daughter will be nothing to you. Who knows, maybe you're already married? It wouldn't surprise me if you were. Either way, that's not my concern. My concern is Courtney and you leaving her alone."

"You know nothing about me," I interject. "Not that it's any of your business, but I love your daughter very much and—" I'm cut off by Courtney's mother's laughter at my admission. "And I don't appreciate you telling me who I am or how I feel. You don't know me; you don't know anything about me. Courtney and I are in love and will have a life together, whether you accept it or not. I'm not here, Mrs. Mason, to get your permission because I don't need it, nor does Courtney. I'm here for Courtney, and Courtney only!"

"You realize that Courtney has a history of making men believe she's in love with them. Surely, she's told you about her fiancé Dylan, who, by the way, has been by her side since she found out about her father's health. Where were you, dare I ask?"

I open my mouth to respond, though we're interrupted by the sound of a loud truck approaching from the east. I can see Courtney in the passenger seat, and her eyes meet mine before the truck comes to a stop. The look of shock I was hoping for is definitely present, however the look of happiness, or even relief, is harder to find in her expression.

Chapter 31

Courtney

After leaving the hospital, I walk straight to Greensly Cemetery, where my brother Adam is laid to rest. This was one of my last stops before I left over a year ago. For some reason, I had been avoiding it since I returned. Perhaps it was partially out of self-preservation, not ready to feel the loss of my brother, which always comes in full force anytime I visit this place. Or maybe it was because I was ashamed. I'm not ashamed that I came back to see Dad, considering his health scare, but ashamed that it took so little time before I was being drawn back into staying. Between my mom, Dylan, and the strange pull of familiarity and nostalgia, I find myself wondering what it would be like if I stayed.

My mind, which is now shrouded with guilt, quickly jumps to Josh because the aforementioned thoughts of staying here means a life that doesn't include him. That guilt rolls into more guilt, which is layered with guilt my mom gives me about my role as her daughter and only child. Before I know it, my brain is spinning out of control, and I want to run—again.

I'm hoping that by coming to the cemetery today, I can find solitude and comfort beside my brother, who encouraged me in the kindest way. Always simply telling me to be myself and that the rest would fall into place.

After swinging the wrought-iron gates open and walking across the patchy grass to the walkway, I noticed that not much had changed since the last time I was here. There are a couple of new mounds of dirt, signalling that there are some new residents. I walk past them quickly, not looking to see the names etched on the headstones. I'm not here to see them, and now that I'm finally here, I cannot wait to get to my brother.

About halfway down the gravel path that intersects the middle of the square field, I take a right turn. After passing Mrs. Griffiths, Mr. Adams, and Mr. Herbert, I arrive at my brother Adam.

Immediately, I walk to the headstone and brush away the dirt and debris collected on the dark slate top. There isn't as much as the others around us, so I know my mother has been here recently.

Once clean, I let my fingers run over the letters etched into the stone. Following the smooth lines of each letter, I trace the entire length of his name—Adam Christopher Mason.

"Hey, Addy," I whisper, as though I'm worried I will wake his sleeping neighbours, and settle myself slowly down onto the grass. "Sorry, it's been so long."

Taking a moment, I look up at the sky, wondering if Adam can see me right now. I think he can. I watch as a black crow flies overhead and lands on a tree near the back perimeter of the cemetery.

"I'm going to assume you know what's been going on with me, Mom, and Dad, so I won't bore you with a retelling. If you could go ahead and give me some advice, it would be greatly appreciated." I sit quietly for a minute, waiting for a response. I know it's ridiculous, but I wait just the same.

"I feel like I'm being pulled into two directions, Adam." I begin babbling while tugging at a strand of grass. "I'm being pulled in two very different directions. First, of course, is Mom's direction. She wants me to stay home, and as much as I don't want to admit it, I kind of get where she's coming from. She's alone and afraid. I mean, yes, she has Dad, but I know the stroke scared her. Now, she has to take care of him in his recovery; it's going to be a lot for her.

"After we lost you, Adam, Mom wasn't the same. She struggled for control over everything. My life, Dad's life, everything. I felt like she was always pressuring me to do things the way she wanted me to do them, so I did just that. I didn't like seeing her sad or upset, so it was easier to keep the peace.

"Even when I started dating Dylan, she was overjoyed because I think she felt our connection was because of you, which I guess maybe it was. Then, everything seemed to spiral from there—the dating, the living together, the engagement. I've never felt so trapped and suffocated in my life. That's why I ran to Elmerson. Living there was the first time in my life that I was on my own. You would've been so proud of me, Addy." I pause for a moment, leaving my non-existent audience hanging.

"Then I met Josh. I think you'd like Josh. He's funny, sweet, and way too serious for his own good sometimes. He's so supportive of my goals and dreams, which is opposite from the way Dylan was. Josh is practically perfect, and I hate to admit it, but that scares me. We're so different but also exactly the same, which I know sounds crazy. What if he gets tired of me or wants the type of woman his father wants him to be with? The Lindsay-Isabelle type. Ugh. You should see these women, Addy." I roll my eyes and flop onto my stomach, stretching out beside my brother's grass-covered plot. "They're straight out of *Real Housewives*, I swear. But that's the world Josh comes from, and while he swears that it's not what he wants, it's still ingrained in him somewhere. It's kind of like how this life is ingrained in me. The small-town, going-to-church-on-Sundays, baking-pies-for-the-fair kind of life. And it's not a bad life, but I'm not sure it's the life for me.

"Sometimes, I feel like I couldn't get out of here fast enough and forget everything, that I never gave myself the chance to mourn the life I gave up. I know not marrying Dylan was the right decision, and it's not because I didn't love him. He was so sweet at first, you know? Then, he became moodier and bossier. He would be so nice to other people but then miserable to me. When I would ask him about it, he tried to make me feel bad, saying things like he shouldn't have to hide how he really felt with me. I think he was angry about the accident and about losing you, but you know, we were both angry about losing you. We thought we could find comfort in each other, but it just turned into resentment in the end."

I roll onto my back and look up towards the cornflower-coloured sky. There are a few clouds out today, thin ones that are more like wisps of white paint strokes through the sky. The crows caw over by the tree line where the one flew to earlier.

"I don't want any more resentment. What I really want is peace. I want Josh to be happy. I want Mom to be happy. I want Dad to be happy. Hell, I even want Dylan to be happy—and somehow, I feel like their happiness is all contingent on me and my choices. It's a lot of pressure, Addy."

Closing my eyes, I allow the sun to bathe me and continue to lay stretched out beside my brother's grave. I'm not sure how long I lay there before I hear footsteps crunching the dry grass, getting louder with each step. Drawing myself up to a seated position, I place my hand over my brows to block the bright sunshine and look up at the tall figure standing before me.

"I thought I might find you here. Your mom said you left the hospital when she arrived." Dylan towers over me, wearing faded denim jeans, a red T-shirt, and a black ballcap. "Mind if I sit?"

I pull my outstretched legs and tuck them into a criss-cross position, allowing space on the grass beside me. Dylan sits down, trying to cross his legs like mine, but I can tell the length of his legs makes it difficult. Dylan places his hand on the grass of Adam's plot and closes his eyes. I let him have his moment and say nothing.

Sitting in silence together, it feels as if we are both enduring the memories of the accident, the funeral service, and the loss of Adam.

"Do you ever come out here?" I finally break the silence.

"Probably not as much as I should," Dylan replies in a muffled voice while opening his eyes and looking into mine. "I miss him, though, every day."

"Me, too. What do you think he would be doing now if he were still alive?" I ask Dylan.

"You know Adam and his love of cars. He'd probably be working at the garage with your dad, fixing up a 1971 Corvette or a 1965 Mustang. He always had a thing for Mustangs."

"Yeah, you're probably right. He'd be married to someone like Allison Henth, with how she always mooned over him when she saw him." We both begin to laugh, and it feels nice.

"Remember when he was supposed to come and watch the new *Star Trek* movie with me but backed out at the last minute when he heard Allison needed a date for her cousin's wedding, so he decided to take her?" Dylan recalls.

"Yeah, and so you made me go with you to that terrible movie?"

"Hey, it wasn't so bad. You got to see Kirk and Spock finally fight over a woman."

"Ugh, don't remind me." I roll my eyes with exaggeration.

"But Adam was always the nice guy, wasn't he?" Dylan hangs his head slowly. "It should have been me."

"Don't say that, Dylan," I say with shock and look at him with disbelief. I've never heard him speak this way. Dylan wipes a tear that has fallen over his flushed cheeks onto his chin.

"Come on, Court. What good have I done in my life? Since I lost you…"

"Dylan, don't," I urge him as I feel my own eyes dampen.

"You were everything good I had left, and I messed it up. I understand why you left, Court. I really do. If I could go back in time and fix this, I would."

"Do you even know why I left, Dylan?"

"Because I was rushing you into marrying me?"

"Partly. Also, I felt trapped. Remember when I told you I wanted to see the world and travel? I wasn't joking. I was hoping that one day we would get out of here together, but then, after a while, I could see that that was never going to happen."

"I'll leave with you now if that's what it takes," Dylan replies with boldness as he looks up, meeting my eyes.

"Dylan, you don't want to do that. You love it here."

"I would do it for you. I love you, Courtney. I'm sorry for everything, and I can prove to you that I'm good enough for you. We can go wherever you want and—"

"Dylan, stop," I abruptly interrupt before taking a few deep breaths. "It would never work. We want different things, and honestly, I'm not even sure I know what I want anymore."

"Is this because of that old guy?"

Remembering now that Dylan was the one to tell my mom about Josh and that I had yet to call him out on his actions, anger fills my thoughts.

"You had no right to tell my mom about him."

"I was worried about you. I think he is taking advantage of you."

"You don't even know him, Dylan! And now I have to deal with Mom's guilt trips and judgment."

"I just think if he were the stand-up guy you claim him to be, he would be here with you right now."

"I told him not to come."

"Why?"

"It's hard to explain."

"It sounds like maybe you two don't have anything figured out. I would never leave you on your own while your father is sick. What kind of a man does that? I would take care of you, Courtney. I would be there for you!"

"Stop! This is none of your business. You don't know Josh, and you don't even really know me anymore. I don't need Josh here to be okay, and I don't need you, either!" I look up at the sky for a moment and notice a bank of dark clouds gathering to the west. "I don't want to talk about this anymore. We should probably go in case it starts to rain."

Dylan stands up and brushes away the stray bits of grass stuck to his jeans before extending his hand toward me. Despite my anger towards Dylan, I reach up and take his hand, the first time we've touched in so long. His skin feels familiar and comforting but not igniting like the way Josh's skin feels to me. With a pull of my arm, Dylan helps me up to a standing position. We each take a moment to look back down at Adam's grave, still holding hands.

"I love you, Adam," my voice cracks as the words get stuck in my throat.

Dylan squeezes my hand before offering his best friend his goodbye.

"Later, bro. Rest easy."

Together, we walk to Dylan's truck at the edge of the cemetery, no longer holding hands. The sound of our shoes crunching against the dry grass and gravel is the only sound between us. After getting into the truck, Dylan drives me towards my home. The entire trip is spent in silence as we immerse ourselves in our thoughts of Adam, each other, and where we go from here.

Chapter 32

Courtney

We approach my parents' house slowly and two figures come into view before my eyes. The first I know to be my mother. Her long braid is swaying in the wind that has since picked up as the dark cloud creeps closer. Standing several feet from her with arms crossed is a tall and solid man. It doesn't take long for my brain to register that Josh is standing on my lawn. My mom and Josh turn towards the truck as it pulls up in front of the house, and Dylan puts it in park.

"So, that's the guy?" Dylan breaks my concentration on the situation in front of me.

I don't bother replying to Dylan but rather jump out of the truck and approach my mom and Josh. Despite the scent of distant rain, the air is thick with tension. I walk over to Josh, who has now cracked a tiny smile upon my arrival. His eyes are painted with worry, probably trying to gauge my reaction to his unexpected presence.

"What are you doing here?" Are the first words to tumble out of my mouth, and instantly, I feel ashamed of my reaction. I haven't seen him in weeks and have missed him terribly; however, seeing him in this particular scenario is bothersome.

"I was worried about you," Josh replies with a hint of frustration.

I reach over and take his hand in mine, the same one that had been attached to Dylan only a short time ago. The touch of my skin to Josh's is electrifying, and tingles of excitement develop in my stomach. Giving me a slight squeeze of my hand with his, Josh finally smiles a full smile. My excitement is short-lived when my mom interrupts our moment.

"Courtney, you should properly introduce us to your friend."

For a brief moment, I had almost forgotten that Dylan and Mom were standing on the other side of the yard.

"Well, it would appear you two have already met. Judging by the showdown, it seems we have something going on here. What is going on?" Turning towards my mom I don't let go of Josh's hand.

"Nothing," My mom states, though I don't miss the quick glare she shoots towards Josh. I know she will not give up the details of their conversation.

"Dylan, why don't you come inside and help me start supper? Let's give Courtney and her friend some privacy."

Dylan follows behind my mom, but he does not miss the opportunity to side-eye Josh as he walks past. I notice Josh doing the same to Dylan.

Once we are alone, I finally turn towards Josh and look up into his rich brown eyes. God, I've missed them.

"Hi," I whisper.

"Hi," Josh whispers in return before leaning down and slowly pressing his lips to mine. The kiss is brief when tiny raindrops begin to pepper our heads.

Pulling back, Josh nods at the black car parked on the street.

"Want to go for a drive with?" Josh asks.

Nodding in agreement, I'm quickly pulled towards the car as the drops increase in size. With excitement and confusion in my stomach, I remain silent as Josh begins to drive.

"You're going to have to help me out on where I'm driving towards," Josh remarks.

"Oh, let's see. We could drive to Willow Park, and if it stops raining, we can sit by the trout pond, or we could just talk in the car."

Josh nods at my suggestion, and I give him directions to the park. The car ride is spent in complete silence except for the woosh of the windshield wipers as they bat away the raindrops.

By the time we arrived, the rain was coming down harder than it had been at my house. Josh parks the car and turns off the ignition. Neither of us moves to exit the vehicle due to the storm outside.

"Is it okay that I'm here?" Josh asks in the most timid voice I have ever heard him speak. "I mean, you told me you didn't really want me here."

"It's not that I didn't want you here, Josh. It's just..." I trail off, trying to collect my thoughts. "I wanted some time to sort stuff out."

"What kind of stuff?"

"Stuff with my family, my responsibility to them, and where I go from here."

"I thought you had already decided where you were going from here. You were going to be with me." I can hear the frustration rising in his voice.

"It's not that simple anymore. Not with my dad sick and my mom needing help."

"What did your dad say?"

I remain silent. I told Josh about how my dad had always encouraged me to leave and follow my heart. Now, of course, it is no different.

"It's not that simple," I finally mutter.

"But I think it is, Courtney. Your dad doesn't want you to lose your dreams. If you're worried about care for him, I can help with that. Financially, I mean. That's not a problem. We can come back here anytime you want to see him and—"

"Josh, just stop it!" I shout with anger.

"Stop what?" Josh matches my tone with his.

"Trying to fix this for me. You don't understand. The pressure and expectations my mom puts on me. She did this to me first after Adam died and now with my dad. She can't do this without me. Do you know what it's like to have a parent expect so much from you all the time?"

Josh laughs slightly. "Are you kidding me? I have lived under my father's rule my entire life, always trying to become exactly who he wanted me to be—crushing any part of myself that didn't fit his mould of the perfect son. So, please, don't tell me about pressure. I know all about it."

"It's not the same. My mom isn't a bad person, she's just…"

"What? Manipulative? Self-serving?" I can feel the swell of tears forming in my eyes as Josh continues. "Listen to me, Courtney. I know it's hard, but you can't live for someone else. Maybe you're too young to understand this, but…"

"Please don't throw my age in my face, Josh. I'm so sick of being treated like a goddamn child. It's bad enough that I get this from Mom and Dylan, but you, of all people, should know I'm anything but a child."

"Speaking of Dylan, exactly how much time have you been spending with him?"

"Oh, don't give me the jealous asshole routine, Josh. I'm sure you're far too mature for that." I roll my eyes, causing a few tears to escape.

Josh clenches his fists tightly around the steering wheel.

"Has he begged for your forgiveness yet? Told you he's changed? That things will be different if you stay?"

My silence acts as my admission.

"Yeah, I thought so. Don't you see, Courtney, they're trying to manipulate you into staying because it's what they want? It's not about what's best for you; it's about what's best for them."

"What about you, Josh? Isn't that the same thing you're doing right now? Trying to get me to go back to Brighten with you because it's what you want, what's best for you?"

"For Christ's sake, don't you get it? It's what's best for both of us. I'm not going to deny that you are what's best for me in every possible way. But you know damn well I'm what's best for you, too. You and me, remember? We were there together—and if you'd stop being so stubborn for two damn seconds, you would remember that."

My arms are crossed as I glare out the passenger window, refusing to make eye contact.

"But it's obvious that you won't stop, so I'll remind you. We are good together, Tiny Bird. Hell, we are more than good. We are the best versions of our broken selves, so much so that we're whole."

"Josh," I whisper as tears stream heavily from my eyes.

"Let me save you from yourself and from all this."

"I don't need you to save me, Josh," I hiss at him.

"After all that, those are the words you choose to hear?" Josh shakes his head, starts the car without saying another word, and drives us back to my parents' place. Once we are parked on the street in front of the house, Josh finally speaks again.

"I'm staying at the Greensly Motel tonight in room 202. I'm leaving tomorrow morning at seven a.m. If you can get your shit figured out by then, you know where I'll be. If not, well, I'm not doing this again, Courtney. I can't do this again."

"So, that's it, then. Is it your way or nothing? Geez, now who's being stubborn?"

"I'm serious, Courtney. I can't…my heart can't take this," Josh's voice cracks during his admission. "I've shown you everything that I am, and if that's not what you want, then there's nothing else I can do."

"Josh, I…" But Josh doesn't allow me to finish my sentence.

"Seven a.m," Josh says again sternly, this time without the slightest crack or hesitation.

I take that as my cue to exit the car. Neither of us offer any good-bye. Almost as quickly as the passenger door latches closed, the car begins to drive away.

Chapter 33

Josh

My hands are gripping the steering wheel so tightly that it feels like the bones in my knuckles might break through the skin. I'm both furious and terrified.

Driving back from where we had parked and inevitably fought, my mind races. I flipped back and forth between wanting to lash out at Courtney for her indecision and stubbornness or pulling over and begging her to choose me. Of course, I did neither of these things and gave her an ultimatum, which sits in a ball of regret in my stomach.

I think back to my conversation with Landry a few days ago, and his words radiate in my mind— *Then you have to fight for her, Josh. You have to fight until you die because on the other side, it isn't even death; it's only a muted existence. An existence that isn't without its pain but isn't with much else.* Seeing the shell of a person he has become, I fear that that could be me if this ends poorly. I don't know how I became so immersed in another person—the person I used to be would never have let this happen. In fact, the old Josh would have probably told Courtney to forget about everything and head straight back to Brighten immediately. I would have left the memory of Courtney somewhere with all my other failed relationships. Yet, there is this other side of me that has grown since finding Courtney, and I feel like maybe it always existed somewhere inside of me. Now, I want to hang onto whatever hope I have left of having a life with Courtney. No, I *must* hang onto that feeling; I *must*.

My nausea hasn't subsided by the time I pull into the parking lot of the small motel. The thought of going straight into my room and staring at the clock all night sounds unbearable, but I'm relieved when I notice a small tavern across the street from the green and white motel.

After I check in and get the keys, I don't bother going to the room but walk directly across the street to the old brick building with the neon sign. The smell of stale beer and old cigarette smoke bombards my nose when I walk into the bar. Once the door closes behind me, the small amount of natural light disappears, and my eyes take a moment to adjust to the dank room. There is an unoccupied pool table in the back and a couple of other patrons sitting at some of the small, circular tables scattered throughout. I decide to sit at the bar—as much as I would like to drown my sorrows right now, I know I won't be able to stay away from my motel room for too long, just in case.

Once seated, I order a neat scotch from the old bartender with a grey beard and matching ponytail. An old country song croons throughout the bar, but luckily, it isn't too loud, so I can easily ignore it.

To occupy my mind, I pull out my phone and scroll through some work emails, relieved that it appears that I'm not missing anything too pressing. Quickly losing interest in work, I find my fingers tapping on my photos and swiping through pictures of Courtney and me together. If I believed in God, maybe now would be the time to pray that all this works out. However, I don't believe in anything, so instead, I gulp down the rest of my scotch and ask for another.

***

Hours later, the sun disappeared, and darkness took over. I left the tavern shortly after my second drink, but not before talking the bartender into selling me the rest of the bottle. I ended up paying a top-shelf price for a bottom-shelf bottle, but that's the least of my worries.

There has been no sign of Courtney, and despite my lack of self-control checking my phone every five minutes, there have been no messages or calls either. The feeling of regret over my demanding ultimatum is growing with each minute.

I'm sitting on the double-sized bed with a yellow-striped blanket in the small motel room. It's dated with its wicker furniture and shag carpet, but it's clean, which was all I was really worried about when I checked in. The TV is playing a basketball game, and considering we are into the playoffs, I should be glued to the screen. I can't bring myself to pay attention to the game—the fear of losing my Tiny Bird is not only occupying my mind, but also radiating panic through my very core. My heart hurts, my eyes are sore, and I do the only thing I know to do at this moment—pour another drink.

Chapter 34

Courtney

It's still raining hard when Josh drops me off at home. I run the entire way to the front door and don't look back towards Josh's car. There is no point; I hear him speed off almost instantly.

When I enter the house, I keep my head down so my mom won't notice my tear-stained cheeks. Trying to maneuver quietly, I attempt to make a break for my bedroom. Before I can fully retreat down the hallway, my mom's voice rings through the air, beckoning me.

When I enter the kitchen, smells of garlic and onion fill my nose. While the frying pan sizzles the vegetables, my mom stands at the sink, scrubbing away on a dirty pot.

"Where's Dylan?" I ask, noticing that he's not here anymore.

"He left not long after you took off with *that* man."

"*That* man has a name, Mom. His name is Josh," I huff as I take a seat at the kitchen table.

"Yes, I'm aware of that. However, after the conversation, we are about to have, I would rather this be the last time his name is spoken in this house again." My mother's words come out seething, though she doesn't look up from the soapy water in front of her.

"Mom, please don't," I plead and rest my head in my hands.

"The nerve of that man thinking he can just show up here to our house, looking for our young daughter, who he's obviously manipulated into thinking there is some sort of relationship..."

"There is a relationship between us, Mom. Or at least, there was, and it was very much real."

"Courtney Ann, he's in his thirties and has no business with a young person like yourself. There is nothing for you two to build a relationship on, nothing in common."

"Mom, why won't you listen to me? I love him!" My words come out as a shout.

"Pfft," my mom scoffs. "You don't have the faintest idea of what love is, especially with a man like that. You think that because he buys you stuff and tells you you're beautiful, that means it's love. Open your eyes, my child; he's using you."

I want to argue back, but tears have overtaken my eyes, and sobs have closed my throat. I am so tired of crying, and I'm exhausted.

"You have everything you're ever going to need right here," my mom continues despite the obvious distress I'm in. "Your family is here. Dylan is here, and he's someone who loves you. He's been here waiting for you to come home while you're out there being selfish, running around with no consideration for anyone else but yourself."

"Dylan and I aren't meant to be together," I croak.

"Why, because he doesn't have lawyer money? Because he doesn't indulge you in your silly dreams of seeing the world? Let me tell you something: the real world doesn't work that way. You don't get to do what you want just because you want it. Eventually, you have to grow up. You don't get your silly fairytale; you get the life God gave you, and you are grateful!"

My mother's hard words pound through my skull. Anger is rising in every inch of my body, and yet, I feel paralyzed. Staring at each other from across the room, my face is damp with tears, and hers is red with rage.

"What if I don't want the life God gave me here? What if I want a life of my choosing, with whomever I choose?" My words fall out of my mouth with a lack of conviction.

"If you can't accept your gifts from God with gratitude, then you have no place in my home."

"Just like that?" I reply with shock.

"Just like that," my mother replies without hesitation.

I break our stare when I stand and walk straight to the back of the house to my old room. Closing the door softly, despite the volcanic anger coursing through my veins, I find myself gulping for air once the door latches closed. Finally, after catching my breath, I try to unpack everything that has happened in the last couple of hours. Between my mom and Josh, I feel like I have been put through the ringer. Eventually, I fall onto my bed with a thud. There are no more tears. I feel completely drained and broken. I'm unsure how long I lie before I succumb to sleep and my dreams take over.

Adam and I are sitting side by side on the stoop of our house. It's a late summer evening, as the warm air blows softly. My mind doesn't fully register that I'm sitting with my brother, the one I haven't seen in years. A breeze causes Adam's brown hair to dance to the side, but he hardly seems to notice.

"You know, I always thought that birds flew south every fall to avoid the cold," Adam says while looking up towards the sky.

"Don't they?" I ask.

"I suppose technically, but I like to think they go south because they are free to go wherever they choose. I mean, who's going to stop them?"

"I guess," I shrug. "But I think they're only doing what they know how to do, what they've been taught to do."

"Aren't you the buzzkill? Next, you're probably going to explain that rainbows are simply the way the light reflects through the raindrops," Adam nudges my arm with a grin.

"It's science, isn't it?"

"Okay, but hear me out, sis —what if rainbows are a gift from nature and Tiny Birds are free to fly away to wherever they choose?"

I sit up with a startle, Adam's voice still lingering in my mind. My room is completely dark now. I listen for a moment and there are no sounds in the house. Everything is silent. I grab my phone nearby to check the time, and I'm surprised to see it's after midnight. My mom must have gone to bed.

I consider calling Josh, but I would much rather see him right now. I know deep down that it's him that I want. I want to achieve my goals and dreams of a career, and I want him to be there with me through it all. I want us to be there for each other because I know we are both the best version of ourselves when we're together.

I know deep down that Greensly isn't home for me anymore. I love my family, I do, but this isn't where my heart belongs. It belongs somewhere out there, somewhere where lilies can be beautiful again, I can fly without being caged, and I can love without fear.

For a moment, I think of the disappointment my mom will feel when she learns of my choice, but I quickly remind myself that she's the one making it a choice. It shouldn't be one life or another; it should be support no matter what I choose. That's what families are supposed to do for each other. I started to see that maybe Josh's father and my mother weren't all that different. Maybe both Josh and I are lost birds needing to find our way, and we'll fly in whatever damn direction we choose, as long as it's together.

I pack up my clothes hastily, not wanting to waste another moment away from my Bluebird. As I tear through the clothes in my closet, a silky white fabric catches my eye from the back. It's my wedding dress. The one I was supposed to wear when I married Dylan. I shuffle the other items out of the way and pull out the long gown.

I hold it in front of me. The gown is simple. White satin is the base with a thin lace overlay. Two spaghetti straps hold the dress from the hanger. I turn it around to look at my favourite feature, the long line of faux pearl buttons that run from between my shoulder blades to my waist. As I run my fingers over the pearls, I have flashes of what my life would have been like if I had married Dylan. I know that life isn't for me. However, I know there is a life for me, and he's waiting.

Chapter 35

Josh

It's a good thing I fell asleep with the sports channel on mute, or I wouldn't have heard the knocking on the motel room door. It takes a moment for my eyes to adjust before I can read the red digits on the tableside clock. It's 12:51 a.m. When I remember where I am and who I'm waiting for, I feel a jolt of energy permeate my body.

Dressed in grey sweatpants and an olive-green T-shirt, my bare feet carry me over the soft carpet to the door as the knocking continues. *Please let it be her.*

I take a deep breath as my fingers embrace the cool chrome handle and open the door. In front of me stands everything I've been waiting for: my Tiny Bird. Her long, dark hair hangs loosely over her shoulders, and her wide eyes look up at me with eagerness and hope. Instantly, I feel relief, though my heart pounds fiercely in my chest. Courtney has a long black coat wrapped tightly around her body, held in place by her shaking arms.

"Can I come in?" her voice whispers.

"Of course," I reply and step aside, opening the door wider. As Courtney walks in, I look out into the parking lot below, noticing there are no extra cars in the vicinity. "Did you walk here?" I ask while shutting the door.

"Yes," Courtney's voice is still quiet as she walks towards the bed, stopping just short of the mattress before she turns around to face me, removing the long black jacket. I'm taken aback when I see Courtney standing in front of me in a long white gown, the bottom of the dress is stained with dirt.

"What are you doing?" I ask, thoroughly confused over her attire.

"This is my wedding dress. The one I was supposed to wear to my wedding with Dylan."

Still standing near the door, I cross my arms over my chest in search of some armour. Seeing her in a dress she had for another man is unsettling.

"What is this about, Courtney?" I grit through my teeth.

"I was thinking about everything after you left. Well, after you left, and after my mother told me how it had to be, I felt sick. I felt like no matter what I did, I would let someone down. And then I heard from Adam—"

"Adam? Your brother?"

"Yes."

"Your dead brother?" I raise my eyebrows.

"Yes."

"Courtney, this isn't making any sense."

"Hear me out, Josh. I decided I wouldn't do what either of you wanted me to and would do what I wanted to do for myself. No matter my decision, it would be my decision, and if it were the wrong one, then it would be my fault. No one else to blame, no one else to depend on; only me."

"Okay?" I say hesitantly.

"I don't need you to save me, Josh." Courtney's voice is confident and firm as she takes a few steps toward me.

"Yes, you've made that very clear. So, is the point of the dress to let me know that this is your choice? Seems a bit over the top and dramatic, don't you think?" I can't help but sarcastically grumble.

"Not exactly. It may be a bit over the top, but I wanted to make sure you really understand what I'm choosing."

As she continues to move towards me, Courtney doesn't stop until we are only inches from each other. The familiar smell of tangerine is wafting from her hair, though I refuse to look down at her in case a certain doom awaits me with her next words.

"By all means, let me have it," I mutter with fear forming in my gut.

"I don't *need* you to save me, Josh," Courtney places her hands on my shoulders and raises herself to her tiptoes until her lips barely touch the flesh of my earlobe. "I *want* you to save me."

Everything inside of me takes note of how the words *I want you to save me* fall from her lips. A combination of relief and glee fills my chest. My head instantly falls forward so that my nose burrows into her hair.

"Are you sure about that, Tiny Bird?"

"Yes, Bluebird—s*ave me.*"

The words barely have time to escape her mouth before I slide my hands up her spine, feeling a hundred rounded buttons underneath them. They're smooth and cold to the touch, but I hate what they represent: a barrier keeping my Tiny Bird in the cage of her past.

Without a second thought, I find the top of the silky fabric, and with each hand gripping tightly, I do away with all the forces keeping her in. The sound of tearing material fills the room, along with the sound of Courtney's voice letting out a gasp. I allow my hands to press against the warm flesh of her back as my lips search out the first sign of bare skin to press against. They end up finding the round of her shoulder. My lips dance in delight over the smooth skin, and my heart finally feels like it can breathe a sigh of relief before the sensation of arousal begins to set in.

"Are you here to stay, Tiny Bird?" I growl against her arm.

"Yes. I—"

I don't allow her to speak further as I lift my face to meet hers and collide our lips with a desperation I didn't know I had. Her voice lets out a slight moan in the meeting.

My hands roam over the torn fabric to the straps of the shoulders before pulling on them until they give way to my force. I hate this dress and everything it represents— a life without me in it. I will tear it to shreds and burn it to ash if I must, if it means that she will always be mine and that the life she is leaving behind will forever stay where it belongs, far below us in the shadows of our wings.

With Courtney standing in her torn dress in front of me, I reach around her waist and lift her against my body; never letting our lips separate, I carry her to the bed and gently place her on top of the mess of blankets. The glow of the flickering TV causes shades of blue and white lights to dance over her body. Standing above her, I remove my shirt and toss it carelessly to the side of the bed. Courtney's eyes peer up at me; her hair is fanned out all around her.

"I love you," Courtney's lips mouth the words without any sound exiting.

I remove whatever is left of the tattered dress and toss it next to my shirt.

"Tomorrow, you're coming home with me."

"Yes," she replies, even though it wasn't a question.

"Back to our home." Again, I state it as a fact.

"Yes." And again, compliance.

"And..."

"And?" Courtney questions, unsure of what comes next.

I don't answer her until our lips are mere inches from each other and her legs are wrapped tightly around my waist.

"And I love you, too," I say before I consume her once again, only this time, I have no intention of stopping until every part of me becomes every part of her.

Without Courtney, I am nothing at all. As much as I didn't want to admit it, even to myself and my ego, she didn't need me to save her. I needed her to save me. To bring me out of this darkness that shrouded my life. To help me find that lost bird inside of me, the one that didn't only allow me to feel but the one that allowed me to soar.

Courtney and I lie together an hour later, trying to regain our ragged breaths. Her head is tucked into the dip of my shoulder.

"I'm glad you came," I break our silence. "I was afraid."

"Me, too," she quietly admits. "I don't think my mom will ever speak to me again."

"What about your dad?"

"He and I will be okay. He wanted me to leave."

"I don't understand them as a couple. How can they be so different?"

"I don't know. He's never talked about that stuff before, but I think he sees himself in me, or at least what he could have been," Courtney remarks.

"I'm sorry that it has to be like this, Courtney. Maybe one day, your mom will accept us."

A small laugh escapes her.

"Sure, we'll have your dad and my mom over for supper any day now."

"You've got a point there," I mumble before pressing my lips onto her head. "You bring out the best version of me, the part of me that I didn't know I had inside me. You know you'll always have me, Tiny Bird."

"And that's all I'm ever going to need, Bluebird."

Epilogue

Josh

After a whirlwind trip from here to New York in less than seventy hours, I'm happy to finally be flopping down on my grey couch in our high-rise condo in downtown Brighten. The same one we've lived in together for the last seven years.

I feel like I can barely move a muscle. Meanwhile, Courtney is fluttering around the kitchen like she hasn't been on her feet for the last three days, assisting with the grand opening of the newest five-star Lux Hotel. I simply went along for the trip. Since our little blip of time apart all those years ago, we can hardly stand to be apart anymore. Isaac calls us co-dependent and pathetic—we call it twin flames.

"Baby, come take a break with me," I beckon her to snuggle with me as I pull the knot of my tie loose and kick off my shoes.

"There's no time. Did you forget that Landry and Hollynd are coming for supper? Oh, and Isaac, too. You remembered to text him this time, didn't you?"

"Yes, I did," I grumble as I stretch my legs out on the sofa, cursing myself for going along with the idea of planning a family supper the same night we arrive back from New York. However, Hollynd is due any day now, and Courtney insisted that we do it as soon as we arrived home, "just in case."

It's hard to believe that after all this time, we are having a family supper, like a real family. Of course, with our father now being a senator and, for the most part, out of our lives, save for Isaac, who still seems connected to his leash, our family suppers are actually enjoyable. However, it's also been strange not having Rob here; he seems to find any reason to leave the country, travelling everywhere. He wants to be anywhere but here. Not that I can blame him.

Over the last few years, my relationship with Landry has improved. We are in a good place, and it turns out that Hollynd and Courtney have become close friends, almost like sisters. With Courtney losing touch with her mother over the years, I know she has relied heavily on her relationship with Hollynd, and I am grateful that the two found each other. Courtney and I are both excited about the arrival of our niece or nephew, and though we have decided not to have children, we know that we will love this baby as if it were our own. Hollynd and Landry deserve this blessing more than anyone else I know. The person Courtney is for me, Hollynd is for Landry; of this, I am certain.

Then, there is Isaac. Still gruff and stubborn as always. He works too hard and never allows himself to find what he truly wants. I blame my father for this, as I have done for the last twenty years. The last time I saw Isaac truly happy was shortly before the last time I saw him truly broken. Since then, it's as though he has vowed never to let either happen to him again.

Despite the sounds of rustling dishes from the kitchen, I feel my eyelids getting heavy. I allow sleep to overtake me, thinking that a quick power nap will do me good. A short time later, I felt fingers running along my hairline.

"Time to wake up," Courtney's voice softly wafts through my ears.

A groan escapes from my throat as I stretch my body over the surface of the couch.

"Come on, Bluebird. Your family is going to be here soon."

"Call and cancel. I want you to myself," I mumble, still without opening my eyes as I slide my hand over the curve of her thigh.

"Nice try," Courtney says before pressing her lips to my forehead. "Come on, my old man."

"Hey, who are you calling old?" I sit up with a scowl.

"I knew that would do it," Courtney says with a grin.

"You might actually be the death of me, Tiny Bird," I mutter as I nuzzle into her neck, nipping at her skin. We are interrupted by the ring of the oven timer.

"So dramatic," Courtney says with an eye roll and walks back to the kitchen to tend to the alarm.

I can't help but feel a smile tug on my lips as I watch her whirl around the kitchen. A sight I have never tired of. While I joke about her being the death of me, it couldn't be further from the truth. My Tiny Bird could never be my death, not when she is why my heart has finally found *joy*, my soul feels *seen*, and my bluebird is finally *free*.